"I want to kiss you."

Adan's mouth was near her as he said it. "Which doesn't make a bit of sense," he added.

"I know," Sofia said on a raspy protest that fizzled and faded. He somehow did feel the same way, which gave her hope and scared her silly. "I know."

"We have to keep moving," he replied, not moving.

"Yes." She snuggled closer.

"Don't do that."

"What?"

"Look at me like that, touch me like that."

"You're the one holding me."

He grunted then pulled her closer. "Let's get this out of the way."

His lips moved over hers in a blazing heat that would surely melt a spot in the snow. Sophia returned the kiss with a deep longing that pooled into liquid warmth with each touch of her lips to his. Had she ever really been kissed before?

No. Not like this.

D0595230

Dear Reader,

Some people carry a secret with them to their grave. But most of us usually tell our secrets to someone we can trust, if for no other reason than to get it off our chest.

Adan Harrison comes to Crescent Mountain, Arkansas, right before Christmas to find a dangerous criminal. But before he can finish his mission, he gets all tangled up with Sophia Mitchell and her well-meaning but interfering neighbors. Adan soon learns that everyone on this remote mountain has some sort of secret. But he believes Sophia has the biggest secret of all. Could she be harboring a fugitive?

Sophia's worst fear comes back to haunt her as she realizes Adan is trying to find the man she believed to be dead. A man who has come to the mountain to get his revenge on Sophia. And now on her protective friends, too.

I loved the quirkiness of this story. It seemed to take many twists and turns before Adan and Sophia realized they could trust each other and help each other. The tight-knit community of Crescent Mountain turned out to be like any community where the neighbors watch out for one another and sometimes just watch each other. But this story begs the question—do we ever really know our neighbors or what they are plotting behind closed doors?

I hope you enjoy Adan and Sophia's story. It's all about mystery and secrets but it does have a true Christmas story tied into all of that, too. I promise.

Lenora Worth

New York Times and
USA TODAY Bestselling Author

LENORA WORTH

—

Cowboy Who
Came for Christmas

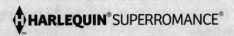

If you purchased this book without a cover you should be aware that this book is stolen property. It was reported as "unsold and destroyed" to the publisher, and neither the author nor the publisher has received any payment for this "stripped book."

Recycling programs
for this product may
not exist in your area.

ISBN-13: 978-0-373-60935-2

Cowboy Who Came for Christmas

Copyright © 2015 by Lenora H. Nazworth

All rights reserved. Except for use in any review, the reproduction or utilization of this work in whole or in part in any form by any electronic, mechanical or other means, now known or hereinafter invented, including xerography, photocopying and recording, or in any information storage or retrieval system, is forbidden without the written permission of the publisher, Harlequin Enterprises Limited, 225 Duncan Mill Road, Don Mills, Ontario M3B 3K9, Canada.

This is a work of fiction. Names, characters, places and incidents are either the product of the author's imagination or are used fictitiously, and any resemblance to actual persons, living or dead, business establishments, events or locales is entirely coincidental.

This edition published by arrangement with Harlequin Books S.A.

For questions and comments about the quality of this book, please contact us at CustomerService@Harlequin.com.

® and ™ are trademarks of Harlequin Enterprises Limited or its corporate affiliates. Trademarks indicated with ® are registered in the United States Patent and Trademark Office, the Canadian Intellectual Property Office and in other countries.

Printed in U.S.A.

Lenora Worth writes for Harlequin's Love Inspired and Superromance lines. Her books have won national and regional awards. Her Love Inspired Suspense book *Body of Evidence* made the *New York Times* bestseller list. With more than fifty-five books published, she writes Southern stories set in places she loves such as Atlanta, Georgia, the North Georgia and Arkansas mountains, Texas and Louisiana, including Dallas and New Orleans. Lenora is married and has two grown children.

Books by Lenora Worth

HARLEQUIN SUPERROMANCE

Because of Jane
A Southern Reunion
The Life of Riley
That Wild Cowboy

LOVE INSPIRED SUSPENSE

Fatal Image
Secret Agent Minister
Deadly Texas Rose
A Face in the Shadows
Heart of the Night
Code of Honor
Risky Reunion
Assignment: Bodyguard
The Soldier's Mission
Body of Evidence
The Diamond Secret
Lone Star Protector
In Pursuit of a Princess

LOVE INSPIRED

The Wedding Quilt
Logan's Child
I'll Be Home for Christmas
Wedding at Wildwood
His Brother's Wife
Ben's Bundle of Joy
The Reluctant Hero
One Golden Christmas
Easter Blessings
"The Lily Field"

Blessed Bouquets
"The Dream Man"
Christmas Homecoming
Mountain Sanctuary
Lone Star Secret
Gift of Wonder
The Perfect Gift
Hometown Princess
Hometown Sweetheart
The Doctor's Family
Sweetheart Reunion
Sweetheart Bride
Bayou Sweetheart

In the Garden

When Love Came to Town
Something Beautiful
Lacey's Retreat

Sunset Island

The Carpenter's Wife
Heart of Stone
A Tender Touch

Texas Hearts

A Certain Hope
A Perfect Love
A Leap of Faith

STEEPLE HILL

After the Storm
Echoes of Danger
Once Upon a Christmas
"'Twas the Week Before Christmas"

To my Arkansas friend
Valerie Hansen with love.

CHAPTER ONE

THE BARREL OF a shotgun pressing into his back stopped him in his tracks.

"Don't take another step."

The feminine voice surprised Adan Harrison. He had not been expecting that. What he had been expecting was a wanted fugitive he'd been tracking for three long, cold days.

"I'm not here to harm you," he said, hoping she'd put the shotgun down. He held his hands up and went to reach inside his sheepskin-lined coat. "I'm…an officer of the law. I'll show you my badge and ID."

"Don't do that."

Adan stopped, waited. He could hear her shifting in the slush and the snow. Freezing in his boots, he didn't dare turn or make a move for his own gun. He'd been around enough prickly females to know you didn't mess with a woman with a loaded shotgun. Especially if you were in the deep woods of a treacherous mountain terrain in western Arkansas.

"Let me show you my badge," he said. "Look,

I got lost and it's cold and I didn't think anyone was inside the cabin."

"Did you bother knocking?"

She was so close he smelled something clean and fresh through the scent of wet, frozen trees and decaying wood.

"I did knock, yes, ma'am." He took a chance at looking over his shoulder. "Can I turn around so we can talk face-to-face?"

She made another movement, quick and sure. "Okay, but slowly. And keep your hands up."

Adan did as she asked, pivoting in the snow and dirt to face her. Another surprise. She was young and pretty, but she was so covered in her big coat and dark blue scarf that it was hard to tell anything else. Her eyes matched the scarf and bits of stray hair hung in light auburn tufts around her face and ears.

"Show me your badge," she said, the gun now aimed at his heart. "And I won't hesitate to shoot if you try anything."

Adan didn't argue with her. He believed she'd shoot him in a heartbeat. Something about her stance and the dark fierceness in her eyes told him this woman was either hiding something or running from something. Or someone. Maybe she was hiding someone, now that he thought about it.

The someone he wanted to take back to Texas?

He slowly reached to unbutton his heavy jacket. She stepped closer, her unyielding eyes burning him to the spot. The damp hulking trees dripped with softly falling snow as night begin to descend on Crescent Mountain. If he didn't get himself out of this soon, he'd be stuck here in a December snowstorm.

Keeping his eyes on the woman with the gun, Adan opened his coat and showed her the badge attached to the left pocket of his flannel shirt. "I'm a Texas Ranger, and I'm looking for a man," he said. "A very dangerous man."

She got all skittish and then her gaze moved from his face to the badge. "What if that's fake? What if *you're* a dangerous man?"

Was she trying to deflect attention away from herself by accusing him?

Aggravated and losing patience, Adan stepped closer. And found the barrel of the gun digging deeper into the middle of his chest.

"Look, lady. It's cold and I'm tired. I thought the cabin was empty. I'm here for one reason, to find this man before he hurts someone else. I have it from a reliable source that he might be either headed here or already here, hiding out on this mountain."

The fierce gaze he'd seen earlier was replaced with what looked like fear. He could feel the gun trembling against his ribs. And because he knew she was afraid of something besides him, he took advantage of that slight distraction by grabbing the barrel and holding tight as he pushed it up enough that she had to either shoot into the sky or drop the shotgun.

She stared into his eyes with a white-hot anger while they stood so close he could smell that sweet, fresh scent tickling against his cold nose. She pulled the trigger and sent scatter shots into the trees before he was able to wrench the gun out of her control. The woods vibrated with the sound of the gun going off and the trees shook down patches of snow and leaves.

Adan's eyes held hers as they stood nose to nose. He saw a certain horror there in her startled gaze. She held onto the gun with surprising agility, but Adan was stronger. He wrestled the gun away and stared over at her.

"Okay, now that we've settled that, I'm not here to hurt you," Adan said, holding the twenty-gauge down. "If we could just go inside and talk this through, I can prove to you that I'm who I say I am."

"You never said your name," the woman replied, a kind of triumphant gleam in her eyes.

In the next second, Adan heard the whack of something hitting him. And then he felt the intensity of a hard sharp pain. Her face was the last thing he saw before the world went black.

SOPHIA GRABBED THE gun back and stared down at the tall man lying at her feet. "Miss Bettye, I hope you didn't kill him."

Sophia's seventy-year-old neighbor, Bettye Scott, stood over the big man, her hands tight on a cast-iron frying pan, her braided gray hair falling around her shoulders. "He ain't dead. I see his chest rising and falling. Is he the one?"

"The one?" Sophia was used to her neighbor's strange ways and quirky attitude on life, but sometimes Miss Bettye really didn't make any sense. Then at times like this, the woman zoomed in on the glaring truth.

Miss Bettye tugged at her moth-eaten wool hat and smiled over at Sophia. "The man you're hiding from, honey."

Sophia had shared lots of secrets with her feisty neighbor but Bettye didn't always remember the details. Sophia decided now was not the time to jar Bettye's memory. But Sophia hoped the man she'd gotten away from wasn't the man this Ranger might be looking for. Because as far as she knew, that threat had been neutralized. She thought. She hoped. She prayed.

She shook her head and gave Bettye what she hoped was a calm glance. "He says he's a Texas Ranger, and he *is* wearing a badge."

Bettye squinted, her chin dipping as she pushed her hat back. "Is his badge over his heart?"

Sophia glanced down at the unconscious man. His heavy jacket lay open to expose his plaid flannel shirt. The round badge with the star-shaped Texas Department of Public Safety emblem winked at the growing dusk. And scared her into backing up a few steps.

She nodded to Bettye. "Yes. Is that a good thing?"

Bettye stomped one of her booted feet. "Dang, I done hit a Texas Ranger over the head. And he's a mighty pretty thang, at that. I guess I'll be hauled off to jail." She shook her head and held down the frying pan she'd used to hit him, her attitude resigned and nonchalant. "You don't ever mess with a Texas Ranger."

She said that with a little too much assurance. Sophia had learned to never ask any of her neighbors about their past and in return, she didn't have to tell anyone much about hers. It was an unwritten rule of this isolated mountain of misfits and outcasts to keep things to themselves and to protect each other. They'd helped her when she'd first arrived. Helped her and welcomed her, no questions asked.

"What should we do?" Sophia asked, glancing around.

If the Ranger was telling the truth, then she had to be on watch. She should have asked him the name of the man he'd come looking for before she'd let Bettye knock him out.

But it can't be him. He's...he can't hurt me again, ever.

"Let's drag him inside your cabin," Bettye

suggested in a meek voice. She sounded as if they'd just discovered a kitten.

"Why?" Sophia didn't like that idea. She'd stared into this man's golden-colored eyes and… well…there was something about him. Something that made her think of a big tiger about to pounce, and that could be even more dangerous than running from your crazy ex-husband.

"We gotta hide him until he wakes up," Bettye said. "We need to convince him that we meant him no harm. After all, we're two innocent, helpless women living in a wild and wondrous world."

Sophia would have laughed if the situation hadn't been so serious. But with a shotgun and a frying pan, they didn't look all that innocent or helpless. "I tried to shoot him and you knocked him out. How do we explain that?"

Bettye stared down at him, then kicked one of his snow-encrusted boots with her foot. "I got a plan. Let's get him inside where it's warm and I'll explain."

ADAN HEARD A band beating a marching tune somewhere close to his ear. Over and over the thump, thump struck at his consciousness until he could feel the hit of a big bass drum inside his brain. He really wanted it to stop. Now.

He woke up with a killer headache and two women staring down at him. One of them was old and scrawny and full of what looked like a daring glare.

The other one was young and pretty and full of what looked like apprehension.

And then he remembered.

He tried to speak and realized his mouth had been taped shut. He tried to sit up and realized his hands were tied with rope to the old iron bedposts just above a sagging mattress.

Had he been dropped into a century gone by? That movie *The Beguiled* with Clint Eastwood came to mind. That thought did not bode well for Adan. He'd left Austin in a hurry to get this man and get home to his five-year-old daughter by Christmas Eve. Adan didn't intend to break the promise he'd made to Gaylen.

The women kept staring at him, their hands held down in a prim manner that belied the assault they'd landed on him. Okay, so this was a first. Tricked and hog-tied and now at the mercy of two obviously determined women.

This was why he didn't go on blind dates.

Adan closed his eyes and willed the pounding pain and this bad dream to go away. Neither did. So he opened his eyes again and grunted. Crescent Mountain had not been kind to him.

He'd left Austin during a massive winter storm that covered the whole state of Texas, and now he'd managed to get stuck on this mountain in the middle of a brutal chill. The icy roads and a raging snowstorm full of daring, crazy drivers had stalled him for hours. He'd slipped and slid his pickup right through that and taken way more time than he'd planned, but he'd at least found the last road up the mountain before nightfall.

Only to take a mean slide toward the left and into a towering rock face that dented and banged his truck, and then he got stuck in a snowdrift. So he'd walked uphill the rest of the way and spotted a cabin that appeared to be empty. He'd come up here to see if he could get help or at least get in out of the cold until he could continue to look for the fugitive he'd been tracking. Maybe he should have asked a few more questions in the process.

Now he'd been attacked and accosted by two fierce women.

It was about time for him to retire.

He tried to speak. Tried to sit up. Gave up and grunted again, his gaze passing between the two crazy women before he pinned his eyes on the young, pretty one.

SOPHIA WATCHED HIM, her heart doing that warning clang as her pulsed picked up tempo. "I'm gonna take off the tape," she said. "But first, we need you to understand something." She got closer. "You have to remain quiet and calm. Nod if you can do that."

He nodded, glared, struggled with his ties.

Bettye grinned, the shotgun in her capable hands.

"We didn't mean to hurt you," Sophia said, hoping he'd believe her. "We live close by and we watch out for each other. We have a few other neighbors but we're not used to strangers showing up. Usually we just get long-lost relatives or a few lost tourists, but not during the worst winter storm of the season. Do you understand?"

"You shook us up," Bettye said, bobbing her head. "She was over visiting me and saw you snooping around her cabin."

He grunted and gave Sophia a stare down.

Ignoring those tiger eyes, she continued. "Good. So if I take off the tape and untie your hands, you aren't going to haul us in or report us for assault with a deadly weapon or an attempt to shoot an officer of the law, are you?"

Bettye patted the shotgun, still grinning.

He grunted and shook his head, his golden-green eyes sending a different message from the docile grunt. He was probably bluffing, but she couldn't keep the man tied up inside her cabin. Her very small cabin.

Sophia looked at Bettye. Bettye nodded and leaned over the man. "Just for good measure, I'll shoot you if you try anything."

"Do you understand that?" Sophia asked, hoping they had properly handled this situation.

"We need you to understand we're just trying to protect ourselves."

She didn't intend to let Bettye shoot the Ranger, but she wanted him to know this was serious. "Okay?"

He nodded, tugged at his restraints.

Sophia placed one hand on his face and felt the brittle caress of his five-o'clock shadow. Her fingertips tingled with an awareness that skidded right up her arm. In an attempt to ignore the unusual, long-dormant feeling, she smiled and gave him a reassuring glance. "This might hurt a bit."

Then she pulled the duct tape off his mouth.

ADAN GRITTED HIS teeth but to save face, he refused to scream. As soon as the tape was off, he let out a string of colorful words.

"No need for profanity," the old woman said, her smile as serene as a nun's.

Adan glanced from her to the woman now untying the ropes from around his wrists. "Don't you think y'all took this just a little too far? I mean, giving me a possible concussion, then taping my mouth shut and tying me up. What is wrong with you people?"

"We don't trust nobody," the old woman replied, still smiling.

He could hear that theme song, the one where the mountain people murdered the newcomer and buried him in an old well. His weapon had been removed and his cell phone had been confiscated. He hadn't reported in all day, so hopefully someone would realize he'd gone missing. Or there was the other possibility—because he was known for going off on his own to do his job and he always turned back up eventually, he might not even be missed until it was too late.

Nor found until the spring thaw. He'd either be frozen solid under a snowdrift or chewed into pieces by some hungry mountain varmint. Not exactly a noble death.

Too late to worry about that now. He'd have to find a way around these two overly zealous defenders of the universe so he could get back to finding his fugitive. Obviously, if the criminal Adan was searching for had been here, they'd helped him escape while Adan was out cold. Or maybe thrown him into an old well, too. He couldn't be sure, though. They didn't seem all that cagey now. More like worried that he'd haul them in.

"I'm sorry," the pretty one said as she stepped back to look at him. "About the…shotgun and about Bettye hitting you with her cast-iron skillet. She thought you were an intruder, so she was just trying to protect me."

"We're tight, me and Sophia," the older one replied, her thumb hooking toward the pretty one, her eyes squinting inside the crow's-feet stretching out around her face.

The older lady wore so many layers, it was hard to tell where the coats and scarves ended and her actual skin began. Her gray-streaked braid of hair was woven around her head to match the old gray scarf woven around her neck.

Adan let out another grunt. "You think? Tight like Thelma and Louise. Do you always greet strangers with a gun and a skillet?"

"Only the tall, good-looking ones," the lady called Bettye said on a chuckle. "Just our way of saying welcome to the neighborhood."

Adan wondered again if he'd stumbled into an alternative world. But this was Ozark country in Arkansas. Anything could happen. "Well, thanks for the welcome. Don't I get cookies and coffee, too?"

"Yes," the one called Sophia replied. She put her hand on his arm. "Can you sit up?"

"I'm fine," he replied, testy because two spry women had gotten the best of him. "I can sit up and I can stand up." He tried to do both and saw double.

And he really didn't need two of either of them.

"Lie back down," Sophia said. "Rest and I'll make some dinner. Bettye, you will stay and have dinner with us, right?"

Adan saw something quiet and secretive pass between the women. Were they still aiding and abetting a fugitive?

"Wouldn't miss it for the world," Bettye replied. "I'll keep our guest company while you get dinner going." Then she turned to Adan and hooted with laughter. "We've had ourselves a very exciting night, don't you think, Mr. Texas Ranger?"

Adan glared at her and willed his eyes to quit showing him two of her. "I couldn't agree more."

But once his head quit spinning, he'd be up and out of this bed and then he'd decide what to do with these two enchanting and entertaining petty criminals.

Thinking he could persuade the older one, he said, "I'm just here trying to do my job. And I did try to show you my credentials."

Bettye gave him a sharp glare. "Just remember, you were the one trespassing."

CHAPTER TWO

"DINNER'S READY. DO YOU feel better now?"

Adan glanced up at Sophia and studied her for signs of betrayal and deceit. But the woman only appeared concerned and certainly worried. She was making nice now that he'd lived.

"I feel fine," he said, his mood anything but fine and dandy. He was dirty, hungry and frustrated. At this rate, he wouldn't make it back to Austin in time for New Year's Eve with his parents and his daughter, Gaylen, let alone Christmas Eve.

How many times had he let that girl down? Being a single dad was hard on a normal day. Being a Texas Ranger didn't provide for many normal days.

And being accosted by these two just proved that point.

He stood and made it out into the hallway then surveyed the tidy little mountain cabin. It was square and long, with a kitchen-dining area across from a small living room in the front and what looked like a bath between two bedrooms on the back. The furnishings were sturdy and colorful. Old furniture painted in bright primary colors—flowers and leaves, stars and the moon—and a Christmas tree with sparkling little odds and ends of all colors and shapes decorating it. Two entryways, one out the front toward the woodsy view of the Ozarks and the other probably backed up to a bluff overlooking one of the many flowing streams in the foothills that moved down from the mountain peak.

A man could sure hide out in those snow-capped hills. But a man could also freeze to death out there tonight, too.

"Nice place," he finally said. He ambled toward the round oak table with the mosaic tile top, his pulse tapping at the sore spot on the back of his head. "You live here alone?"

"Who wants to know?" the older woman standing in the kitchen asked, her eyes going into double question marks.

Adan gave Sophia another direct glance. "I'm one of the good guys, so tell her to let up on being so ornery and suspicious. Or I will reconsider how I'm gonna handle being attacked and held hostage."

"We are not holding you hostage," Sophia said, motioning to him to sit down. She gave her partner in crime a warning glare. "We overreacted, but we have to be careful. This mountain is off the beaten path, and it's isolated."

"And don't I know that." He sat down and sniffed the beef-and-vegetable soup cooling in a chipped blue bowl. "How 'bout we start over while we eat." He waited for the ladies to sit down.

Bettye giggled and pushed at her gray hair and then pointed a finger toward Adan. "A gentleman."

She sat down with a prim and proper air. Sophia placed biscuits on the table and found her seat. Adan followed suit, his stomach growling in joy. It had been a long day and he'd skipped a meal or two.

He grinned, then grimaced because it hurt to grin. "I'm Adan Harrison. I live in Austin and I'm a Texas Ranger."

"They grow them Rangers everywhere down in Texas, don't they?" Bettye asked, her expression full of wrinkles and curiosity. She grabbed a flaky biscuit then shoved the straw basket toward Adan. "Tough lot, all of you."

"We *are* a proud lot," Adan admitted. How strange to be sitting here having dinner with the two women who'd tried to do him in. But he wasn't so dumb that he couldn't twist things around on them. "And we pride ourselves on getting the job done. So I'll make a deal with you two lovely ladies. I won't press charges against either of you. But you need to do something in return for me."

"And what's that?" Sophia asked, her blue eyes widening as she set the biscuit basket next to her plate. She put down her spoon and waited as if she were afraid to take her next breath. Guilty? Or scared? Or both?

"You need to tell me if you were harboring a wanted felon. And if you were and you let him escape, you need to come clean. Or I won't be able to help you later."

SOPHIA'S APPETITE WENT as cold as a lone snowflake. "I don't know what you're talking about."

Did he think she'd hide a criminal here? Did he know something about her already? What if he'd come here looking for her? He couldn't possibly know what had brought her to this mountain over four years ago. Or what she'd done after she'd arrived here.

"Me neither," Bettye said. "I don't know anything about anybody."

She passed the biscuits again, her actions twitchy and nervous. Sophia gave her friend another warning stare.

Bettye took the hint and asked the Ranger, "Want some homemade mayhaw jelly with that biscuit?"

"I'm good, thanks." Adan kept his eyes on Sophia, making it hard for her to breathe, let alone eat. "So I know your name—or at least your first name—Sophia. Want to give me your whole name?"

"Not particularly," she replied, her bravado a false front. "I don't like strangers."

"Again, I get that," he said in that wry Texas tone that seemed to be his way of getting people to talk. "I can find out, you know. Run your plates—"

"She ain't got a car," Bettye said. Then she put her hand over her mouth. Grabbing her spoon, she took a big gulp of soup. "Mmm. So good."

Adan gave Sophia another too-close stare. "Did you let him take your vehicle?"

Sophia was caught in a vise. She couldn't tell this man her worst fears because if she did, she'd have to tell him the rest of the story and she wasn't ready for that. Not even Bettye knew the whole story. No one ever would.

"I don't know what you're implying—"

"I'm not implying anything. I'm stating the facts," he said, his tone getting dangerously low and growling. "If you two let a known felon escape with your vehicle, then that makes you both accessories. Do you want to take the fall for a man who'd as soon kill you than look at you?"

"I don't want to take the fall for a man like that," Bettye said, her eyes glued to Sophia in shock. "I don't know anything about a felon who's *that* dangerous."

Sophia wanted to shout to her friend to stop

talking but Bettye wasn't the most tactful person on earth. Now seventy, Bettye had been through her own horror story, and past events had left her a little dazed and confused.

The Ranger zoomed in on Bettye's declaration. "Well, do you know *any* criminals? Maybe one who pretended to be the victim and talked y'all into harboring him for a while?"

Bettye glanced over at Sophia, and Adan's sharp gaze moved between them like a roaming flashlight. "I don't think I know anybody like that, but—"

"We haven't been hiding anyone in this cabin," Sophia interjected, trying to salvage the situation. She could not be hauled off this mountain. This was the one place she felt safe and secure. Or at least she had until he'd shown up.

She stared him down, but it was nearly impossible to intimidate a man who was six feet tall and solid muscle. A man she and Bettye had huffed and puffed and dragged up onto her porch and inside her house.

He didn't break the staring match but his eyes, so golden brown and burning, seemed to soften and shift. "Look, I understand you were scared when I got here, but I can help you. If you're in trouble, tell me the truth and I'll do what I can."

She jumped up and put her forgotten soup in the sink. "I'm fine. Or at least I was until you arrived here. How'd you even get up the mountain anyway, and why were you on foot?"

"I'm on foot," he said on a slow, let-me-explain-so-you'll-understand note, "because my truck slid on some black ice and rammed into a snowdrift and got stuck and I wanted to find either some help to get it out or a shelter to provide me with some warmth until morning."

"That does make a lot of sense," Bettye said in a pragmatic tone. "I mean, it ain't a fit night out there for anybody."

"Of course it makes sense," he said, his voice rising with each word. "You have my badge and my gun, so why don't you just tell me the truth?"

"The truth? You want the truth?" Sophia took in a breath and willed her next lie to sparkle into sounding real. "The truth is that I was visiting my friend here in her cabin. We were making Christmas cookies and didn't realize how bad the weather had turned. I was on my way home and looking forward to getting all settled in with my soup and a good book and I heard a rustling on my porch. So I got my shotgun and I came around the back way to see who was out there."

"Were you expecting someone else?"

"No." Frustration coursed through her like a mountain spring. "I was expecting some peace and quiet and a nice long sleep while the storm passed outside."

"She likes her private time," Bettye explained. "Took me a while to understand that."

"I think she does at that," Adan said. Then he shoved a spoonful of soup into his mouth and chewed the beef, his eyes still on Sophia. "But tonight, she won't get any, because I can't leave here in that storm. And I won't leave y'all, since this man could show up here or return back here. If that happens, y'all will have more than me to worry about."

Sophia's pulse skidded and slid with each snowflake that fell outside her door. What if he did get snowed in and she had to deal with him for a week or so? She'd go mad. The man stared through her with those captivating eyes and made her think he could see all of her secrets. She'd get cabin fever and spill her worst sins to him. Then she might truly go to jail.

ADAN WAITED, GIVING them every opportunity to chime right in. But neither said a word. Sophia busied herself with offering more soup, but something about her demeanor worried him.

"Have you seen any strangers around here recently?"

"Just you, Mr. RangerMan," Bettye blurted out.

His gut told him that one wasn't lying about this, but they both had secrets about something. He could give them a description of the criminal to see how they'd react but he didn't want to give away too much too soon. If they'd been involved with Joe Pritchard, they'd let something slip sooner or later.

"Y'all are sure making this harder than it needs to be."

Bettye snorted a retort. "I thought Rangers could handle just about any situation."

"I can," he said, his frustration mounting with each breath. He watched Sophia for signs of stress or any sign that she might be willing to talk to him. "I would. I'm not worried about the storm. I'm worried about what y'all might be trying to hide."

"We ain't got nothing to hide," Bettye replied. "Not from you, that is."

He leaned his elbows against the table and gave Sophia a measured look. "Then who are you hiding *from*?"

Sophia's head snapped up. "We're living here, trying to mind our own business. And that's the truth."

She got up and started clearing the dishes. Adan took that as a sign dinner—and the conversation—was over.

Adan had never had anything like this happen before. He was going to have to walk a line on this one. He couldn't deal with having these two hauled in because the man he'd tracked to Crescent Mountain was still out there on the loose. And while they'd tried to do bodily injury to Adan, he figured it was more out of fear than any criminal intent.

Still, he'd have to make it a point to be on his best behavior and ever watchful while he was around them. They were hiding something, all right, only he couldn't be sure they'd been involved with hiding the man he'd come looking for.

But he couldn't leave two slightly innocent women alone if that man was out there somewhere. So he stood in front of the fire and listened to the sounds of feminine chatter and a few cryptic whispers coming from the kitchen across the room. They had never actually answered his question. After snapping that curt retort, Sophia had busied herself with the dishes. Bettye had offered him homemade fudge and coffee. The rich chocolate was now stuck in his gut and the coffee had him too warm.

Sophia finally approached him. "Bettye needs to go home, but I'm not sure she'll be able to find the path. I thought I'd walk with her."

She left things hanging, so he jumped right in. "I'll walk with both of you and I'll check her cabin."

"And what do you plan to do after that?"

He thought he saw a plea there in her interesting dark water-blue eyes. She pushed at her rich auburn curls and stared up at him, waiting again.

"I plan to stay close by until this storm is over. I'll figure out the rest in the morning."

"You mean you want to stay here?"

"Do you have any other suggestions?"

She glanced at the fire, looked out the window, stared over at Bettye waiting by the back door. Then she turned back to him. "No, I don't have any other ideas. Unless you want to stay at Bettye's place."

He looked at her then turned to do a quick glance at her friend. "To be honest, I'd be afraid to fall asleep with her in the next room. My head is still throbbing from that darn frying pan."

The older woman let out a whooping laugh. "My aim is still good."

Adan rubbed the back of his sore head. "I agree with that, at least."

He was rewarded with a pretty smile from Sophia, followed by a firm reminder. "I'm the one with the shotgun, though, remember?"

"I don't think I'll ever forget," he said, mirroring her grin in hopes of gaining her trust. "But I doubt I'll sleep no matter where I stay."

"You can sleep on the sofa," she finally said. "I have a spare room, but it's full of my art supplies."

He nodded on that, saving the information to mull over later. "I won't be a bother, I promise."

"I know," she said with a smile. "I always sleep with my shotgun right by the bed."

He let out a chuckle and shook his head. "I've never met anyone like you two."

Sophia didn't give anything away with her Mona Lisa smile. "Let me get my coat and hat. Bettye lives right around the curve so it's not a long walk, but I don't want her to fall in the snow. It's brutal out there tonight."

He checked the windows, wondering what was hiding in those woods. "We'll get her home. Think she'll be safe?"

"She's been living on this mountain alone since her husband died about fifteen years ago. She can take care of herself, but...if there is someone out there lurking around, I'll be worried about her."

His mind raced ahead as he did another visual. It was near impossible to see beyond the banks of thick white snow. "Should she stay with you, too?"

"She won't. Bettye likes her privacy, same as me. Most of the people who live up here keep to themselves unless we plan to have a dinner or get-together. But Bettye has been a good friend to me."

"I'll keep watch between the two of you," he said on a decisive note. And in the meantime, he'd try to decipher who was telling the truth and who wasn't.

"You two gonna stand by that fire all night or are you gonna walk a feeble old woman home?"

"Coming," Sophia called.

He watched as she wrapped her bright blue scarf around her neck and tucked it into her coat. "Oh, she also has a dog that usually tags along with her. She won't let him out too long in this weather, so he didn't come over here with her tonight."

"He mighta bit you," Bettye added. "Only he can't see and he can't really hear good. A lot like me, I reckon."

"But he protects you," Sophia said on an empathetic breath.

Bettye nodded. "Bandit's his name. He can still bark warnings."

"Good." Adan took that comment as a personal warning to him. Or maybe to anyone in hiding around here.

He mulled it over and then put on his own coat and opened the door. The storm was full-blown now. Fat white flakes danced around under the porch light like bits of lost lace. The soft sound of snow hitting the woods didn't bring him any peace. It was a bitter, unforgiving night.

And it didn't help that a man who'd long ago given up on any decency might be somewhere out in those woods. If he was, he probably wouldn't survive for long. And like a dangerous animal, he'd turn on anyone who encountered him or tried to stop him.

They all stood on the porch while Bettye got her bearings.

"I shoulda marked the way," she said, squinting into the night, her flashlight beam hitting dark tree trunks and thick hedges. "I guess we'll find our way if we hold on to each other. That's what my Walter used to say to me. Too bad it didn't work out for us."

"We'll make sure we get you home," Sophia replied. She leaned close to Adan. "She says that no matter the weather."

Adan took Bettye's flashlight, pain throbbing in his temples. "Let me lead and y'all hold to each other and follow." He waited for them to huddle behind and then turned to search them with the light. "Just shout the directions to me as we go."

"What are you doing?" Sophia asked with a frown.

"Looking for frying pans and shotguns," he replied.

Bettye let out a hoot of laughter. "It's gonna be a good Christmas this year. I just know it."

CHAPTER THREE

SOPHIA HUGGED BETTYE and petted her big hound dog. "Bandit, take good care of Bettye for me, okay?"

The chocolate-colored hunting dog whimpered a reply and then pushed his nose against Bettye's worn overcoat.

Bettye nodded and kissed Sophia on the cheek. "You'll be all right, sugar pie." She sent Adan a stern glance. "I don't know a thing about a criminal on the loose around here, Mr. Ranger-Man. But this girl means the world to me and she's been a friend to me since she moved up here a few years ago. Be kind to her."

"We'd better get back inside," Sophia said before Adan could form a reply.

Bettye meant well, but she could take care of herself. This man showing up had confused and surprised Sophia even though she should have known someone would find her sooner or later.

"I'll check on you in the morning," she told Bettye.

The older woman stood silent and waved, a

knowing smile beaming on her withered face. "I'll be right here, honey."

Adan said good-night to Bettye, then followed Sophia, his hand on her elbow making her too aware of the fact that he would be in her tiny cabin all night. And making her all too aware that his presence did make her feel safe in spite of her fears.

She didn't need him or anyone else taking care of her, though. She'd been on her own for so long she wouldn't know what being taken care of might mean...and she wasn't even sure she deserved anyone's attention or concern. She turned and hurried off the porch before Bettye could add any more information.

"Keep your porch light on," Adan called to Bettye. "Just in case."

Bettye chuckled and nodded. "I'll do that, Mr. Ranger-Man."

Then she shut the door and turned off the light.

As they shuffled through the ankle-deep snow, he turned to Sophia. "So who else lives on this mountain besides two stubborn women?"

Sophia didn't want to trust this man, but even though he hadn't charged in on a white horse, she could tell he was one of the good guys. She wished she could ask him who he was looking for, but if she showed too much interest he'd see the truth in her eyes. But she could be honest with him about Crescent Mountain.

"This spot was named by a trapper who traveled the summit of the hills and decided he'd walked in a curve that made him think of a crescent moon. That somehow stuck and so this curved hillside became Crescent Mountain."

Adan had studied several maps of the area. "It circles west of the lower White River. I can see how it got that name."

"Yes, and it also has a reputation for being a kind of retreat since it's so near a big national forest. Few people know about our little community. We're pretty self-sufficient. We take turns going down the mountain to town for supplies and groceries and if someone is in need, we either take care of them or get them help at the regional medical center about forty miles from here."

Adan didn't respond. Maybe he thought she was issuing him a warning. Good. He needed to back off and leave her alone. She'd only give him as much information as she thought he needed.

They followed the beam of his flashlight and stayed on the path, retracing their earlier footsteps. When they reached Sophia's yard, he moved the light over the path and out into the nearby woods. The eerie yellow glow shined brightly against the stark ghostly white curling around the trees, making Sophia feel as if shrouded fingers were reaching for her.

Sophia shuddered, the cold wet wind piercing her skin. How could anyone survive out here tonight? The temperatures had dipped well below freezing.

"We don't normally get snow this heavy," she said, glad to have a warm place to stay. "A rare winter storm right here before Christmas."

She was about to go inside when she thought she saw a moving shadow just past Adan's beaming light. He must have seen it, too. He stopped, held up the light again. Then he walked toward the encroaching woods and held the light up and out.

Nothing but trees and snow. The blanketed woods held no sounds except that of the occasional dripping of snow off drooping branches.

Sophia didn't want to think about who might be out in those dark woods. She'd escaped death once and this isolated mountain community had taken her in, no questions asked. The Crescent, as the locals called the mountain, was known for accepting quirky characters who wanted to get away from the world. She wasn't all that quirky, but she did want to stay hidden. She had no other choice.

Now a mountain of a man had come pushing into her quiet, safe world. And he was a man of the law. Which could only mean trouble was sure to follow. If Adan Harrison found out the real story about her, he'd haul her off in hand-cuffs without another word.

"What did you see out there?" she asked, try-ing to sound brave. But her teeth chattered from the cold. And from that deep fear she'd tried to hide for so long.

"I don't know. Probably nothing." Adan stomped the snow and mud off his boots. "Just the wind pushing at a tree."

Sophia cast one last look out into the darkness. The hills and valleys beyond the level lane glis-tened in an eerie shimmer against the dark night. The woods were hushed and still and the snow fell in soft lacy threads that covered the ground like an icy white blanket.

How could anything evil be in such a beauti-ful setting?

"Let's get inside," Adan said, his hand on her arm.

Sophia normally didn't allow strangers to touch her, but she didn't push his hand away. They'd reached a tentative unspoken truce and she intended to keep it that way until this storm was over and she could decide what to do with this cowboy who'd invaded her space.

They shook off the snow then went inside to take off their coats and scarves. Sophia took Ad-an's big still-warm coat and hung it on a peg by the door, her actions making her think of the kind of life she might not ever have. A life that included a husband and a family. A real Christmas.

"Want some more coffee?" she asked, tongue-tied now that she was alone with Adan Harrison.

"Yes."

He did a quick visual of her cabin, his gaze sweeping and serious. Whoever he was after, he seemed intent on getting the job done. And intent on finding out her secrets, too.

"Can you talk about this man, the one you're tracking?" she asked after she brought over two cups of fresh coffee.

They settled by the fire, him on the sofa and Sophia in her favorite old leather chair between the Christmas tree and the fireplace.

"That depends," he responded. "Can you tell me if you've seen anyone suspicious around here?"

She shook her head, her fears about her past at bay now that things had quieted down. "Like Bettye said earlier, you're the first stranger we've had all winter. We usually get lost hikers or vacationers thinking they can rent a cabin for the night, but most of us live here year-round except for one or two couples. The Burtons—one of those couples—are here now, at least through Christmas."

"How many people?" he asked, his expression serious now.

"Bettye and me," she said. "Jacob Miller—he's

got a bad crush on Bettye and she doesn't even realize it. David and Karen Harper. Mostly retired people or...people who're single. It's a mixed bag. I'm an artist and Bettye is a collector—mostly junk, as you saw if you looked in her cabin— and Jacob builds stuff and helps us keep up the cabins. The Harpers fish and go for long walks, and the Burtons—Maggie and Arnie—they go on more rigorous hikes all over the mountain. We have a few more who rent part of the year, but they usually only show up in the summer. We come together for meals and picnics and holidays and we leave each other alone other times."

"No odd person lurking about?"

Sophia got that uneasy feeling in her gut again, a stabbing, sick feeling. "No. We'd notice that, trust me. We're all accounted for and we watch out for each other."

Something snapped outside.

"The tree limbs are starting to crash," she said, hoping that was all they'd heard. Her stomach clenched in a jittery snap of its own.

When another snap echoed against the porch, Adan got up. "Limbs, maybe, but I'd better check." He set his coffee cup down and put a finger to his lips. "Don't move."

Sophia's heart hit her chest and caught against her ribs. Was someone out there? She didn't want to have a panic attack, but between this rugged Ranger and whomever he'd been tracking, she couldn't help but fear the worst. And if her fears overtook her, she'd get that racing heart feeling and lose her breath. Taking a deep, calming gulp of air, Sophia willed herself to go into a silent strength.

And then another sound outside. A tap at the back door, maybe?

Adan's hiss hit the air. "Where did you put my gun?"

She rushed into her bedroom and came out with his big, heavy handgun. "And here's your badge, too."

Taking both, he checked the gun then stashed his badge in his pocket. Grabbing his coat, he glanced back at her. "Stay here," he said. "I'm going out to check."

Sophia's emotions ran the gamut between scared and anxious to sad and full of regret. She'd only known Adan Harrison for about three hours, and in that time, she'd held a gun on him, watched her friend knock him out and they'd tied him up and put tape over his mouth. Now, she was so glad he'd come to Crescent Mountain. The man exuded confidence and power and made her feel secure. But those traits didn't hide the one glaring thing Adan's presence had brought out in her—the solid fear she'd managed to keep at bay by sheer force and willpower.

For the first time in years, she didn't feel safe here.

ADAN SLID ALONG the rough plank walls of the square brown cabin. He'd checked around the big front porch and found nothing. But here on the side of the house, he hit the ground with a penlight and saw fresh footprints by the back window of one of the bedrooms.

Someone snooping, or someone leaving through a window. He checked the windowsill but it didn't look as if the window had been opened. Fresh snow was encrusted over the bottom of the glass and the thick wood casings. He did see a couple of imprints. Looked as though someone had placed a hand against the outside sill. Then he heard a crunching sound out in the woods.

Adan cut his light and turned to stare into the swaying trees. Something was definitely out there. Or someone. Had ol' Joe seen his truck down on the road and followed the path Adan had taken to get up to the cabin?

Or had the man he'd come to find been here all along? He waited in the shadows, his breath hitching in the cold, his hands freezing against the steel of his gun. A shuffling and rustling in the distant woods had him on the move again. He reached the edge of the cabin's garden and stood silent behind a giant oak tree.

More thrashing about and then the woods went quiet. Deciding to circle back around, he trotted from tree to tree, hiding behind snowdrifts and limbs heavy with ice and snow until he thought he'd cleared the area in the woods where he'd heard the noise. But the heavy snow and the midnight darkness kept him from finding anything. Following his own footsteps, he could imagine how easy it would be to get lost out here at night. Maybe whoever'd been snooping around had gotten confused and crashed into a ravine. Or they'd purposely caused a distraction to lure him away from the cabin.

When he heard a scream, he started running through the knee-deep snow, falling and getting up again until he hit the porch and rushed inside the cabin.

Sophia stood there staring at a piece of paper, her face as pale as the night. Adan hurried to take the paper from her. "Where did you find this?"

She pointed to the back door. "Inside the screen. I heard someone and I thought it was you." She shuddered, took in a breath. "When I opened the door I found this."

Adan stared at the artist's rendering of the man he was chasing. "Do you know this man, Sophia?"

She sank down on a dining chair, shock evident in her eyes. Holding her chest, she gave him a frightened stare. "I… I don't know. I mean, I just got scared when I saw that someone had left that there." She gulped in air and shot a worried glance at the door.

Adan's gut told him she was lying. This woman who'd been so strong and sure was now shaking and uncertain. Fear colored her skin white. Her hands were cold, her actions jittery and unsure. She kept staring at the mug shot in the picture with a shocked expression on her face.

"You know this man, don't you?" Adan asked again. "Sophia, did you help this man escape earlier tonight?"

She hurtled out of the chair and crossed her arms as if to stop the shaking. "Why do you keep asking me that?"

He grabbed her, his hands rubbing her arms over her heavy sweater. She stared up at him but she couldn't seem to speak.

Finally, she asked, "The man you're tracking? You said he's a wanted felon. What did he do?"

Adan decided it was time to come clean. Someone had left that poster on this woman's door on purpose. That same person had obviously broken into his truck and found the flyer. If Joe Pritchard was here, the battle had just begun, but Adan had to take on that battle.

"He robbed a gas station near the Texas border and killed the cashier. He's been robbing people left and right all the way from Austin to the Arkansas border and some locals had him cornered, but he escaped. Based on maps we found in a vehicle he stole and abandoned, we believe he was headed here. He's got a long rap sheet that stretches over years, but this time he's committed murder and I need to find him."

He held her there and looked into her eyes. "If you know him, if you've aided him in any way, you need to tell me now. Before he hurts someone else."

She gulped a sob, held a hand to her mouth. "He killed a store clerk?"

"Yes, a woman. A single mother with two children."

She let out another sob then pulled away from Adan. "I need to check on Bettye."

Adan watched her, his instincts to protect her too strong to ignore. "We'll check on Bettye. But you have to tell me what's going on with you. Right now, Sophia."

When she kept moving toward her bedroom, he grabbed her and turned her around. And that's when he saw the sheer terror in her eyes.

Without thinking, Adan gently tugged her into his arms. "It's okay. It's all right. I'm not going to hurt you. No one is going to hurt you."

She felt small and stiff, like a frozen doll. But he held tight and kept reassuring her while his mind raced with the possibility that there was a killer out in those dark, snow-covered woods. He'd protect this woman because that was part of his job. But from the terrified expression on her face and the way he wanted to wrap her in a cloak of warmth, Adan decided he was in this for the long haul. He shouldn't feel this way about a woman he'd only known for a few hours.

And he had to ask again. "Sophia, did you recognize this man?"

She shook her head, but the look in her eyes told Adan differently.

Disappointment coursed through Adan. Had she helped this man escape? But if she had, why would he risk coming back to stick that poster in her door? Maybe as a warning or a threat? Or maybe to taunt Adan? To show him that he'd managed to let yet another criminal get away?

"Have you seen anyone matching this description?" he asked, his hands still on her shoulders.

"I'm not sure," she said, a plea in the words. "I don't know him and I didn't help him, Adan. I've…never seen that man on Crescent Mountain."

She turned and walked to the table and stared down at the grizzly face on the white paper. "I… I don't know him and I don't know why someone would leave this on my door."

Adan put his hands on his hips and watched as she paced from window to window. For someone who repeatedly said she didn't know this man, Sophia sure seemed nervous and agitated. She'd just said she'd never seen the man in the picture here on the mountain. But had she seen him or known him before?

She was lying through her pretty white teeth.

And Adan wasn't leaving here until he found out the truth.

CHAPTER FOUR

ADAN STEPPED BACK and took a breath, his eyes watching Sophia with a big-cat precision. "Sit down."

Sophia did as he told her, too weak and afraid to do anything else. No gun could protect her from the trail of lies she'd had to tell. But she'd stall as long as she could.

She had to protect Bettye and the others. She'd brought this trouble on all of them when she'd shown up on the mountain late one night, scared and in shock. The cluster of people who'd become her neighbors had helped her without asking too many questions, and she didn't want to pull them into any kind of trouble with the law.

What if it's him? Sophia's stomach roiled each time she glanced at that sketch. *What if you don't have a choice?*

Adan went to the stove and turned up the heat on the kettle, then searched through the cabinets until he'd found the tea bags.

She watched him, amazed. "How did you know...?"

His chuckle was quiet and sure. "My mama always makes hot tea when she's upset."

Sophia latched onto that tidbit, a wistfulness filling her soul. She ached for a family of her own but for now, Bettye and her other neighbors would have to do. "Your mama and you—are you close?"

He turned and gave her a quick glance. "Yep. I'm close to both my parents. They live in Austin, not far from my house. They help me take care of my daughter, Gaylen."

So he was married. Good. Sophia could put yet another wall between them. And she could let go of that sizzle of attraction that seemed to spark her back to life each time he touched her.

"Where's your wife?" She'd asked it before she could think it through. "I mean, won't she be wondering where you are?"

He didn't turn around, but his hand went still on the teakettle. "She's gone."

So much for trying to focus on the positive. So did that mean he was still married and his wife had left? Or did that mean his wife was dead? Sophia refused to ask.

"She left when Gaylen was eight months old," he finally said. "I'm a divorced single father."

Sophia's heart went out to him and his little girl, but she didn't want to make him uncomfortable by saying that. "So you're a single father who chases criminals in the snow."

"Yep." He opened a tea bag and dropped it into a big floral mug. "And I need to be done with this and home by Christmas Eve."

Sophia hoped that would happen. "You think you'll find him around here?"

"I think so. He's here for a reason, but he'd have to hunker down tonight or risk freezing to death."

She decided to feel Adan out and get a few details in the process. "I wonder why he decided to come to Crescent Mountain."

Adan left that statement out there floating on the air between them along with the scent of chamomile tea. Finally he said, "I wonder that, too." He brought her the tea, his gaze sweeping over her face. "It sure would make my job easier if you'd just tell me the truth."

Sophia didn't know what to say to that. She wanted to shout that yes, she knew who Joe Pritchard was but...she thought he was dead. She thought he would never hurt her again. So how could that possibly be him out there?

But she couldn't find her voice. She couldn't speak his name. So she sat there and watched Adan while he watched her drink the herbal tea and she hoped against hope that Joe wasn't on this mountain.

But Adan didn't pressure her anymore. He pulled out his cell phone and tried to make a call. "No bars," he finally said, frowning down at his phone. "Guess the storm is messing with the reception."

"We never have good reception up here," Sophia told him. "It comes and goes even on good days. If we have important calls to make, we go down into town and sit on a bench or do our business in the Crescent Diner. They have free Wi-Fi there."

"I see." He tapped his phone and put it away. "I wanted to check in with my parents and tell Gaylen good-night."

He sat for a moment, his gaze on his phone. Sophia chanced a glance when he put it on the table and saw a picture of a pretty blond-headed little girl. His daughter?

Before she could ask, Adan picked the phone back up and started tapping away.

"Notes to myself," he said by way of an explanation. "So I won't forget the chronological order of things."

Sophia couldn't believe her world had shifted within the space of an hour. The Christmas decorations Bettye had helped her make and put on the tree now held a garish shimmer that only reminded her of other Christmases she'd rather not remember. Days and nights that had involved overly decorated rooms and expensive catered dinners. And a facade that crumbled like dry bricks.

Sophia didn't miss that kind of fake holiday.

Nor did she miss the disconnected misery of growing up moving from pillar to post and sometimes living with strangers.

She'd looked forward to a quiet Christmas on the mountain with real people who cared about her. She'd planned on baking all kinds of goodies for her friends over the next week or so before they all celebrated with a Christmas Eve get-together.

But all of that had changed. Now, she had one very good-looking, very serious man questioning and doubting her and one very dangerous, very angry man out there possibly searching for her. Tonight they'd both found her. Would there be a battle between them? She got the impression that Adan Harrison wouldn't give up until he had Joe Pritchard in custody. But would he give up on questioning her? No doubt on that one, either.

She sank down on an old side chair and grabbed a turquoise-colored chenille throw and held it tight to her chest. She didn't realize she was shivering until Adan bent in front of her and lifted the blanket from her. With slow, deliberate gestures, he carefully took the throw and tucked it over her lap and around her sweater leggings and old cowboy boots.

Sophia didn't like men touching her, but this gentle giant did it in a way that made her want to cling to his hand and thank him. His eyes held no malice, no intentions other than to bring her comfort. When was the last time a man had been this kind to her? Especially a man who'd seen the business end of her shotgun?

"There," he said, his eyes going a gentle burnished brown. Then he turned to a side table. "Here's your tea."

She nodded her head, still not used to this kind of reaction from a man. Or her reaction to that man. "Thank you."

His gaze stumbled over her heated skin. "You don't look so hot."

She almost smiled at that. "Well, I wasn't exactly expecting company tonight."

He sank back on a stool made out of old floorboards and straightened the embroidered yellow cushion. "And I wasn't exactly expecting to show up on your porch."

She forced a smile. "Funny how life works, huh?"

He nodded. "Ready to talk now?"

Sophia looked down at the frayed threads of the secondhand throw. "About what?"

He gave her a long, hard stare. "You'll have to tell me sooner or later."

Sophia sipped her tea so quickly she burned her tongue. "Tell you what?"

"Why you reacted so strongly to this poster."

He held it up, his intentions obvious and deliberate.

Sophia glanced at the drawing then looked

away. "I just got scared when I saw it hanging on my door. I mean, someone was out there prowling around and whoever it was came up onto my back porch."

"I was out there prowling around and you came at me with a shotgun."

She shrugged, tried to put on a neutral face. "I guess two prowlers in one night sent me over the edge."

Adan pulled out his phone. "Mind if I ask you some questions?"

"Haven't you been doing that since you showed up here?"

"Part of my job, especially when I need some answers and I think you can give them to me."

Sophia didn't want to give him any information, so she pointed to his phone, thinking he was going to haul her in. "I told you, you might find it hard to get any service out here."

"It's okay. I have a password to protect any work-related information so I take notes on my phone's notepad. But if you're uncomfortable—"

"No, I just don't have anything more to say." She tried to swallow away the dryness tightening her throat. Then she lifted her chin and stared him down. "Even if it means you have to take me to jail, too."

ADAN RUBBED A hand down his face. This day had not turned out the way he'd planned. "Okay then. I hope I don't have any reason to take you to jail. The best thing you can do for yourself is tell the truth, understand?"

"Yes," she said on a soft note. "I… I'm sorry I held a gun on you. I'm not a criminal."

He glanced at the ever-present shotgun then pivoted back to her and decided not to tell her how many times he'd heard that comment over the years. "I don't know about that."

"I have a right to protect myself," she said, her hackles definitely rising, her freckled skin flushing while her eyes became a fire-tipped blue.

Ignoring the current of heat running through his body, he said, "Yes, you certainly do. Why do you need to protect yourself?"

"I shouldn't have to tell you that. It's pretty obvious."

Adan tried again. "Do you recognize the man in the sketch?"

She lowered her head, her gaze cutting to the floor. Adan couldn't be sure if she was about to lie to him or if she really was agitated by seeing that wanted poster on her door.

"Sophia?" Adan wasn't always patient, but he'd learned to be whenever he was trying to drag information out of someone. He waited for her to look at him and hoped she'd be honest.

She finally let out a long sigh and gave him a direct glare. But he didn't see anything but sincerity and stubbornness in her blue eyes. "I haven't seen him around here."

Adan let out a grunt and got up. "That's not what I asked."

SOPHIA DECIDED SHE'D had enough questions for one night. "I'm going to see about Bettye," she said, already reaching for her heavy coat and her gun.

"Hey, wait a minute," he called after her.

But Sophia was tired of waiting, tired of looking over her shoulder and very tired of being afraid. "I told you, I haven't seen that man around here, but somebody left that mug shot for a reason. I'm going to check on my neighbor, so you need to just back off."

"I'm coming with you," Adan called, his boots hitting the old hardwood floors as he chased after her.

Sophia opened the heavy latched door, a gust of cold wind and wet snow taking her breath away. She needed this blast of cold air to clear her head. After four years here on the mountain, she'd become happy again and she'd gotten her strength back. She wasn't about to have a midnight confession with a Texas Ranger.

I'll figure out something. I always do.

"Hey, wait up."

The driving wind caused the heavy flakes to dance in a straight line across the woods. She gasped to catch her breath then motioned to Adan. He'd just come after her if she didn't let him go with her. And to be honest, she didn't want to be out here alone. Not if Joe Pritchard was roaming around.

Adan followed her down the slippery wooden steps and took hold of her arm to link it with his. "We need to stick together."

"I agree."

"Why do you feel this sudden need to check on Bettye? We just left her place."

Sophia lifted a gloved hand in the air. "The weather, a criminal on the loose, because I can."

"You're sure stubborn," he said on a hiss as the wind cut them both to the bone.

"Yes, I am." She nodded. "Her cabin is dark, but she has a night-light. The power might have gone out." Taking a glance back at her own cabin, she said, "I still have electricity, so she should, too."

"Must be asleep," Adan called over the driving wind.

Sophia nodded, her skin tingling as the icy flakes hit her and clung to her hat and hair. This was the worst snowstorm she'd ever experienced while living on Crescent Mountain.

How would Adan ever be able to get out of here?

Worried now that she'd have to contend with him for more than just tonight and wondering where Joe had gone, she steeled herself to deal with both of them. She wouldn't let Ranger Harrison intimidate her and she wouldn't let Joe Pritchard—or whoever it was—scare her. She was long past being afraid of anything.

Except the truth.

She'd worry about how to handle that later. She had to make sure Bettye was okay—she was spry and in good shape, but she was still getting on in years. If Joe knew Bettye was Sophia's friend, he'd zoom in on her just to bring out Sophia.

When they reached Bettye's porch, Adan pointed to the snow going up the steps. "No fresh footprints, but the downfall could have hidden any."

"We left her about an hour ago," Sophia replied. "I'd feel better checking the back porch and all the windows."

Adan grabbed her by the arm. "Why are you so worried about Bettye?"

Sophia didn't know how to explain that now. Telling him the truth would save her a lot of grief, but she didn't want to give Adan something to pin on her, a bargaining chip to make her talk even more. Or evidence that could put her in jail.

"I care about her," she finally said. "She's helped me a lot and…she's the only real family I've ever had."

Adan's eyes widened but he seemed to accept that explanation. At least that much was the truth.

"Let's go around back," he suggested, his gun now drawn.

Now he was taking her seriously.

"Will her dog alert?" he asked.

"He should if it's a stranger," she said, her voice carrying through the ferocious wind and clinging snow. "But he knows me, so he might not bother with us."

Adan shined the flashlight at the side window, but the heavy bushes were so covered with fresh snow it was impossible to tell if anyone had been near the place. No sign of new footprints on the back porch, either. Not even a peep from Bettye's devoted companion.

"Her bedroom is on the other side," Sophia said, pointing to the right corner of the porch.

Adan nodded and helped her down the steps. They slogged through almost a foot of snow before they reached the other window.

And saw that the screen was not on the window. It was lying ripped and torn on the snow-covered grass.

Sophia turned and tried to run. "I have to get inside."

Adan hurried and caught her by the arm. "Hold up. Do you want to scare her?"

Angry that he was wasting time, she shouted, "You saw that screen!"

Adan nodded. "Yes, and I saw the window. The glass is intact. No one went through that window."

"He could have closed it."

"He would have broken out a pane to get inside. The glass is intact."

When they heard a dog barking from inside the house, Sophia yanked away from Adan. "I'm going inside."

"How?"

She lifted the key ring from her coat pocket. "I have a key."

She didn't wait for him to ask her about anything else. Sophia's heart was churning and shifting in the same blustery confusion as the wind's unforgiving gusts. Her safe, quiet life was now in an uproar and her fears for her friend had multiplied twofold after seeing that busted window screen.

She was fighting two very determined men. One evil…and one good. She just wished she knew which one would win.

CHAPTER FIVE

BY THE TIME they'd made it back around the house, the rear porch light flickered on and Bettye cracked open the door enough to push a rifle barrel through it. "Who's out there?"

Letting out a held breath, Sophia ran up the slippery steps. "It's me, Bettye. I was worried about you."

The door peeled back like a creaky old trunk lid. "I'm fine, honey. You sure scared Bandit, though." She motioned them inside with the gun down and her left hand in the air.

Sophia smelled the faint scents of vanilla and lavender. A burning candle? Then she heard a man's cough.

Adan shot her a confused glance before they entered the back door of the cluttered, cloying cabin. "What's going on?"

Bettye gave them a sheepish grin. "Jacob saw y'all with me earlier and…came over to see what all the commotion was about." She motioned to Adan. "Jacob, this is the Ranger-Man I was telling you about."

Jacob? Sophia's relief was followed by a bemused confusion. She'd always known Jacob Miller had a huge crush on Bettye, but Bettye had never indicated that she felt the same about the grizzled, cantankerous older man. He had to be at least eighty. He could barely walk!

Adan introduced himself and walked over to shake Jacob's hand. "Hello, sir."

Jacob pushed up off the chair and shook Adan's hand. "Hear you're tracking a nasty criminal."

"Yes, sir." Adan explained what he was doing here. "Have y'all seen or heard anything?"

"Not a peep until you two showed up," Jacob said on a grin.

"Hey there," Jacob said to Sophia after grasping Adan's hand, his ever-present pipe hanging like a leafless tree branch out of his whiskered mouth. What little bit of hair he had stood out around his head in white tufts that reminded Sophia of snow caught against limbs. "We're just sitting here enjoying the fire."

"Without any lights on, apparently," Adan replied on a dry note. He turned to Bettye. "Sophia was concerned and when we went around to the side, we found one of your window screens lying in the bushes."

Bettye brushed at her braid. "Been meaning to replace that."

"Remind me when spring comes and I'll take

care of it," Jacob said, his gray beard dancing. "A mite too cold out there tonight."

Bettye eyed Adan and Sophia. "It's late, but you're both welcome to come in and sit awhile."

She didn't offer up anywhere to sit, however.

"Uh, no, we won't stay," Sophia replied, unable to hide her smile. "As long as you're okay, Bettye."

"She's just fine," Jacob said with another big grin and a strong bobble of a nod. "We were reminiscing about when we were young and in love."

"With other people," Bettye replied in a rush of words. "We both were married long ago, before the mountain claimed us." She glanced down at her house booties, a sly smile hanging off her cheery face. "Now we enjoy sitting by the fire."

"Uh-huh," Adan replied, his lips twitching. He glanced at his watch. "It *is* late. Sophia, I think we should leave these two young'uns alone."

Bandit meandered out of the bedroom, his ears flopping and his nose in the air. After sniffing at Adan and then stopping in front of Sophia for a fur rub, he sauntered over to the hooked rug in front of the fireplace and plopped down.

"Some watchdog you are," Sophia said, walking over to bend and pet him again. After giving Bandit a thorough belly rub, she stood and said, "Okay, now that I've embarrassed everyone, I'm going back to my own cabin."

Bettye came over to give her a hug. "Jacob

and I'll sit a bit longer, then I'll send him on his way." She leaned in. "I did hear a noise earlier, honey. I used the old-fashioned message system. I flicked the porch light three times. Jacob saw it and came over straight away."

"You should come home with me," Sophia said, her gaze scurrying toward where Adan was making small talk with Jacob. She'd wondered if Jacob had been climbing in and out of that window, but that image just didn't jive with his arthritic arms and legs. Maybe he was a back-door man.

Bettye shook her head then lifted a hand toward Jacob. "Are you kidding me? I been waiting for this man to catch me—this man sitting in the rocking chair, that is—for about three years now. Fate has a way of working in our favor sometimes." She shot a covert glance at Adan. "Bad guy on the loose, nice-looking Ranger in the house, Jacob in my rocking chair. Fate."

"I don't need this kind of fate," Sophia retorted, her gaze hitting on Adan. Then she looked Bettye in the eye. "Maybe we can talk in private tomorrow."

"Sure thing," Bettye said, stepping back. "Sorry about scaring you," she said a bit louder for Adan's benefit.

After a few more questions from Jacob about Adan's being a Ranger, Sophia and Adan left to face the brutal cold once again. Adan had given them a description of Joe Pritchard before urging them to be alert. He did one more thorough check on the bushes around Sophia's cabin, but turned up nothing.

Maybe the prowler was gone, or worse, frozen in the snow. Sophia could hope that, right?

When they were safely inside her cabin, she turned to give Adan a solemn stare. And found him standing there with a wide grin on his face.

"What's so funny?" she asked, completely captivated by his beautiful smile. Too captivated. The man dazzled her with gleaming toughness, but she needed to remember this was not a social call. He was here to do lawman business and she had to keep that in mind at all times.

He lifted a dark eyebrow. "Did we just walk in on a...senior hookup?"

Sophia gasped then clamped a hand over her mouth. "No. I mean, no. I don't know. I... I don't think so. Not yet, at least. Bettye isn't that kind of girl."

"You're blushing," he said, his smile dying on his lips while his eyes heated to liquid gold. "And you're smiling."

Trying to deflect the sizzle of his eyes moving over her, Sophia shook her head. "So are you. I didn't think Rangers knew how to smile."

His eyebrows lifted while he stared her down. "And what exactly do you know about Rangers?"

"Not nearly enough," she said on a sassy huff.

"Or in your case, way more than I ever wanted to know."

Such as, he would arrest her if he knew the truth. Or maybe that his smile could definitely change her attitude from standoffish to *come closer.*

No, never mind that!

"But I still don't know a lot about you," he said, his gaze melting her chill away. And scaring it right back in a shivering slide down her backbone.

"You know enough."

He grinned and headed to drop another log on the fire. "What a night."

"Full of lots of revelations," Sophia said, reminding herself to be careful. He was being charming now that they were alone. Did he plan on tormenting her with his commanding presence until she gave in and spilled her guts?

Even that thought made her blush.

"And full of lots of secrets," he retorted, his grin tapering off to a solid, unyielding poker face.

The man was truly like a dog with a bone.

"So we have a snowstorm, a criminal on the loose and two old people making eyes at each other."

Not to mention her being here with Adan in a cabin in a snowstorm, alone. Trapped.

He stepped so close she could smell the snowdrift all around him. "And…one very pretty woman who isn't telling the truth."

Sophia started making the sofa into his sleeping quarters, probably to avoid the accusation in his words. After fluffing blankets and tucking sheets, she said, "So you're back on that?"

Adan watched her face for lies but in the flickering golden light from the fire all he saw was a secretive confusion. Was she hiding something? Was she hiding someone? Would the snow ever melt?

The snow she had around her heart, that was. This woman obviously had something to hide and she seemed to have a major distrust of law enforcement.

Not so much a hard heart, but maybe a bruised one.

"I'm good at my job," he replied, once again taking in the bright colors and quirky artwork that filled every surface of her little home. "I'll get the truth out of everyone around here, sooner or later."

"I figure you'll have to go back to Texas— sooner than later, I hope."

Adan decided to mess with her a little bit. "Until that storm clears, I got nothing but time, darlin'. And you got nobody else to talk to tonight."

She whirled to give him a feminine frown. "And what makes you think I'm lying? Haven't

I tried to cooperate with you and answer all of your questions?"

He had to grin again at that. "You held a gun on me and tied me up but yes, you've been very cooperative. But as I said before, I couldn't help but notice you got scared, extremely scared, when you found that wanted poster on your back door."

She lowered her head then crossed her arms over her stomach. "That was silly and I shouldn't have reacted that way. Probably one of our neighbors went down the mountain and ran into someone passing those out. Any one of my friends could have left that on my door just to warn me."

"A passable explanation, but not on a night like this."

She peeked out the kitchen window. "Criminals don't care about the weather."

"True. But why would a neighbor wait until so late in the day to leave posters on doors? And why didn't Bettye mention having one on her door?"

Sophia whirled around and took her time putting fresh pillowcases on the two pillows she'd pulled out of the hallway closet. "I don't know. I just reacted to seeing *that* right after you showed up here. Too much excitement and you with all your talk of some dangerous man on the run."

Adan stared over at her with purposeful intent. "A dangerous man who obviously came to Crescent Mountain for a reason."

She got that fearful look again but quickly cleared it and gave him a defiant chin lift. "Maybe he knows someone around here."

A roundabout confession? "Maybe so."

The room grew uncomfortably quiet.

Deciding to back off for now, Adan stifled a yawn. "Sorry. I guess I'm more beat than I realized."

"Me, too," she said on an eager sigh. "I hope this will be okay."

He nodded toward the blanket and fluffy pillows. "Looks like heaven." He took off his hat and laid it on the coffee table then shrugged. "I've slept in worse places."

She gave him an appraising glance. "I guess you have at that."

"I'll be fine."

He wanted to say more, but it had been a while since he'd been in a forced confinement with a woman. Adan's rule was to keep moving fast so no woman would ever try to tie him down the way his ex-wife had. And yet this one had already tied him up. He'd have to bear that in mind until the snow stopped falling. No telling what she'd try if he actually fell asleep.

"Okay, then, I'm, uh, going to bed." She motioned toward the bathroom. "I'll just be a minute then you can take a shower if you'd like. Towels underneath the sink. And I think I have several unopened toothbrushes from our many trips into town. Jacob always brings everyone a new toothbrush. He's a retired dentist."

Adan nodded and grinned. "He did have white teeth."

She put a hand to her mouth and reminded him of his daughter, girly and giggly. But this particular girl was all grown-up and way too enticing.

"I guess I have missed a few clues around here," she admitted. "Did not see that one coming."

"I think they make a cute couple," he replied. "But I'll have to question them again. And everyone else on this mountain, too. I need you to understand that, Sophia."

"I guess I don't have much of a choice," she replied, her playful expression changing as an aggravated frown arrowed its way up her forehead. "You do what you need to do. And we'll do the same."

"Is that a threat?"

"I have no reason to threaten you."

"Then be honest with me so I don't have to threaten you."

"I'm tired," she replied. "And I'm going to bed."

And the moment was gone.

In a whirl worthy of an award-winning actress, she turned and strutted into the bathroom and slammed the door.

But the warning had been very clear.

Sophia and her merry band of followers would not make his job easy. He'd have to do some investigating when this weather cleared. If this weather cleared.

Something wasn't right about Sophia's reaction to that poster. Either she knew the man in the picture or she'd seen him recently. Why would she withhold information on a dangerous man?

Maybe because she might be the reason that man had come to this mountain?

Adan grunted and sank down on the sofa and removed his boots. Sometimes, his job really got the best of him.

But at no time on a case had a woman ever gotten the best of him.

Not yet, at least.

CHAPTER SIX

Adan dozed with one eye open.

He must have finally fallen into a deep sleep only to wake up to sunshine and the smell of coffee. With a grunt, he sat up on the sofa and looked around. In the light of day, this place was cozy and comfortable even if it wasn't much bigger than a horse stall. The room was colorful and full of little *woman* things—embroidery and lace, fluffy pillows and crocheted quilts, vases and picture frames. Dainty things. Which only made him feel like a stallion in a henhouse.

When he heard noise in the kitchen, he first checked his hands and feet for any ropes or tape. None there. Then he checked her for signs of a weapon. Nothing there, either. She wore a too-big flannel shirt and slim gray sweatpants and fuzzy boots. Her hair, caught up in a haphazard twist, was a loose rich auburn that burned bright in the light of day. Sophia looked earthy and right at home as she scooted around the small U-shaped efficiency kitchen.

He hitched a breath then got aggravated at

himself. This woman was lying through her pretty white teeth and somehow, he had to get around all that cuteness and find the truth. He didn't like lying women. Only reminded him of Gaylen's absent mother, Helena. She'd lied to him from the day they'd met and she'd lied even as she'd walked out the door, never to return. Helena hadn't wanted a baby and she sure hadn't wanted him. She'd used him as a means to an end—to get out from under her powerful father's thumb. Well, now she was living high on the hog with the rich man she'd always wanted. Good for her.

He missed Gaylen with the kind of ache that brought a man to his knees. He'd get home to her soon. Somehow.

Adan scowled over at the woman in the kitchen, trying to associate that pretty countenance with that of a liar.

Hard to do.

"You're up," she said, her smile not so sure-footed.

Adan realized he'd been staring and pushed at his hair and grunted. "Yes, and… I'm still alive."

"Don't worry, I thought about doing you in but decided against it since I didn't want to drag you out there and leave you like a frozen lump." She smiled and brought him a huge cup of steaming coffee. "I have biscuits and ham in the oven."

Her serene attitude threw him. It was completely opposite of her skittish, worried mind-set last night. If she was hiding something she sure didn't seem too worried about it this morning. Or maybe she'd successfully helped Pritchard escape and she was bluffing until she could figure out how to get rid of Adan. In the meantime, he'd bide his time and get some answers out of her. And watch her like a hawk.

He took the coffee with a grateful nod. "Do you always get up at the crack of dawn?"

"Most days," she replied. "I like to work in the early light."

He glanced around at the various forms of artwork. "So you're an artist?"

"Yes. Mixed media."

"Mixed what?"

She went back to the kitchen and opened the oven. "It's just using several different ways of creating an art piece. Layering different textures and materials onto one canvas."

"Right."

She laughed and pointed to a big structure hanging over the fireplace. "I made that piece out of old fence boards, buttons and jewelry."

Adan studied the piece of art and decided it did look like part of a fence. Then he saw it. "It's the mountain. A vista." He moved closer, amazed at the striking piece of art. "I don't know art from Adam," he said, "but this is real pretty."

She smiled, obviously pleased that he'd guessed

right and probably glad she'd managed to distract him. "There's one spot down near the stream running behind the cabins where the view is incredible. I go there a lot for inspiration."

"And so you recreated that view of the mountain with old wood and other things?"

"Yep. I go into town once or twice a month and leave a couple of pieces in the art gallery. Sometimes I go with Bettye to the arts-and-crafts shows held in several of the towns around the Ozarks and we set up a booth. She makes quilts and does embroidery on pillows and hand towels."

That explained all the dainty stuff exploding in this room.

"Is that how you make your living?"

She stilled at that. "Yes. And I saved up before I came here."

Okay, there it was again. A subtle evasiveness that he immediately recognized. She wasn't telling him everything, but he only needed to know the part where Joe Pritchard came into the picture. Adan knew patience wasn't his virtue but decided to take it easy since she was slowly opening up to him. He needed to get Pritchard and get back to Texas. First, he wanted to check on his truck and maybe move it back here near the cabins, and then he'd figure out what to do next.

He waited to see what Sophia was doing.

When she started toward him with two biscuits on a plate, he stood. "I can eat that at the table."

She shook her head. "No, here by the fire."

"Okay." He took the plate and stared at it for a full minute.

"Is something wrong?" she asked as she curled up in a big, broken-in leather chair, her legs tucked up under her.

"Just checking for glass or maybe poison mushrooms."

She looked confused. "Oh, you think I'm still out to do you in?"

He sniffed at the wonderful smells coming from the plate. "Aren't you?"

She shook her head. "If that were the case, I had all night to do it. And yet, like you said, you're still alive."

He leaned back and took a sip of the coffee. The taste was rich and dark and fresh, like that head of hair cascading around her face. Then he bit into the biscuit.

"Hmm, pretty good."

"Bettye taught me how to cook," she explained, her blue eyes going soft. "She knows how to cure ham in a smokehouse. She grew up on a farm in Alabama."

"How'd she wind up here?"

"I'm not sure. She doesn't like to talk about it, but I think after her husband died, she went into a deep depression. She told me once that she got in her car and drove until she found this mountain."

"This sure must be a special place," Adan said, his gaze taking in everything and seeing nothing out of the ordinary other than him sitting here among exotic paintings and twisted doodads eating a biscuit.

She nibbled at her own breakfast. "It's a quiet, unassuming place. It's peaceful and secure and… comfortable. I like a certain schedule and I like order. I've had enough chaos in my life."

He zoomed right in on that last comment. "Care to talk about it?"

She looked so shocked, he figured she just now realized she'd mentioned her past. "No."

"What brought you here?"

She glanced around as if searching for a good response. "Art. I like how everyone here is involved in folk art."

"How did you find out that everyone here is an artist?"

She gave him a blank stare and shrugged. "Artists tend to find each other."

"Why is everyone around here so tight-lipped?"

"You haven't met everyone around here."

"You have a way of answering a question with a counterstatement. Were you ever a lawyer?"

Shock again. "No. I just don't like to talk about myself."

"And why is that?"

She got up and threw another log on the fire. "You might be able to get out and walk around today. The snow and ice will be here awhile, so I doubt you'll be able to get down the mountain today, but you can at least search for...that man."

"You mean Joe Pritchard?"

Her hand stilled on a log before she tossed it into the fire. "Whoever he is."

Hmm. A bit of defensiveness and deflection. She sure didn't like to talk about herself and apparently, any wanted criminals, either. Adan's burning gut told him Sophia knew more about Joe Pritchard than she was letting on. If he had any service on his phone he could run a check on her, too.

"I intend to get out and search for him," he replied with a cool assurance that didn't calm his stomach. Then he polished off the last of his second biscuit. "Thank you for breakfast."

She turned and took his plate before he could set it down. "Want more coffee?"

"Sure."

He got up and followed her into the tiny kitchen and, too late, realized this space wasn't made for two people. They bumped together when she whirled to take his cup.

"Excuse me," she said, a becoming blush moving down her cheeks. She lowered her gaze and held her head down.

"I can get my own coffee," he said to fill the space.

"Let me get it."

She took the cup right out of his hand, her fingers brushing his in a soft sizzle that surged through him all the way to the tips of his boots.

Adan backed up, regrouped and reminded himself he didn't like entanglements of any kind. Even while he envisioned his hands entangled in all that rich auburn hair.

SOPHIA GRIPPED THE sink with one hand and scrubbed with all her might with the other hand. She hated stains.

And she also hated having Adan Harrison in her home. And she hated lying and hiding things.

But she had no other choice. Did she?

When she'd come into the kitchen earlier and seen his too-big body curled up on her too-small couch, she'd had to swallow back a shard of longing. She'd always imagined having someone special in her life, and she'd tried so hard to make that happen. Once. But once was enough for Sophia.

Having Adan asleep on her couch was one thing. Getting all fuzzy hearted and sentimental was quite another. So she'd reminded herself to stay away from the sleeping giant and to keep her hands and her daydreams to herself. After a sleepless night of trying to figure out what her next move could be, she'd decided she had to be nice to the big Texas Ranger. For now.

This man wasn't here for a fling.

He'd come to this mountain to find a killer.

And she'd come to this mountain to escape. Just to escape.

Why was he here now and when would he leave? Who was out there taunting her? Her mind skittered over memories still too fresh to tuck away completely. Did someone know her sins?

Sophia stared at the sink and decided it was clean enough. She rinsed away the cleanser and washed out her dish towel, then dried her hands and grabbed her lotion bottle to moisturize them. Then she turned to tidy up the living room. Adan had folded his bedding and pillows and left them on the sofa. She touched a hand to one of the pillows and remembered his head touching that same spot.

The bathroom door opened, causing her to jump back like a kid caught with her hand in the candy jar.

Adan walked into the room, chewing up space with each step. "I'm gonna walk down the mountain to check on my truck."

Relief flooded through her. He'd be out of her hair for a couple of hours so she'd have a chance to talk to Bettye. Trying not to sound too happy, she said, "Oh, okay. Be careful."

"You're going with me."

Panic scurried across Sophia's nerve endings. "What? Why?"

He stood by the fire, his hands in his pockets. "Don't look so scared. I need you to be my guide and to help me with spotting any signs of activity out there. You know these woods better than me." .

She did know these woods. She also knew how to steer him away from places he didn't need to go. Her heart beat in little skips and jumps, but she didn't have a choice in this matter, either. She would have to serve not only as Adan's guide, but his guard, too.

She ran a hand over her hair. "I'll get my gear."

He gave her a puzzled glance. "I figured you'd protest and stomp your foot and come up with some good excuses."

Sophia quirked an eyebrow. "Would that have worked?"

He laughed at her remark. "No. I'd still take you with me."

"Even if I refused to go?"

"That would only make me suspicious."

"You mean even more suspicious than you already are?"

"Yeah. Even more."

She went about putting on her hat, gloves and

coat so she could hide the fear and disappointment his words brought out. "Why don't we get going while the morning sun is bright and shiny? The snow won't melt completely. Too cold out here."

"Fine."

That sun might shine a light on things she wanted to hide. But if she kept him on the road and out of the woods, they should be okay.

She should be okay.

He grabbed his coat and hat. Then he turned to holster his gun. "Let's go then."

Sophia felt as if she was about to go on a death march. How could she keep up this charade until the winter mix had melted completely? Until she could wave goodbye to Adan? Until she found out for sure if a criminal who wanted her dead was still out there somewhere?

With weak cell signals and frozen roads below them, Sophia figured he'd be here for a couple of days, at least. No snowplows or tow trucks would dare come here, anyway. This mountain was too remote for any kind of county maintenance.

She was juggling a lot of snowballs and they could all come crashing down on her if she wasn't careful.

THEY WALKED DOWN the curving mountain road in silence.

Adan wondered what Sophia was thinking.

She'd been a bit too keen on escorting him to his truck. Probably afraid he'd stumble on the place she'd obviously hidden a criminal. Or possibly, she was trying to stall him while the others helped that criminal get away.

But he still couldn't figure out how anyone could have found a hiding place out here in this whitewashed world. The only visible cabins were up the ridge on a flat incline. He'd checked around the area when they'd first walked outside. Sophia had pointed out the circle of cabins and mentioned again the people who lived here year-round.

"The last cabin's vacant. The owners usually come up here in the spring and summer."

Adan should have searched more last night, but the driving snow and the possibility of getting lost in whiteout had held him back. "I'll want to check the cabins before we head down the road to my truck. He could have broken into one."

She'd obediently followed him, her gaze cutting here and there through the ice-covered trees. When they'd searched around the vacant cabin and glanced in the windows, Adan decided he could rule out anyone hiding inside. No signs of forced entry in the windows or doors.

So what would he find on down the road?

Now they were headed past the little community and down the sloping road, the way slippery with ice patches and thick with snowdrifts. So far, they hadn't seen a soul. The woods were quiet and settled in a blanket of fresh, powdery snow.

"It rarely snows this heavily here," Sophia said, her breath wispy around her. "I need to take some pictures."

"It's cold," he said, hoping to rouse her into more small talk. "And beautiful."

"Yes."

She said that in a way that implied he might be stupid.

Adan smiled at her attitude. If he could trust her, that kind of sass might be cute. But since he couldn't trust her, it only managed to irritate him.

He tried again. "Did you have any big plans for today?"

"No."

"So do you try to work every day?"

"Most days, yes." She actually cut him a glance. "I like to take long walks and find different things to include in my work. Twigs and leaves, old buttons and scraps, feathers. I never know what I'll find."

"My job is kind of like that, too," Adan replied, glad for the comparison. "I have to put together bits and pieces of different things to come up with a way to solve a case."

She slanted her gaze toward him again. "Are you comparing your job to art?"

"I guess I am. It requires a certain amount of artistic persuasion to find out what I need to know."

"Oh, is that what you'd call this? You questioning my every move and badgering me to come clean on something I don't even know about? That's your kind of art?"

"I am painting a picture in my mind, yes."

"Are you always this funny?"

"I have my moments."

She gave him a harsh glance followed by a wry smile. "At least you're not boring."

"You might change your mind on that after I've been around a few days."

She stopped on the snow-packed road so fast ice chips flew out around her boots. "Are you staying that long?"

He gave her a frown. "Ah, tired of me already?"

"Yes," she said much to his surprise. "I want my nice, quiet life back. You're annoying."

"You make me laugh in spite of myself," he admitted.

Then he decided while he had her out here in the open, he'd level with her. But he made sure they were in the middle of the slippery road and not near a plunging ravine before he confronted her. "Sophia, we really need to talk."

She looked up at him, concern filtering through her poker face. "This is no laughing matter, is it?"

At least she knew the situation was dangerous. But she also needed to know he was serious.
Dead serious. "No. Pritchard is desperate and he's
mean. That's a dangerous combination."

Her face went pale again. "Are you sure he's
still here?"

"If he came to this mountain with a purpose,
he won't leave until he's fulfilled that purpose."

She held a hand to her mouth and then dropped
it to her side. "We need to check your truck and
then get back. I don't like leaving the others."

Adan stopped on the side of the road and
breathed deep, his words coming out through a
cold mist. "Sophia, I'm not leaving this mountain until I have my man. If I have to drag Joe
Pritchard back to Texas in a body bag, I'll do it.
I always get my man."

Then he gave her one of his surefire Ranger
glares. "Or my woman."

CHAPTER SEVEN

SOPHIA TRIED TO calm the panic in her stomach, but the butterflies hitting at her insides caused her heart rate to jump and sputter. "What makes you think I'm involved in this?"

He squinted and gave her an unyielding glare. "You tied me to the bedposts. What other conclusion should I come to?"

"Maybe I had something else in mind?" she said on a sarcastic breath that belied the sharp pulse bumping against her temple.

"With Bettye there? Right." The bemused look in his eyes didn't change his frown.

"Look, I told you I was scared and… Bettye was just trying to help me. I didn't do anything to you last night. So give me a break."

"I want to give you a break," he replied as they started carefully making their way down the road, sticking toward the more level side that butted up against the rock face of the mountain. "I can understand protecting your property, but y'all tied me up and gagged me for some reason."

"We were scared," she repeated. "And frankly,

you're scaring me now." She lifted her gaze back to him, hoping she could convince him. "Look, Adan, we don't get many visitors up here. Especially not Texas Ranger–type visitors."

"Well, maybe you should," he retorted. "I've been at this job long enough to know a thing or two, and my gut's telling me y'all aren't being completely honest with me."

Maybe if she just told him a little bit of her history, Sophia thought. Would that be enough to shut him up and get him off her trail?

"Adan, I…"

"What in the—" He held up a hand and instantly drew his gun. "Get behind me."

Sophia didn't have time to act. He shoved her behind him so fast she almost slipped on a sliver of icy rock. "What is it?"

Adan lifted his chin. "Look at my truck."

Sophia glanced a few yards downhill and into an embankment near a sharp curve. A black double-cab pickup sat at an odd angle against the snow-covered mound, all four of its tires flat.

"I don't think the storm caused that," she said, fear coursing through her in a cold rush that rivaled the freezing winter temperature. "He's still out here."

He's alive.

Those two words hit her with the force of a ton of snow and drifted over and over in her mind with a twisting clarity.

He's still alive.

"He must have doubled back and found my truck," Adan said, oblivious to her terror. He stepped forward, his gun still drawn. "If he's still here, he must be the dumbest criminal ever. Now I'm stuck here until I can get these replaced."

Which meant she'd be stuck with both of them. Sophia didn't know what to do now. How could she stall telling Adan the truth while Joe Pritchard stalked her at the same time?

"Do you think he's in the truck?" Sophia asked, her hands automatically clinging to Adan's heavy canvas jacket. Dumb or not, this man *was* still dangerous.

"I don't know," Adan whispered. "But it would bring him some shelter. I don't get why he let the air out of the tires, though." He edged into the snow-covered woods. "Could be an ambush."

Sophia hoped not. If Adan got shot, she'd be out here on her own with a killer. A killer who was no doubt looking for her. She shuddered as memories rushed through her mind like a howling wind.

Sophia watched the truck for signs of life. "Did you lock it?"

He kept his eyes on the truck. "I don't remember. I hit the embankment and tried to back up but I spun deeper into the snow and mud. Then I got out of the truck to see if I could dig away some of the slush. That didn't work, so I started walking." He checked his pocket. "I have the keys."

"Click your key fob and see," she suggested, hoping no one was inside that truck.

Adan pulled her into the woods on the level side of the road. "Stay here," he said. "I'm gonna move closer and try the locks. If anything happens, you run back to your cabin, you hear?"

"I'm not leaving you," she said, surprised that she'd blurted that out. But she wouldn't leave him. Not if a crazy criminal was in that truck. Especially since she was the reason Joe Pritchard was here.

Adan gave her a stern glance. "Just do it, Sophia."

She stood behind a snow-encrusted pine sapling, thinking she should have brought her shotgun. What if Adan got hurt and she tried to make a run for it? She'd be killed.

Adan crouched low and made his way toward the truck then used his key fob to hit the unlock mechanism. Sophia heard a distinct click and breathed a sigh of relief. Maybe Joe Pritchard had moved on.

But when a dark head popped up, she gasped. "Adan!"

Adan went down low and hurried to the passenger side of the truck. "Come out with your hands up!"

ADAN'S ADRENALINE HIT a rush as he hastened to open the door of the truck. "Out of there, right now."

"Okay, okay."

He blinked and slowly stood up. "Who are you?"

A young woman with dark brown hair uncurled out from under the old army blanket he kept in the drop seat of the truck. She wore a black nylon coat with a fur-trimmed hood, tall boots and jeans.

With her hands up, she dropped to the ground and immediately started shivering. "Don't shoot me, please."

Adan lowered the gun. He could hear Sophia hurrying toward them, but he made sure he was still between this stranger and Sophia. "Who are you and what are you doing in my truck?"

The girl's big brown eyes widened in apprehension. "I… I hitched a ride from Hot Springs but…uh…the driver let me off at the foot of the mountain. I had to walk the rest of the way and I was so cold. When I saw this truck, I… I crawled inside and fell asleep."

Adan's gut clenched again. Did everyone on this mountain lie and withhold information? The girl kept glancing at her feet and refused to make eye contact with him.

Sure there had to be more to her story, he checked the surrounding area, halfway expecting Joe Pritchard to charge out of the woods. "Are you sure that's all that's going on?"

The girl's scared expression turned into a scowl. She glanced around, her gaze darting here and there. "Why would I lie? That guy was a jerk and I wanted out of his stinky car."

"How'd you get in the truck?" Sophia asked, her gaze darting from the girl to Adan.

"The door was open." She pointed to the driver's side. "That window was shattered."

Adan glanced over and for the first time saw that she'd stuffed his old hunting jacket where the glass should be, probably to stay warm. Good thing he never cleaned out his truck or she could have frozen to death.

Adan searched the vehicle but only found his duffel bag still intact in the small backseat. Grabbing it to take with him, he turned back to the girl. "Did you break into my vehicle?" he asked, his gaze pinning her to the spot.

She shrugged and tugged her hood up on her head. "No. I guess somebody hit it with a rock or something."

"Are you telling the truth?" Adan asked, thinking he was getting mighty tired of having to ask that.

"I didn't break that window if that's what you're asking—again."

"What's your name?" Adan asked, his tone less intimidating this time since this kid seemed to be streetwise and unyielding. Any other time, he'd have forced the truth out of her, but he had bigger fish to fry.

"Melissa Curtis," she said, stomping her feet against the bitter chill. "My grandma Bettye Scott lives on Crescent Mountain."

Well, now, that was a new twist. Adan couldn't help but wonder if this mountain didn't hold more secrets than the Pentagon. Before he could question the girl again, Sophia let out a gasp.

"Bettye?" Sophia rushed toward the girl. "I know her. She's a good friend of mine. She's never mentioned a granddaughter."

"She doesn't know she has one," Melissa admitted. "Can I see her?"

"Did you run away from home?" Adan asked, still not sure he could trust this girl. For all he knew, Joe Pritchard had set the girl up as a decoy. The more he thought about it, the more he had to wonder. "Who was this person you hitched a ride with?"

"That's none of your business," the girl retorted, her hands crossing over her stomach. "I just want to see my granny."

Adan let out a long sigh. Just what he needed. Another noncommunicative, stubborn woman. "It is my business since you spent the night in my truck."

"I came to see my grandma," she said, her chin jutting forward. "I just couldn't go any further."

Adan could tell the girl was frightened and cold—and still way too evasive. He'd deal with how she got here later.

"Did you see anybody else on this road last night? Or near my truck? Somebody took the time to let the air out of all of the tires."

The teenager gave him an incredulous look. "I told you, man, I had to walk up this stupid icy road in the dark. I didn't see anyone and I didn't notice anything wrong with the tires. I got inside this truck to keep from freezing to death."

"Let's get her back to Bettye's," Sophia suggested, reaching an arm out toward the girl. "You can interrogate her there."

Adan frowned and stomped and after grabbing some of his supplies, he locked up what was left of his truck. "Nothing to be done with this for now. Let's go then."

Sweet Melissa yanked away from Sophia. "Just tell me how to get there."

Adan shook his head. "That's not how this works. How old are you?"

"Old enough to get myself here," she replied, her eyes blazing black. Her attitude was now wide-awake.

Adan took her by the arm. "C'mon. We'll take you to your grandmother—if she really is your grandmother. But you'd better show her some respect, you hear me?"

"You can't boss me around," Melissa said on a snap.

"Do you want me to do a search or send out a missing person bulletin on you?" Adan countered. "I can put you on a bus right back to where you came from."

The girl's eyes glazed with shock and fear. "No, don't do that. I'm sorry. I... I can't go back to Hot Springs."

Adan started to speak, but Sophia gave him an imploring glance and shook her head.

Adan wanted to protest but realized the girl was stuck here just like him. He'd get her story soon enough.

For now, he decided his best move would be to shut up.

What did he know about women? About as much as a thimble could hold. He'd grown up mostly in a man's world, but his sweet mama had tried to guide him on the feminine mystique. He'd married well into his late twenties after he'd fallen hard for a spoiled Texas princess and that had ended badly about two years later when she decided she didn't want to be a wife and a mother. Now he was remembering why he'd been so cautious since. He wasn't good with the opposite sex.

So he grunted and started up the mountain with the girl and Sophia in tow. "Don't make me regret this," he said.

He'd get the girl into a safe, warm place and then find out if she was on a missing person or runaway list and get as much information as he could on her. That was, if he could get any bars on his infernal phone.

AN HOUR LATER, they trudged into the circle of cabins.

"So much for searching for Joe Pritchard," Adan mumbled, aggravated with Sophia and Melissa since his instincts shouted that they both had big secrets.

And probably about the same man.

Ol' Joe must sure be a charmer. Adan planned to show him some charm once he had him in his custody.

Sophia motioned toward her cabin. "Melissa, I live here and your grandmother lives right there a few yards from my place."

The girl stopped at the edge of the clearing. "Wow. This place looks like...outta *Cold Mountain* or something."

Impressed, Sophia smiled. "You've read *Cold Mountain*?"

Melissa rolled her eyes. "Duh—saw the movie twice."

"The movie. Oh, well, that's good," Sophia replied, glad that at least the girl had some sense regarding mountains.

"Do y'all have wireless up here?" Melissa asked.

Adan grunted. "Yeah, as in if it ain't wired up to something, it ain't going out over the airwaves." He tapped his phone. "I have almost half a bar."

Melissa looked panicked. "How will I call Sean?"

"Who's Sean?" Sophia asked.

"Uh…my boyfriend. He's supposed to meet me here this weekend."

"And how old are you again?" Adan asked, his Ranger frown front and center.

"I'm sixteen," Melissa retorted. "And it's really none of your business."

Adan towered over the girl. "It is if—"

"Hey, why don't we get you inside and find you something warm to drink?" Sophia asked with a warning glance toward Adan. "Then we'll go see your grandma."

"I'd rather just see her now," Melissa said, already stalking toward Bettye's cabin.

But before Adan or Sophia could stop the girl, Bettye's front door opened and she came out on the porch. The older lady stared at them for a moment then put her hands to her mouth in a gasp.

Sophia watched as Bettye grabbed hold of the porch railing and tried to get down the steps. She pulled Melissa forward. "Bettye, this is—"

"Martha!" Bettye reached out a hand as if she wasn't sure whether to touch the girl or not.

Melissa glanced over at Sophia, tears in her

eyes. "Martha was my mama. She died when I was a baby."

"Oh, I'm so sorry," Sophia said, her heart hurting for both of them. "She thinks you're your mother."

"Grandma?" Melissa stepped closer. "Grandma, I'm Melissa. Martha was my mama."

Bettye looked confused. "What?"

"I'm Martha's daughter," Melissa said, rushing toward Bettye. "My daddy used to say I look just like her. He left, too, after she died."

Bettye reached out both hands now. "Mercy, child, come here and let me look at you."

Melissa rushed into her grandmother's arms. "I didn't mean to scare you. I didn't know if you knew about me."

"I did, I did," Bettye replied, her hands smoothing Melissa's long hair. "I never got to see you, though. Never did."

"I… I read about you in Mama's journals," Melissa replied, tears streaming down her face. "She said y'all used to come here when she was little. I had to come and see if I could find you."

Bettye bobbed her head, stray grayish-white hair floating around her face in lacy waves. "I'm so glad you did, too. I thought I was seeing a ghost but…you're real."

"I am," Melissa said. She leaned back to wipe at her eyes. "Can I stay for a while?"

Bettye smiled and patted Melissa's face.

"Honey, you can stay as long as you want. Let's get you inside outta this cold."

They turned to head up the steps of Bettye's cabin.

Adan glanced over at Sophia. "I guess we should give them some time alone."

Sophia nodded, her appreciation for his thoughtfulness rising above the aggravation of having to deal with him. "Yes, I think that'd be best. We can catch up with Bettye later."

"And I need to ask Melissa some more questions." He started toward her cabin. "What a morning. What else is gonna happen on this dang mountain?"

Sophia didn't know how to answer. She wished she could open up to Adan and tell him the truth. But that truth might net her a long stay in jail. She couldn't risk that. She wouldn't risk that or getting all of her friends in trouble, either.

She gazed over at him. "I don't know. What's your plan on trying to find Joe Pritchard?"

Adan turned and did a scan of the woods. "I don't know whether to wait him out or search the entire area." He let out another grunt. "He's either dead by now or long gone."

"You don't like failing, do you?"

Adan glared at her with a comical shocked expression, as if he'd never heard that question before. "What do you mean?"

"I mean, you're like a bulldog searching for a lost bone."

"The man is a wanted criminal so, yes, I intend to do my job no matter how many people around here try to stop me."

"What makes you think we're trying to stop you?"

He shook his head. "Are you serious? I get stonewalled at every turn."

Sophia pointed toward Bettye's cabin. "You honestly believe that girl had anything to do with…you not finding Pritchard?"

"She showed up right after he did—or maybe even when he did," Adan retorted. "I'm just putting two and two together."

"You're just being paranoid."

"I'm being smart," he replied. "And you'd be wise to help me instead of hindering me."

She would be wise to do that, yes. But Sophia wasn't ready to give up yet. She didn't want to involve herself in this. She wanted to run inside her cabin and lock the door and hold her gun close. But if she wanted to get Adan off her back so she could get on with her life, she'd have to help him search for Joe. Or at least get him out of her way long enough for her to come up with a solution for this whole mess.

"There's a small stream and waterfall down the path a way. We could search there. I'd think if he survived last night, he'd be looking for water this morning. Or he'd at least follow the stream back down to town, right?"

"Have you had experience with this sort of thing?" Adan asked, his gaze making her get all tingly and exposed.

"No, just assuming," she retorted. "Did I assume wrong?"

"No, you guessed right. That's exactly what a criminal would likely try."

Sophia didn't like that statement. "Does that make me a criminal?"

His gaze danced over her face with a questioning intensity. "I don't know. You tell me."

Sophia's disappointment must have shown on her face. When she turned to go inside her cabin, Adan reached for her and tugged her back around. "Hey, I need to quit ribbing you, I guess."

"Is that what you'd call this—you accusing me and doubting me at every turn? You're just having fun at my expense?"

"I'm trying hard to give you the benefit of the doubt."

"I appreciate that," she said, her eyes moving over his warm hand on her coat sleeve. "But you sure do have a funny way of doing things."

He let go and smiled. "I'll try to trust you more," he said on a soft note. "And sooner or later, you'll have to try trusting me."

Sophia had to turn away. His eyes told her the

truth. He really did want to trust in her. And he might be beginning to like her.

But he'd be so wrong to do that. She wasn't trustworthy at all. Not when she had to lie to him at every turn.

Maybe she was just as criminal as Joe Pritchard after all.

CHAPTER EIGHT

SHE WAS WAY too quiet.

Although Adan had only known Sophia for twenty-four hours or so, he knew enough to wonder what was going through her mind. Back there on the road, he'd sensed a need from her to say more, to finally open up to him. Maybe if he backed off and made her feel safe and comfortable, she'd let him into her pretty head. Right now the tension between them radiated enough to melt the ice on the trees outside.

But that tension wasn't all about hunting a criminal or Adan catching her in a lie. He didn't want to admit it, but he was attracted to the woman. She was voluptuous and cute and just quirky enough to be enticing. And just enticing enough to be dangerous. But so far, she'd been helpful in getting him around this curving, rock-clustered mountain.

By the time they returned to her cabin, the afternoon sun was high and the snow was changing into a messy slush. But according to the only two channels available to watch on the tiny television, more snow was on the way tonight and the temperature would go back below freezing. With a windchill of around ten degrees. Not good for anyone.

That meant the mountain road would ice over again. Not that that mattered too much to him now—his truck wasn't going anywhere until he could get his tires fixed. And by that time, Joe Pritchard would be long gone.

Unless someone on this mountain was hiding him.

Adan glanced over at Sophia again, thinking she sure didn't act like a woman who was hiding a wanted felon. But then, he'd learned that people could put on a good show when they were desperate and being chased by the law. After her initial reaction to that wanted poster, Sophia had managed to settle down and get back to being perky and cute.

Which only made him doubt her even more. There was a definite desperation to her laugh, a hint of worry in her tone, a shade of hidden urgency in her every move. She'd been frightened when they'd found his tires flat and spooked when the girl had popped up in his truck.

Had she been expecting someone else to be in that truck?

Hard to gauge, since they hadn't had time to talk about things after finding Melissa there.

Thinking of the girl, he tried his phone. "I have two bars. I'm doing a trace on Melissa Curtis."

Sophia turned from getting lunch together. "Are you sure that's wise?"

"Uh…she's a teenager who hitched a ride with a stranger from Hot Springs in the worst snowstorm of the winter. What's *not* wrong with that picture?"

"I see your point," she replied before she turned away. "I just think it will do Bettye good to have her here for a while."

"Well, with this weather she'll likely be here for a couple of days at least."

"Good," Sophia said, her tone full of pep.

Okay, so at this moment, she seemed perfectly normal. Adan watched her while he waited for someone in Austin to answer. It was close to Christmas, so maybe she loved having company for the holidays. Even sorry on-the-run criminal types? Even him?

His phone went dead before he could get through, so he gave up and decided to study Sophia.

She looked right at home in her colorful kitchen. The blue cabinets matched the blue in her long, bulky sweater and complimented her vivid eyes, while the bright pink-and-red tablecloth matched her captivating blush.

And when had he turned into a poetic sap?

Better to focus on what was going on in her

mind than what was happening with her curvy, becoming body.

It had been a while since he'd been intrigued by a woman. This one could either be a saint or a criminal.

Which only made things more interesting.

Adan didn't get all tangled up in messy relationships—not since Helena had left him high and dry with a baby girl. And he never would have been able to raise Gaylen without his parents there to help out.

No, sir. His job was a day-into-night kind of deal, with lots of hours on the road, away from home. He'd already missed out on so much in his daughter's life. He didn't want to add a love affair to that and disappoint yet another ready-to-settle-down woman. And he couldn't add to Gaylen's disappointment by parading a bevy of would-be stepmoms in and out of her life.

Not a problem with this one.

She bristled like a porky-pine if he looked at her wrong.

But it might be nice to soften that rigid stance.

He needed to remember that as far as he could tell this particular woman certainly didn't seem to be the settling down type. Sophia obviously had made a life for herself here on Crescent Mountain, but he wanted to get out this afternoon and talk to some of the neighbors to see just how settled she really was. Or how settled any of them really were.

Crescent Mountain was an eclectic, strange little community that could easily harbor vagabonds and criminals right along with artists and creative free spirits.

"What are you thinking over there, Ranger-Man?"

Adan blinked and glanced up to find Sophia standing at the table. A pot of steaming soup sat on a big trivet and the scent of bread wafted toward his hungry nostrils.

"Well, since I can't get a call out of here to save my life, I was just going over the particulars of finding Joe Pritchard. This weather has seriously aided and abetted that criminal." He gave the soup an appreciate sniff. "That is, if he's even still hanging around."

Her face went as neutral as the beige dish towel in her hand. "What's your next plan of action? After you eat this late lunch I fixed?"

Adan had a moment where he thought his next plan of action would be to walk across the room and kiss the cook. But he blinked that notion right out of his thick skull.

"I'm going back out there to look for signs that he's been here. To track him until I find him."

"You mean you might not be back here tonight?"

Adan pulled out a chair for her and smiled down at her. "Missing me again, darlin'?"

Something sizzled between them with all the power of a loose electrical wire.

They both stood back in surprise.

"I'm sorry," he said, silently kicking himself. "That was highly inappropriate."

She plopped into her chair and started dipping soup. "I will miss you. I'll miss that accusing tone you use and that questioning look in your eyes."

Adan took in her words while he watched soup splatter all around the plate underneath his bowl. "I make you uncomfortable. I've never been a ladies' man, but I have tried to be professional and courteous around women."

"I appreciate good manners, but I don't appreciate everything else you've done." She tore into a corn bread muffin and then meticulously dropped little pieces in her vegetable soup. "I feel like a prisoner in my own home."

"Fine," he retorted. "I'll bunk on the porch or go back and sleep in my truck."

Her eyes widened, her gaze hitting on him with what could have been a fierce concern. "You'll freeze to death."

Adan let out a grin. "Ah, so you do care."

She stirred her soup. "Only because I'm a

decent, kind person who would never leave anyone out in the cold."

Adan picked up on the flicker of something dark behind that statement. Still wondering what she needed to say but couldn't, he leaned up in his chair. "Then I'll ask Bettye to host me, or better yet, I'll ask one of your other neighbors."

"No, you can't do that!"

The tone of that declaration had his antenna up. "And why not?"

"You don't need to bother them. I have room, and other than Jacob and Bettye, most of them are...couples."

"Well, I'll share with Jacob, then. Two bachelors trying to figure out women. That'll sure fill the time."

"Just shut up and eat. You'll stay right here with me. And that's final."

Adan grinned again in spite of his doubts. Maybe she liked him a little bit after all. Or she wanted to monitor him all the time. "You sure are bossy."

She tossed back a wave of hair. "Well, I've been my own boss for a long time now."

He leaned in, elbows on the table. "Want to tell me about that?"

"Not particularly."

She ate her soup in silence for a moment. "On second thought, I guess you do need to know a few things about me." She shrugged. "If it'll get you off my back."

Seeing the touch of pain in her eyes, he nodded. "I'm listening."

"I...grew up in Waco. In a not-so-great part of town. My father left us when I was young and my mother drank herself to sleep every night." She put down her spoon and held her hands on the table. "I went from family members to foster homes and then back with my mom, over and over, so I learned how to be the responsible one. But no one taught me how to trust or how to judge. So I fell in with a bad crowd. Just so..."

"Just so?" Adan prompted.

"That's enough for now," she replied, a faraway look in her eyes. "You can stay here as long as you want. But don't try to figure me out or analyze me."

She dug back into her soup and shoved a big spoonful in her mouth so she wasn't able to speak. Adan followed suit and tried to taste the warm, homemade concoction.

But he couldn't stop thinking about how her lips would taste.

Adan watched as she slipped out of her chair and dumped the remains of her soup in the trash. Since he'd lost his appetite, too, he tried to finish his soup, but the chunky meat and spicy vegetables seemed to clog his throat.

She'd said she'd never learned to trust.

But he had to wonder who had hurt this woman to the point that she couldn't open up and tell the truth, for her own sake. What was she afraid of?

ADAN HADN'T FORCED her to go out with him this time. But Sophia kept her guard up, watching until he'd gone on up the hill before she ran over to Bettye's cabin. She'd have to put that moment they'd shared there by the dining table out of her mind while she warned the others to stay quiet.

The smoldering heat in his ever-changing golden-brown eyes when he'd called her *darlin'* had burned her worse than any encounter she'd ever had with a hot stove. Sophia couldn't chance that kind of heat ever again. That kind of feeling only ignited a raging fire that led to regret and to getting burned all over again.

"What's all the commotion?" Bettye asked when she opened the door after Sophia had pounded against it with all her might.

"He's out of the house for a while," Sophia gushed as she pushed through the door. "We can talk."

Bettye put a finger to her lips. "Okay, but Melissa is asleep in the other room." She glanced at the closed bedroom door. "Or leastways she was."

Sophia hadn't even considered Melissa being here when she'd sprinted across the woods. She was getting sloppy about being careful and it was all Adan's fault. How could she possibly stay ahead of a Texas Ranger?

"Honey, settle down," Bettye said, pulling Sophia into the kitchen. "Do you need some chamomile tea with wild honey?"

"No," Sophia said. "I need that Ranger to quit asking me about Joe Pritchard. I can't relate with his need for justice right now."

"So this Joe Pritchard is the man you thought you killed, right?"

Sophia had never heard it put quite that way but she trusted Bettye with her life. "Yes."

"Well, now you *can* relate to something with the Ranger," Bettye said on a pragmatic twist. "Apparently, Joe ain't really dead and you got a good man staying in your house. That works for everyone, right?"

"No, not right," Sophia replied, wishing the matchmaking glow would leave Bettye's face. "I tried to kill Joe and then I hid his car on this mountain. That means Adan could haul my butt in for attempted murder and for stealing a vehicle."

She'd never told Bettye the rest of the story and she wasn't about to now, either. Bettye knew too much already. Adan might brand her friend as an accomplice.

"But he won't," Bettye said in a low whisper. "He likes you way too much for that to happen."

"He might like me, but he likes his job a lot more and he's obviously good at it. It's only a matter of time before he figures things out, and then I'll have to go back to Texas."

"Figures out what?"

Both Bettye and Sophia jumped at the sound of Melissa's voice coming from the hallway around the corner. The girl stood all bleary-eyed and curious against the kitchen wall.

"Hey, honey," Bettye said as she hobbled over to Melissa and gave her a peck on the cheek. "Are you hungry?"

"Granny, you fed me four pancakes and a lot of bacon," Melissa replied, her arms wrapping against one of Bettye's old flannel shirts. "I'm fine."

"How about something warm to drink. Hot chocolate for everyone."

"Okay, yes, hot chocolate," Melissa said as she moved into the kitchen, her bright Christmas socks padding against the old, battered wooden floor. "Then will y'all tell me what's up with that wicked good-looking Ranger and what you're both trying to hide from him?"

Sophia nodded. "Only if you come clean on how you wound up in Adan's truck."

Melissa's mouth formed an O and then she shrugged. "Okay, deal. 'Cause I think I know exactly who he's looking for."

ADAN STOOD BEHIND a tree and watched as Sophia hotfooted it over to her friend Bettye's cabin. What was so all-fired important that she'd had to wait for him to leave?

Comparing notes, maybe? On him, since they'd tried to hold him hostage? Or maybe on Joe Pritchard, since that poster of his face had obviously upset Sophia? Or maybe plotting right along with Melissa about what they needed to do next?

He wasn't surprised about any of this, but he was disappointed that Sophia wouldn't level with him. If she'd helped Joe Pritchard escape, it would be bad but not the end of the world. Maybe the man had held her at gunpoint and forced her to help and she was just too scared to squeal on him.

Or maybe she knew Joe Pritchard and had willingly helped him get away.

Adan had hurried back to his truck earlier to get all of his notes on this man's rap sheet. He'd go over those and his phone notes later when it got too dark and too blasted cold to hunt anyone. He'd checked the truck from front to back but nothing other than the deflated tires had stood out. No signs of anyone moving through the woods around the vehicle that he could tell, either. Had Pritchard decided to get away while he could?

Adan wanted to search the area around the cabins for any trace of Pritchard. Or any signs of who might have aided and abetted him. Later tonight, he'd have to try again to reason with Sophia about why she refused to open up to him.

And in the meantime he'd hope he could get a signal on his phone so he could do a background check on just about everyone on this cold mountain.

CHAPTER NINE

ADAN STALKED THROUGH the foot-deep snow, looking for any hints that someone had been roaming around these wintry woods. Late afternoon was fast approaching and he wanted to cover a circular perimeter of these woods before nightfall.

Pritchard might be stupid in many ways, but he was on the run and that meant he'd try to survive any way he could. Maybe he'd hidden in his vehicle somewhere in the woods going up the mountain. The hills and valleys along the paved road offered protection and with a little foresight, even a dumb criminal could manage to stay out of sight. And staying near a water source made sense to Adan.

Adan's trek down toward the stream was arduous since trying to keep track of his whereabouts in the deep snow took extra time and effort. When he started seeing snapped branches and disturbances and indentions in the snow, he followed what became a definite trail. But with all the new snowfall from last night, it was hard to determine what or who had left the tracks in the woods behind the cabins.

He followed a haphazard path until he reached the icy stream that Sophia had mentioned earlier. A shallow band of water meandered like a white snake through the woods. The water was frozen over in spots but cracked and gaping in others. Someone had moved through that water to the other side of the stream, and that someone had done a lousy job of trying to keep their movements hidden.

Maybe it had happened this morning, since any earlier tracks would have frozen over solid again last night. Adan followed the stream and kept his eyes on the cracked ice, then eased into the open path, cold water covering his sturdy boots and worn jeans. He made it to the other shore and climbed up the bluff and searched, the smell of wood smoke causing him to crouch low and tread lightly.

When he saw an opening underneath the shelter of an ancient oak tree, he got down in the snow, the wet slush covering his heavy canvas coat. As he inched his way toward the recent campfire in a belly crawl, he heard voices. Adan pulled out his pocket-size binoculars and centered his gaze on what was left of the campfire.

No one there, but a struggling swirl of smoke told him it hadn't been long since someone had left the area. He scanned the white-blanketed woods, searching for signs of human life. Listening carefully, he traced the voices off to his right. Sounded as if someone was coming back up the incline of the mountain face.

Adan hid behind a copse of brittle snow-covered shrubs and waited to see who would show up, one hand on his gun and the other on his binoculars. He had to wonder if Sophia had hinted at this spot earlier because she knew Pritchard would head this way. Which made no sense. Was she helping the man or hoping he'd be captured? Or maybe hoping Pritchard would take care of Adan for her? The woman was a complete puzzle.

Focusing on his work for now, Adan put Sophia back in the I'll-figure-that-out-later box.

When a man and woman showed up with twigs and small limbs and worked on starting up the fire, Adan hid his frustration and took his hand off his weapon. These two people were buff and fit and apparently having a high old time out here in the freezing woods. Bundled in down jackets and sturdy hiking boots, they obviously didn't have a clue anyone was around, let alone a dangerous man.

He didn't know whether to enjoy the way they exchanged kisses and giggled gleefully or call it a day and go back and try to do the same with Sophia. After he interrogated her again, of course.

That wouldn't be right, so he decided he could at least interview these two lovebirds to see if they'd noticed anything unusual, like a desperate criminal traipsing through the woods.

So he stood and made as much noise as possible, then walked down what looked like a path and waved. "Hello."

The couple broke apart and looked shocked and embarrassed.

"Uh...hello," the young man said, getting up to stand in front of his woman. "Can we help you?"

Adan nodded and showed them his badge. "Texas Ranger Adan Harrison—"

"It's the Ranger," the woman said, getting up to stare at Adan with a kind of curious fascination she might give an unusual bug. "We've heard a lot about you."

Adan did an eyebrow frown, thinking it would be mighty hard to find a criminal when everyone on this mountain knew they were both here. "Is that right? And who told you about me?"

"Bettye, of course," the woman said. "We have a very tight grapevine around here."

Adan approached until he stood directly across from them. "Then you know why I'm here."

The woman shook her head. "Not really, other than you're a friend of Sophia's and...well...y'all need your privacy."

Surprised yet again, Adan put on his poker face. "Well, I guess the cat is out of the bag."

The woman stepped forward and extended her hand, clearly happy to discuss his so-called love life. "I'm Maggie Burton and this is my husband, Arnie."

The man offered his hand, but he didn't look all that thrilled to see Adan. "Hi. How ya doing, sir?"

Adan grinned and shook his head, thinking the vibes with these two set off all kind of alarms in his mind. "I'm fine, I reckon. And call me Adan."

They laughed and both started talking at once.

"This is where he proposed to me," Maggie explained, one hand sweeping the distant vistas. "Such a lovely spot."

"So we come back here every year right before Christmas and remember how special that day was," Arnie added. "Of course, it's not usually whiteout conditions like this."

Adan glanced around. "I didn't expect to see anyone out on a day like this. Surprised you'd want to deal with this cold and snow."

"We're big hikers," Maggie said, adjusting her wool cap for emphasis. "But today, we were cold after our morning hike so we lit a fire and just had the nicest lunch of hot chocolate and trail mix and then we did another quick hike and came back." She pointed to her husband's backpack. "Would you like a granola bar?"

"No, thanks," Adan replied, his mind whirling with all kinds of scenarios. "So you just got back from an afternoon hike?"

"And here we are," Arnie said on a nervous laugh, obviously hoping that explained everything. "Need to build up this fire again."

"Did you get out for some fresh air?" Maggie asked, her tone a bit too perky. Then she looked past him. "Where is Sophia?"

"She stayed behind," Adan replied, glancing past them with the solid assurance that these two were putting on a big show.

"Oh, too bad," Maggie replied, her hand tugging at her hair. "We all love Sophia." She did the hat moving thing again.

A secret code or warning to someone?

"She's a sweet woman," Adan said, not bothering to mention Sophia was pretty brutal with duct tape. "I probably need to get back and check on her."

Then reality set in. What if these two were a distraction so Pritchard could circle back to see Sophia? But why would he do that and why in the world would she still willingly be helping a known felon when she had a Texas Ranger staying at her place?

He'd have to hurry back to the cabin and confront her.

The more he thought about it, the more convinced Adan became that something was up with the friendly folk of Crescent Mountain. The only explanation seemed to point to all of them trying to put on some kind of act for his sake. And these two were front and center right now.

They'd made a big show of kissing and cuddling before they pretended to be rebuilding the fire. Then they'd been so animated their acting smacked of a complete deception.

Or maybe he was just becoming too jaded and distrustful.

"So have y'all seen anyone else today?"

"Who wants to know?" Arnie quipped, slapping a hand on his fancy hiking pants.

"I do," Adan said, done with the comedy routine. "I'm here on official business. Looking for a man—big, bulky and mean, and wanted by the state of Texas." His voice grew louder with each word. "Fugitive, felon, murderer who could be loose in these beautiful, romantic woods. And anyone who might be aiding and abetting him would suffer serious consequences."

He lifted his gaze to the trees and thought he saw a movement up on the bluff. Adan pretended to ignore that movement and then zoomed in on the now cowering but still adorably cute couple. "Know anyone like that?"

"We don't," Maggie said, her voice rising, both

of her hands on her hat now. "We don't. Do we, Arnie?"

"No, we haven't seen a soul. Just out here for our annual smoochfest." He gave his wife a big peck on the cheek for emphasis.

"Cut the charade," Adan retorted, stomping closer. "I need somebody to tell me the truth." He called out to the trees. "And someone better start talking or I'll haul all of you to the nearest police station."

He waited, hoping he'd finally get somewhere.

And heard nothing but the echo of his suspicions.

Maggie and Arnie had both become quiet, which was kind of amazing in itself.

Adan stomped his boots, causing Maggie to jump. "What? Nothing? No words of wisdom, no other explanation for the two of you being out here in the freezing cold?"

Arnie shot a panicked glance at Maggie. "Hey, man, we're renters. We only come up here about twice a year. At Christmas, to celebrate our engagement and anniversary, and a week or two during the summer to get away from Dallas and do some hiking." He shrugged and tugged his down jacket close. "We don't want any trouble."

"We got married here," Maggie added, her hat now firmly on her head. "This is a special place to us. The people here are special. Tight-knit."

Adan took in their meek expressions and quiet confessions and then it hit him. "So you two aren't protecting Joe Pritchard at all, right?"

"No, sir," Arnie replied, clearly relieved to have that notion out of the way. "We're kind of concerned that he might still be here, but…"

"So you've heard of Joe Pritchard?" Adan retorted, his gaze moving between the two of them.

"Only just in the last twenty-four hours or less, even," Arnie said, clearly wishing he hadn't messed up on that one.

"Who mentioned him to you?"

"Uh… I don't recall."

Adan snorted. "Right."

Maggie piped in. "But we had to come to our special spot and we've been extra careful and…"

"And you're actually protecting someone else, right?"

Maggie bobbed her head before she realized she'd been tricked. Then she gave her scared husband a quick, apologetic glance and leaned close to Adan and started in a rather loud whisper, "We also have a lookout." She did a quick point and lifted her head. "Up there on the ridge."

"Who?" Adan asked, thinking his mind was so befuddled he couldn't even spot a sniper in the snow.

"Jacob," Arnie said in a manly whisper, followed by a confused shrug. "It's a way to protect ourselves."

Adan almost laughed out loud. "Jacob?" The man had to have cataracts in both eyes. "How would Jacob be able to stand as lookout?"

Maggie twisted her hat. "Because he's an expert—"

A shot rang out and Adan heard a distinct whiz about six inches from his left ear.

"Marksman," Arnie finished, still ducking.

Adan grunted and waved a hand in the air. "Sorry, Jacob. No offense."

"None taken," a wizened voice called out. "How 'bout we all just go on home now?"

Adan couldn't agree more. "Is it safe?"

Jacob chuckled. "I reckon it is by now."

SOPHIA CHECKED ALL the windows again and went back over her new exit plan. If Joe tried to double back from whatever hidey-hole he'd crawled into, she'd be ready. And if Adan tried to stop her from escaping to save her own hide, she'd be ready.

She didn't know whether to cry because her hopefully dead ex-husband had finally found her or to laugh because she had a Ranger marking her every footstep to protect her—or make her confess.

If she could just figure out how to trust Adan, she might make it out of this predicament alive.

"All okay?" Bettye asked, doing her own covert visual at the back door.

"I think so," Sophia replied. "We've checked every cabin, every shed and every cave close by. Joe is not anywhere in our little area of the mountain. We've hidden any evidence of what I did before. And we've done as much as we can to catch him if he is hiding out here."

She read over the to-do list she had to destroy. While the Burtons had distracted Adan, she and Bettye, along with the newly recruited Melissa, had gone out with guns to flush out anybody who might be hiding in the many outbuildings and caves in the area. They'd also hurried to set up animal traps in strategic places in all of those areas, too.

Melissa watched from her post at the other window. "And you promise you won't tell the Ranger what I had to do?"

"No," both Bettye and Sophia said in unison.

Then Bettye wagged a finger at her grand-daughter. "Not as long as you abide by my house rules, young lady."

"Yes, Granny." Melissa's wide-eyed gaze flashed between them. "As long as y'all don't report me to anyone back in Hot Springs. I can't go back there."

"Agreed," Bettye said.

"Agreed," Sophia replied. Having been through the foster system herself, she'd learned that not all foster families had a child's well-being in mind.

"Now go to your post outside," Bettye said through a proud smile. She watched as Melissa did as she asked. "I'm so glad she found me," Bettye said in a quiet voice.

Sophia thought Melissa's involvement would be just one more fib she'd have to keep quiet. But after hearing the girl's story, she could certainly understand why Melissa needed some help of her own. Bettye loved the girl already, so that was enough of an endorsement for Sophia.

"But his car is still here," Bettye pointed out with an eloquent shrug. "I mean, the car you say you stole when you had to leave him in a big hurry and all."

Bettye was being discreet. Sophia had fought for her life and she'd believed she'd killed Joe in the process. But she'd run away with his car and she'd never looked back.

Until now. Guilt colored her face because she couldn't bring herself to tell Bettye the whole truth. She'd taken more than just Joe's crappy old car.

Would she forever be running from her necessary lies?

"And we took care of that, too," Sophia replied, feeling much better since she'd set her plan into action. They'd added more brush and rocks to cover the big rock overhang under which she'd parked the car all those years ago. And a trap near the passenger side door, too.

She always felt better when she could control her environment. Or at least when she knew her crazy ex-husband wasn't going to try to murder her again.

Now to take care of the good-looking, well-meaning Texas Ranger who'd come to do his duty. If she could stall Adan long enough to get either him or that car off this mountain, she might not have to go to jail after all.

"Alert the media," Bettye said, spinning in a whirl of skirts and socks. "We got company coming."

Sophia worked to control the panic rising inside her stomach. "Where's Melissa? She's supposed to be the immediate lookout."

"She's leading the way," Bettye replied. Then she poked a thumb over her shoulder. "And your perty Ranger-Man is bringing up the rear."

"Do you think he's onto us?" Sophia asked, running to the window to look out at the path behind the cabins.

"He's a smart one," Bettye admitted. "But he's still alive, so that means Jacob didn't have to shoot him."

"I told Jacob *not* to shoot him," Sophia reminded her. "What about the Burtons—are they with them?"

"Right smack in the middle and cooing and cuddling like two doves."

Sophia didn't want to envy her friends their perfect marriage, but a twinge always hit her whenever the Burtons were in residence on the mountain. She so wanted that kind of love for herself. "Are they still putting on a show?"

"Those two are the real thing," Bettye replied. "You could have that, too, you know." She pointed out the window.

"No," Sophia said, her tone level and sure. "No, that kind of feeling isn't in the cards for me. Especially with a man like Adan."

Bettye gave her a good hug. "You sell yourself too short, honey."

Sophia didn't know how to respond to that. She was being realistic. And she certainly couldn't admit an attraction to a man who might have to take her back to Texas and throw her in the slammer.

"I have to face the fact that I'm not good enough for an honest man. If I had been, I would have never gotten involved with the likes of Joe Pritchard."

Bettye gave her a shake of the head. "We disagree on that, but we ain't got time to fuss about it." She fluffed her always falling-down hair and put on her game face. "Let's just have some fun flirting with your Ranger-Man."

Sophia looked out the window and saw Adan's frowning face, her heart doing a drop that felt like falling off a sheer incline. She didn't think there would be any flirting going on tonight.

CHAPTER TEN

HE HAD THEM all lined up like kindergartners waiting for cookies. Only Sophia knew Adan wasn't about to hand out cookies. He was angry. His anger radiated off every pore and showed in the fine sheen of sweat on his brow as he tugged off his jacket and threw off his hat and jammed his fingers through his damp spiky bangs.

"So everyone here is trying to hide something from me, right?"

No one said a word. Sophia held her head high but refused to spill her guts unless she had no other resort. These people were trying to help her, and she didn't want their efforts to be in vain. But she couldn't let them take the heat for her past sins, either. So she held her breath and hoped Adan would understand. At least until she could come up with a good answer.

He stalked in front of the crackling fire, his eyes going a burnished brown. "And no one wants to tell me the truth, either. I let my guard down with you people and now—"

Melissa rolled her eyes. "I really want to call my boyfriend. Can't I please be excused?"

"No," Adan retorted. "You were one of the lookouts, so that makes you an accessory to withholding information and obstructing justice. I'm not done with you yet."

"I got here yesterday," the girl shouted, her hands across her midsection in standard teen defiance. "I don't have a clue what you're talking about."

Sophia lowered her eyes on that one. A sure sign the girl had a lot of clues but she wasn't going to share them with him. Adan would go into another angry spin if she did that.

This situation was getting out of hand.

"I asked Melissa to help," Sophia admitted. "But we were scared that man might come back—I mean—show up again."

"So he was here?" Adan asked, zooming in on her words like a hawk after a rodent.

"I don't know," she admitted. "Someone wanted us to see that poster, and that scared me into action." She had to start trusting him, so she left out a breath of air. "I... I've always taken care of myself so today, I put an action plan into place so no one—and I mean no one—will harm anyone on this mountain."

"So you put a young girl out there right in his path?" Adan asked, his tone full of a fuming rage. "How is that in any way a good action plan?"

"I didn't think about it that way," Sophia replied, mortified. "I guess I need to leave that up to you since you're the pro."

The look on his face changed from condemning to understanding mixed with a bit of sheepishness. "I'm sorry, I shouldn't have said what I did. If you're scared, Sophia, then let me help you." He took a step toward her. "Please?"

The room went silent and to Sophia it seemed as if she and Adan were here alone. She couldn't speak, so she just nodded. Having a real man willing to apologize and tell her he'd help her touched her more than she realized. No one other than her friends here had ever offered that. Could she trust Adan in the same way she trusted the Crescent Mountain folks?

"I am scared," she admitted. "But not for the reasons you think." She plunged ahead. "But don't blame my friends for trying to protect me. They were only doing what I asked."

Adan broke the thread between them and the moment of hope was gone. "I need someone to start talking so we can get to the bottom of this."

Bettye shot her a covert glance, her head down, one hand on old Bandit, who also looked guilty even though he'd slept through the whole affair. Jacob stared straight ahead with a noble silence that implied he was sitting on the chopping block. Poor Maggie and Arnie kept sending glances toward each other with the desperation of two people who were about to go down for helping a friend.

Sophia only hoped the last neighbors left—Karen and David Harper—were safe inside their home. No one had seen them much today but they tended to stay to themselves a lot.

Adan went back to stomping and glanced around. "Don't look so glum. I can't prove anything and if no one is going to tell me the truth, I'll just have to keep digging." He rolled up his shirtsleeves. "But we won't leave here until I'm through."

Bettye pursed her lips. "I guess I'd better start supper then. We can't confess to anything on an empty stomach."

She got up off the stool where she'd been perched and ready for flight by the back door. "I can throw something together, I reckon."

Adan held up a hand. "Bettye, I appreciate that, but please sit down."

Bettye did as he asked with a resigned shrug. "We gotta eat. Even if we are being held against our will."

"You are not being held against your will," Adan replied through a grunt. He pointed to the Burtons. "Look, these two have already admitted they were protecting Sophia. I'd just like to know why they felt it necessary to stall me while Jacob held a gun on me and shot past my ear to prove a point."

"I didn't try to kill you," Jacob said on a gap-toothed grin. "If I'd'a wanted to do that, you wouldn't be standing there and we'd all be eating supper by now."

Adan slapped his hand against his jeans, causing Bandit to lift his head and open one droopy eye. Sophia's heart did more than lift. It shot against her ribs. She was sweating droplets of fear and exhaustion. She couldn't keep up this farce much longer.

"That is the kind of attitude that *has* all of you sitting here," Adan explained in the tone of a disappointed parent, his gaze back on Sophia. "Tricking me, consorting behind my back, lying to me."

"We didn't lie," Arnie said in a hoarse gulp. "It really *is* our anniversary and we *do* love each other. We *did* take two hikes today and we built that fire just as we said."

"And you *did* try to distract me," Adan reminded them with the same inflections Arnie had used.

Only they sounded more ominous coming from Adan.

"You were interrogating us," Maggie retorted, her short dark hair tousled and windblown. "I mean, we were simply doing what we always do. Minding our own business and helping out a neighbor."

"But why do you need to help Sophia?" Adan

asked, his eyes now centered on Sophia. "What are you afraid of?"

She tried to smooth things over with a partial truth. "I don't like law enforcement people."

"Because?"

She also didn't like the way his gaze burned hot on her, his expression caught between a big question and a huge disappointment. "Because... I don't trust people in positions of authority."

"Because?" he repeated, clearly glad to be on this track. Until he seemed to absorb some of the meaning behind her words. "Sophia—"

"Because she got a traffic ticket once and she's a good driver," Bettye said on a not-too-convincing sputter of a lie.

"Oh, I see," Adan replied, his hand on his hip. "You know what, if I can ever get any signal on my not-so-smart smartphone, I'll do a background check and pull up that ticket. We can clear that up right away."

Sophia made a mental note to hide his cell phone charger.

"Good luck with getting through," Melissa said, holding up her phone with a groan. "Stupid mountain. Sean will never find me now."

Sophia had to wonder why Melissa was so worried about her boyfriend finding her. If the kid couldn't make it up the mountain, so be it. Probably trouble anyway. And none of them needed any more trouble.

"Don't matter," Bettye continued, digging the hole of their lie even deeper. "She paid it off and went on with her life 'cause she's a good person."

Before Adan could move his lips to form an opinion on that, Jacob piped up. "We don't get many signals at all. Have to go halfway down the mountain—" After all the shushing in the room, he stopped and rubbed a hand down his whiskers. "Uh, and even then it's shady, mighty shady."

"This," Adan said, pointing to all of them, "this is shady. If I have to walk down the mountain and go to the nearest sheriff's office, I will do a check on each and every one of you. So if you've got any past indiscretions, you'd better confess right now."

Sophia had enough. "You don't have to do that. I—"

"Where's David and Karen?" Bettye said, getting up to rush to the back door. "I haven't seen them all day long."

"We checked on them last night, 'member? They were in for the night," Jacob said, making a big deal out of trying to lift up from the leather armchair. "Best go find them so they can get quizzed by the fuzz, too."

"I'm not the fuzz—" Adan gave Sophia a helpless glance and watched in amazement as one by one they left the building.

Except for Sophia.

Sophia didn't move, but she glanced over at him with an apologetic shake of her head. "I'm sorry. It's like herding cats, but they mean well."

He stalked toward her and leaned down, his finger in her face, his eyes blazing. "This is not over."

"I know," she said, resigning herself to what would have to happen sooner or later. Then she stood and faced him and tried really hard to ignore the fresh-snow outdoor scents surrounding him or the sunset gold in his eyes. "But we do need to check on the Harpers. They always come outside to feed the winter birds, and I haven't seen them all day."

Before he could say anything more, she got up and ran out of the cabin.

ADAN GLANCED AROUND and realized he was alone.

Could he possibly be the dumbest Texas Ranger in history? More like the most appeasing Ranger in history. He'd purposely tried to check his mean streak at the door, hoping these seemingly good people would let him in on the big secret.

Were they all trying to hide Joe Pritchard for some odd reason? Joe could be holding someone they all cared about, maybe forcing them to cover up for him. That was one scenario. Or maybe he was waiting for the snow to thaw so that one of them could get him down the mountain. That was another scenario. Or he could be holed up in one of the cabins that Adan had tried to check out yesterday and again this morning.

Sophia had admitted she was scared and that she had asked her neighbors to help her. The neighbors had practically admitted they'd done things to protect Sophia. But not for the reasons he thought.

Was she scared of any intruder or just this particular one?

That would mean she did know Pritchard and she was terrified that he was on this mountain just as Adan had suspected. But instead of aiding the criminal, maybe she was trying to make sure he didn't bother her or any of her friends.

And that would also mean that Joe Pritchard could have come here with one purpose in mind— to find Sophia Mitchell.

Adan's heart did a funny thing. It beat a lot faster.

He couldn't abide Sophia being in real danger. He couldn't allow her to be the sole target of a nasty criminal.

Grabbing his hat and coat, he hurried after the trail of suddenly concerned cohorts, wondering what kind of confession Sophia had been about to make. And wondering how he'd get back to the place where she wanted to tell him the truth.

The woman obviously didn't trust him with whatever escapades she'd been dealing with, but he wanted her to trust him. And he sure wanted to trust her.

Being attracted to her didn't help his mood one bit and since he'd failed at drawing her or anyone else out with his winning personality, Adan decided he'd try to play along with this haphazard troupe and see what happened.

One thing he could see—she'd probably been all about sacrificing herself for someone else. Her friends or Pritchard? Or both? If she was trying to protect her friends, he could help her. He'd have to find a way to convince her of that.

He was seriously getting a headache. And a bad spell of cabin fever. By the time he was out the door, the others were banging and pounding on the last occupied cabin of the far-reaching semicircle of homes. The snow dripped against the trees and merged into the solid white of the forest, but a cleared, muddy path moved through the back trail behind the cabins.

He followed the trail and found the little posse. Catching up with them, Adan got ahead of Sophia. "Let me handle this," he suggested.

They all followed him without a word, but he didn't miss the secretive glances passing between them.

Two cabins sat next to the Harpers' and the rest of the clan and he'd checked those early today. David Harper had answered right away this morning at their cabin and he and Adan had

had a short discussion regarding Joe Pritchard, but David had said he hadn't seen any strangers other than Adan.

After finding nothing out of the ordinary at that cabin, Adan had gone to the next one—the Burtons' cabin.

They hadn't answered yesterday or this morning, either. Today, of course, they'd been out doing their duty for Sophia.

When no one came to the door of the Harper cabin, Adan hushed all the interested parties and called out, "Texas Ranger. Open up."

He thought he heard a muffled sound. Holding up his hand, he demanded silence from the spectators behind him. "Anyone in there?"

Another muffled sound.

"I think I hear something," Jacob called, his hand to his ear. "Turned up my hearing aids this morning," he explained. "That sounded kinda like a cat. Do they have a cat?"

"No," Bettye replied on a loud note. "No animals. She's allergic. Coughs and sneezes whenever she comes to my house."

Before they could get in a big discussion about animal dander, Adan called out again. "Is anyone in there? Can you hear us?"

A definite muffled cry.

"I heard that," Melissa said, her interest perking up. "That wasn't a cat."

"Someone's in there," Sophia said, rushing past him. "Karen, is that you?"

"Uh-hmm!"

"She said yes," Jacob shouted. "We need to break down that door."

For once, Adan agreed with him. "Stand back," he shouted. Then he lifted his leg and hit the door with his booted foot.

And promptly fell in a pile of pain on the porch floor.

"They have a fairly strong two-by-four latch on that door," Jacob said to the now silent crowd. "But we can sure get in through the back door."

Adan let out a groan. "I really wish you'd told me that before I jammed my leg."

They all hurried around the house, making enough noise to scare away even a criminal. The curtains were closed so Adan couldn't see inside, but they could hear the muffled wails growing louder.

"That's coming from the bedroom," Bettye said. "It's just down from this window."

Adan tried the window. "It's locked. Let's go check the back door."

When they got to the back door, Adan turned to Jacob. "Latch on this one, too?"

"No, they have a key to this one. David always locks things up when he leaves Karen alone here."

Adan tried the door. "It's locked."

"Break one of the panes," Melissa suggested with a shrug.

Adan took an old hammer Jacob found in a toolbox on the porch and hit it against one of the wide panes then reached in and found the dead bolt. "I think I can get it open." He drew his weapon. "Y'all need to stay here."

"I'm going with you," Sophia said against his shoulder.

Adan turned to stare at her, the scent of her spicy shampoo assaulting his senses. "No. You will *all* stay right here."

He yanked his heavy jacket away and dropped it on the floor. Then he put his right hand through the hole and with a little bit of muscle, clicked the lock on the old door. After that he kicked the door back and held his gun in front of him.

"Texas Ranger. Coming in."

Sophia pushed past all of them again. "I'm going in, too," she said on an impatient note, the dare in her eyes telling Adan she met business.

A moment of doubt ticked away in Adan's mind, but he had to trust her at some point. "Okay," he said. "But stay behind me and be careful."

She hurried through the door before he could change his mind.

CHAPTER ELEVEN

SOPHIA CALLED OUT in a loud voice. "Karen? David?"

"Umm."

She hurried toward the hallway to the bedroom, but Adan's hand on her arm stopped her.

"Behind me," he reminded her, his tone firm.

Sophia stepped back but she called out, "I'm right here, Karen. We're coming."

She added that last in case Pritchard was still here.

Carefully creeping toward the bedroom with Adan, she jumped when a hand touched her arm.

Adan. He tugged her close and put a finger to her lips. "Stay here and stay quiet."

Sophia almost followed on his heels to the bedroom but the touch of his finger on her skin threw her into a stupor of longing. How could she think about what it would be like to kiss him when her friend was in danger? Shaking her emotions away, Sophia rushed after him and found Karen on the floor with a gag over her mouth, her hands and feet tied up and her body strapped to a bedpost. When she saw Sophia, tears ran down her face.

Sophia slipped around Adan. "It's okay. We're here. You're okay." She untied the gag.

"He took David," Karen said on a wail. "This afternoon when he saw the Ranger going down toward the creek. He took my husband and made David lock me up inside the house. He was gonna take me but David begged him to take him instead."

Adan got out his phone. "I have to get someone up here. Now we can add kidnapping to Pritchard's many illegal acts."

"He said he'd kill David if we called anyone," Karen said as she rubbed her blistered red wrists. "I've been so worried and I don't know what to do." She wiped at her eyes. "He said he needed to get down the mountain."

"We'll find your husband," Adan said, but the look he gave Sophia said differently. "With unreliable phone service to call for backup, we'll have to do it on our own. The roads are still too frozen to get down the mountain for help and besides, we can't waste time with that now."

Karen stared crying again, her brown eyes red-rimmed, her dark hair tousled. She glanced up at Adan. "He was here when you came by earlier. But he held a gun on me in the old root cellar. Told us if we squealed he'd kill everyone on this mountain."

Her gaze moved to Sophia and then she gave a little nod that Adan probably didn't even notice.

Sophia felt sick to her stomach. Pritchard was here because of her and all she'd done so far was lie to protect herself.

"Adan?"

He looked at her with a new trust, his eyes brightening. How could she tell him here and now, with Karen so distraught and everyone waiting on the porch?

"We'll talk later," he said, understanding passing through his eyes. "Let's get her over to Bettye's place."

Karen moaned in pain when they lifted her, but she straightened and nodded when Sophia took her hand. Adan grabbed a jacket to wrap over her shoulders and together they helped her out onto the porch.

Soon everyone was fussing over her enough to get her off the porch and back in a warm safe place. Sophia watched as Adan stared out over the snow-covered mountain, his eyes dark with a dangerous sheen.

He would go after Joe Pritchard and he'd kill him if he had to. She didn't doubt this at all. But Adan lived by the law, so he'd do his best to abide by that law. And that might mean he'd have to bring Sophia to justice.

She once again reminded herself that she was involved with two very dangerous men.

One who wanted her dead.

And one who wanted her to tell the truth.

She knew the danger in both, but her heart was telling her to trust Adan. She had to stop this, so what other choice did she have? She couldn't put her friends through this just to keep Adan from finding out the worst. Things had progressed way too far for that now.

ADAN STOMPED AROUND the yard in frustration.

He couldn't get a signal on his phone and all of the landlines were down because of yesterday's storm. The best option was to try and drive down the icy mountain road to the sheriff's station in town to get help. But that was at least ten treacherous miles and it left everyone here vulnerable to Joe Pritchard's wrath.

The other option wasn't much better. He'd have to track Pritchard in almost whiteout conditions. And with more freezing temperatures tonight.

He went back into Bettye's cabin and sat down on a chair near Karen Harper. "So…can you tell me anything about where he might have taken David? Do you remember anything at all?"

Karen sipped the hot tea Bettye had offered her, her eyes still swollen. "We heard someone on the porch early this morning. David thought it might be Bettye or Jacob, so he didn't think a thing about opening the door to check."

Adan shot a glance toward where Sophia stood near the window, then returned his gaze to Karen. "And what happened when David opened the door?"

"He, uh, pushed his way inside and then held us at gunpoint for hours. He wanted someone to help him get back down the mountain so he could be on his way, but he was real nervous and he kept glancing out the window." She gulped back a dry sob. "When you knocked on the door this morning, he held the gun on me and told David he'd kill me and everyone on this mountain if we told anyone he was here."

"And he took you down into the root cellar?"

She bobbed her head. "Yes, it's under the hallway there by the kitchen. I could hear David telling you to come inside. I think he was trying to drop you a hint, but then he didn't want me to get shot, either."

Adan shook his head, a memory of David's calm demeanor haunting him. David hadn't let on about anything and because Adan suspected all of them, he'd cataloged that as a good sign. "I looked right inside the front door and never suspected a thing."

"David did a good job of pretending," she admitted. "He was so afraid for me."

"I understand," Adan replied. "Anything else stand out? Something Pritchard said or did?"

Karen glanced toward Sophia. Adan didn't

miss the couple of seconds of that exchange. Everyone was in on this but him, obviously. But for now, he chose to ignore that realization.

"Karen?"

"He said he needed a car, so he took ours. Made David drive him… They left after he saw you headed toward the stream."

"Why didn't I hear them going down the road?" Adan asked Sophia. "The road follows the stream in most places and with these icy conditions, I don't understand how they even made it."

"He took him the back way," Karen hurriedly added.

"The back way?" Adan scrubbed a hand down his face. "We have a back way and no one thought to tell me that."

"Didn't know it mattered," Bettye retorted, her expression laced with a pragmatic blankness.

"Everything matters," Adan replied, his words rising.

Karen started crying again. "He forced David to take him that way. I shouldn't have told you that. He might kill my husband." She rocked back and forth. "I heard him tell David he'd let him go when they reached the main road. But it's been hours now and I'm worried." She started crying again. "I'm so afraid David's had a wreck…or worse." She gave Adan an imploring look. "He seemed agitated about a lot of things."

Sophia stalked across the room. "A word with you, Adan?"

He gave Karen a pat on her arm. "I'll find David, I promise."

SOPHIA TOOK HIM out on the back porch. Jacob and the Burtons had all gone home and Melissa was in her room.

Once they were out of earshot, he turned to face her, the memory of her soft lips against his fingers causing his gaze to drift down to her mouth.

She must have remembered that heated touch, too. Their eyes met and held for a brief moment before she looked away, into the setting sun. Then she held her arms around her as if to ward off the bone-chilling dusk. Or maybe to ward him off.

"What do you want to say, Sophia?" he asked, hoping she'd finally tell him the truth.

She leaned against the porch railing. "Everything. Nothing. I don't know anymore."

He tugged her around and stared down at her. "I'm through playing games. Pritchard came to this mountain for a reason and I think that reason is you."

She didn't protest, so he figured she was about to come clean. But when she shivered and turned away, Adan forgot about getting the truth out of her. He only wanted to protect her.

"What did he do to you?"

She shook her head. "I can't say. Not here, not now."

"When?" he asked, his hand touching her hair. "When, Sophia?"

She wiped at her eyes. "Later. When we're alone."

"I have to go out and find them tonight," he said on a frustrated whisper. "If I don't stop this, David Harper might be dead by morning. Pritchard won't let him live to identify him. Do you want that on your conscience?"

She shook her head. "No. And that's why I'm going with you."

Adan stomped back. "Oh, no. You can't do that."

"He came here because of me, so yes, I can do that. We'll take Jacob's SUV. It has four-wheel drive." Lifting her right arm in the air, she went on a rant. "I've learned how to use just about any weapon. I've learned how to protect myself by using defensive techniques. I won't be afraid anymore."

Adan shook his head, but her words sent a chilled warning down his backbone. "You're trying to save everyone but yourself, aren't you?"

"Yes, yes. Because he took David for a reason and that reason is me. He knows I won't let him hurt any of them. He wants me to follow them and that's what I intend to do." She whirled and met his gaze, her eyes misty. "Maybe they all need saving more than I do."

"Don't talk like that," he said, wishing he could get this woman to truly open up to him. But fear and pain held her trapped inside her own agony. He'd be willing to kill Pritchard for that alone. "Your life is worth a lot—to your friends and to me."

"You don't know me," she replied. "But you will, soon enough."

"And what's the worst thing I should know about you?"

She started back inside then turned to stare up at him. "The worst right now—if we find Joe Pritchard, I'll make sure he's really dead this time."

ADAN AND SOPHIA finally headed back to her cabin. Now his mind was full of even more turmoil. He had to get out there and quick, to try and find Pritchard and David Harper, but he also wanted to grab Sophia and pull her close so they could finally get to the bottom of this.

But duty had to come first. At least she was beginning to trust him and that counted toward solving this case, at least.

After going back over the events of the day with Karen, Adan had a clear picture of Joe Pritchard's whereabouts.

He had tracked him to Crescent Mountain after

Pritchard had stolen a car. Then Pritchard must have ditched the vehicle in town and walked the mountain road. Adan had arrived late last night and taken that turn into the snowbank and wound up at Sophia's door. Pritchard had to have been in the area but before he could do anything, he'd obviously seen Sophia and Bettye knock Adan out and drag him inside.

Pritchard then left that wanted poster on Sophia's door to taunt her before he came after her. But Adan's arrival had put a damper on that little reunion. So then Pritchard must have tracked back down the road and found Adan's truck and deflated the tires to keep Adan from having a way to get around. Then traveled back up the mountain, probably through the woods just off the road, and managed to hide out until he could find an opportunity to get someone in the more remote cabins to open their door to him. The Harpers had fit the bill since they'd kept to themselves over the last day or so. Pritchard was desperate now. He needed to get away and he'd kill anyone who got in his path.

Only one thing didn't make sense. Why besides trying to stall Adan would Pritchard flatten Adan's truck tires? He could have hot-wired the truck and taken it or he could have just left it so Adan could leave. Sophia had wanted Adan to leave, too.

Maybe someone else around here needed him

to stay. What if Pritchard had also threatened another person?

Melissa.

That made sense. The girl was skittish around Adan, but she pretended she was worried about her boyfriend. Adan didn't buy that. Melissa's showing up here at the same time as Pritchard couldn't be a coincidence. Things usually didn't happen that way.

Or perhaps Pritchard had decided to mess with Sophia and Adan before he got away yet again. Another distraction to throw Adan off his trail.

Melissa, meantime, had somehow found the truck and hidden inside for the night. At least Pritchard hadn't taken the girl any farther than this mountain. Adan made a note to question her again. He'd let her slide this morning since Bettye had been so glad to see her.

Now, Adan and Sophia were gearing up for a long cold trek on a slippery road down the back side of the mountain. He couldn't leave her unprotected and she refused to involve anyone else again. Jacob had readily agreed to let them borrow his SUV, but he'd told Sophia to be careful.

"You better take care of her, Ranger-Man," he'd warned Adan.

So she was going with Adan while the neighbors stayed on high alert and used their own judgment on how to handle this situation.

"Is this road passable?" he asked Sophia, his mind on so much more than his job.

"As passable as the old road can be." She didn't look at him but kept her head down while she packed supplies in a dark canvas backpack. "We only use it if the main road is blocked. It's more of a hiking trail now."

"Does David know the area?"

"He should. He and Karen like to walk on the road rather than in the woods. Karen's afraid of bears and snakes." She stopped her packing. "But in this weather and with these conditions, I'm not sure any of us should be out on that road."

Adan agreed with that, at least. "Do you know this road?"

She nodded and looked away. "I've taken strolls back there looking for things to use in my art."

Adan wondered why she wouldn't look at him. "Anything else, Sophia?"

She finally closed the pack and hoisted it up on her back. "It's gonna be a long, cold night, Adan. We've got a lot of time to talk."

He came around the corner and put his hands on her arms then stared into her eyes. "And you will talk. Your friends have tried to protect you, but this is putting them all in danger. Unnecessary danger. Do you really want that?"

"No," she said, guilt darkening her eyes. "That's why I'm going to help you find Pritchard.

He took David to draw me out, so he's going to get his wish."

Adan tugged her close. "And that's why you're going to tell me everything you know about the man."

SOPHIA WAS SO bundled she could barely move. She had on a quilted parka with a fur hood and tight leather gloves, flannel-lined pants and wool socks tucked into sturdy hiking boots. Even with all that warmth and the heater blowing warm air in the car, she couldn't stop shivering. A cold sweat popped out along her shoulder blades.

She glanced over at Adan. He'd insisted on driving. That gave her time to think about what lay ahead. She was going to find the man who'd tormented her for years before she'd taken matters into her own hands. Her ex-husband.

And she now had Adan to deal with because of that man.

In a way, she felt relief that this would soon be over. Adan was right. She'd put her friends in danger by not telling him the truth. And by letting all of those friends convince her that they wanted to help keep her safe in the first place. What would they say if they knew everything?

Now David was out there with Pritchard, and she hoped they weren't too late to help him. David wouldn't know what Joe probably wanted or why he'd lingered on the mountain all night and day. But she knew. She knew exactly why Joe was acting so erratic and indecisive.

"If something happens to David," she said to Adan, "I'll never forgive myself."

He didn't say anything at first. Maybe he was tired of her cowardice or maybe he'd had her pegged from the beginning. Or he could be trying to watch the icy, muddy road.

He downshifted and hit the brakes as they rounded a tricky curve. Then he stopped the SUV. "I'm gonna check for tracks and shine the light down in that ravine."

She watched as he got out then decided she'd help him. But he worked in silence and that worried her. He looked up then held the flashlight high.

"Say something, Adan," she finally pleaded.

Instead of responding, he grabbed her and pushed her into the woods and fell down on top of her.

CHAPTER TWELVE

"I HEARD SOMETHING in the woods," he whispered in Sophia's ear. "Stay still."

"I can't move with you over me," she said against his ear, the scent of his early morning shower merging with the smells of snow and wet earth.

"Stay quiet," he retorted, not bothering to move away from her. His hands cupped her head, cushioning her from the cold ground, but his heartbeat bumped a warm message against all of the layers separating them.

That he was willing to throw his body over hers to protect her touched Sophia more than she could admit. But the strength of his arms around her made her feel safe...and content. Way too content. She couldn't take being so close to him when so many secrets were still between them. She needed to remember that she'd only known this man exactly one whole day.

Besides, when he heard her story he'd turn against her completely.

But she remained still and quiet and savored

his touch in spite of being scared out of her wits. Then she heard it, too. A crashing sound down in the ravine. Footsteps?

"Should we get back in the car?" she asked, hoping they could at least use the SUV as a shield. But she sure liked having him to shield her, too.

"Not if it's David. Or Pritchard. Jacob's SUV is held together by mostly rust." He listened, his head up. "I don't hear it anymore."

"If it's Pritchard, he'll try to take me. And he'll try to kill you."

"Both great choices, but he isn't getting either of them."

She had to smile at his wry humor. He'd been a trouper through all of the shenanigans going on around him. The man had come here on a noble mission and all she'd done was try to thwart him at every turn. But how could she blurt out all that had happened over the last few years? Especially to such a devoted lawman?

"I think it was an animal," he said after several blissful moments of sweet torture.

"Okay." It was a small whisper but Sophia had to remember that she couldn't give in to the crazy feelings coursing through her system each time she was near Adan. Her mind told her to push him away. Her heart told her to pull him closer. The war inside her blazed while she stayed there in his arms. She really didn't want to move.

And apparently, neither did he. Moonlight played across his rugged features, shadowing a day's worth of beard growth and coloring his eyes a rich, dark gold. His hat had come off on the way down and now his hair fringed in a rebellious sweep across his forehead. His lips parted as he stared down at her.

Sophia drank in everything about this moment. She wanted to kiss Adan, which was absolutely, positively not the thing to do.

"I want to kiss you," he said, his mouth near hers. "It doesn't make a bit of sense."

"I know," she said on a raspy protest that fizzled and faded. He somehow did feel the same way. This gave her hope and scared her silly. "I know."

"We have to keep moving," he replied, not moving.

"Yes." She snuggled closer.

"Don't do that."

"What?"

"Look at me like that, touch me like that."

"You're the one holding me."

He grunted then pulled her closer. "Let's get this out of the way."

His lips moved over hers in a blazing heat that would surely melt a spot in the snow. Sophia returned the kiss with a deep longing that pooled into liquid warmth with each touch of her lips to his. Had she ever really been kissed before?

No. Not like this.

Just as she was surrendering everything, Adan pulled away and rolled to the side, then grabbed his hat with one hand and tugged her to her feet with the other. "We need to keep moving."

"You already said that."

"Well, this time I mean it."

She should be hurt that he'd turned grumpy after kissing her, but Sophia couldn't, wouldn't feel bad. Not tonight.

She'd remember that kiss when things got complicated.

She'd remember that kiss when he heard the truth and then hauled her back to Texas to face her punishment.

After he checked the area and listened again, they got back into the SUV and started back down the rut-packed road. Adan did a slow crawl along the treacherous road, stopping now and then to search the area for tracks.

"Definitely some fresh tire marks, but no sign of them sliding off the road."

"At least this isn't too icy," she said to fill the awkward silence. "Not like the main road. That one has only been paved a couple of years but it does ice up during the winter months."

He did a survey of the road behind them through the rearview mirror and then turned back, his slow progress helping them avoid puddles and potholes. "Why don't you tell me how you wound up on this mountain?"

Sophia took in a cold breath. So this was it. This was where her future would get shaky. He'd kissed her in a way that showed he wanted her and now he'd decided he needed to know her before acting on that want. He needed a reason to walk away.

"The short version or from the beginning?"

"Where does your story start?" he asked, his tone low and muted. He glanced over at her, his eyes holding hers for the briefest of moments. "I think I need to hear everything."

"Way back," she admitted. "It starts way back. My parents were divorced when I was young and neither of them really wanted me in the picture." She pulled in a breath for control and hoped she wouldn't cry. "My mother tried to raise me, but I got passed around a lot from relative to relative and sometimes even foster homes, then back to her. It was kind of a vicious cycle."

Adan grunted at that confession. "That's not good for a child. Every child needs a mother."

Sophia sensed a world of hurt in that bold statement.

"Does your ex-wife ever visit your daughter?"

He shook his head. "We're not talking about me, but no...not that much. She's too busy having fun with her highfalutin oil-rich boyfriend. He caters to her every whim."

Sophia took that admission in and figured his wife's betrayal might be behind his distrust of women. Adan would love a woman but he wouldn't do the catering-to-every-whim thing. Only the good whims, like kissing a lot. That would be her only requirement, really. Just being with him all the time.

Telling herself to stop that kind of thinking, she went back to her story. She needed to get this out of the way, too.

"Well, my mama never found a rich boyfriend and…that kind of left her bitter. She's had biker boyfriends, drunk cowboy boyfriends and some not so nice companions. At first, I started to follow in her stiletto and short-shorts footprints."

"What changed for you?"

She swallowed, said a little prayer. "Everything changed for me when I was eighteen and I met Joe Pritchard."

ADAN WANTED TO stop and sit here in the warm SUV with her, but it was too cold and too dangerous for that. Besides, she'd gotten a little too close to his own issues, so he needed to focus on getting to the bottom of her involvement with Pritchard.

Disappointed even though he wasn't surprised, he said, "So you do know him?"

"I married him right out of high school."

"Wow."

Adan's heart sank after hearing her words. She'd married that worthless piece of humanity. And she lied about the whole thing. He shouldn't feel so betrayed since he'd suspected she was lying all along, but her confession stung all the same. One more reason to put some distance between them.

"Did you love him?"

"I thought I did."

Adan couldn't see that happening. He did a check of the woods and whispered low, "How did you wind up with him?"

"He hung out with one of my mom's boyfriends. A younger guy who used her for booze and cigarette money, but he brought his friends along with him. I was lonely and I'd had one too many bad boyfriends, so I enjoyed the attention. Joe was nice to me at first. A real sweet talker. And because he was older and kind of hip and he had a steady job, I fell for him."

Adan could understand her need for security and a new way of life, but he had to wonder what she'd seen in Pritchard. "You didn't have enough gumption to tell him to take a hike."

She shifted her backpack and looked down at the road. "No. No gumption, no self-esteem. No strength. I wanted a way out. I always swore when I turned eighteen, I'd leave. So I took the easiest route."

"By marrying him?"

She bobbed her head. "Yes. I was about to turn nineteen. After a night of drinking and partying, we got hitched." She shrugged. "I regretted it the next night when he went out partying again. Without his bride."

The discomfort in Adan's stomach turned to a burning rage. "He started treating you bad right away?"

"Yep."

"So you left, right?"

She lowered her eyes. "Not exactly, no. I'm not proud of it, but I didn't have anywhere to go. My mother didn't approve since it meant she didn't have me to take care of her anymore, so she told me to get lost. And when I did try to leave, he'd sweet-talk me with promises and all kinds of lofty plans." She shrugged. "Just like my mama."

Adan didn't want to hear this, but he had to. He'd believed Sophia to be a strong, independent woman. And she was—no doubt about that. But what had brought her to this point?

"So what happened to your marriage?"

She watched the headlights hitting the muddy road. "It got worse. He…he became jealous and possessive. Didn't want me to work or have friends." She looked over at Adan. "He didn't trust me and he didn't want anything more than someone to wait on him and sleep with him. I felt so worthless."

"Classic signs of an abusive person," Adan replied, hoping this hadn't gone that far. "He wanted you to feel worthless and useless."

"Bingo," she said, her gaze falling away.

"Sophia…"

"He…treated me like a punching bag," she said, her eyes closed now. "I had to get away."

Adan wanted to kill the man. "How long did you stay?"

"Too long. About six years."

"Six years?"

At her sharp intake of breath, Adan glanced over and saw a shadow of fear on her face. "I'm sorry, but I don't get why you stayed that long."

"Neither do I," she said. "I don't have any excuses except fear—fear of leaving and fear that if I did leave, he'd find me and kill me."

"Did you ever try to get away?"

"Many times. I asked my mother to help me and she just laughed and told me to grow up." She shrugged. "So I did grow up…and I took matters into my own hands."

Adan kept one eye on the road while he gave her a long stare. "What did you do, Sophia?"

She didn't answer.

And he didn't get a chance to question her again. Adan glanced back at the road just in time to see a man standing there waving his arms.

"Adan, stop!" Sophia shouted.

He slammed on the brakes and skidded, then turned toward the skid to right the vehicle. He barely kept it from plunging over into the deep ravine on the left. The SUV stopped just a foot short of hitting the man.

Adan let out a grunt of relief while Sophia took in several deep breaths. "That's David!"

Adan grabbed her before she could open the door. "Hold on. It might be a trick."

SOPHIA WAITED WITH her rifle as Adan opened the driver's side door and got out, his own weapon drawn while he stayed behind the open door.

"Who's there?" he asked. "I'm a Texas Ranger. Show me your hands."

The man held his hands in the air, palms up. "It me. David." He squinted toward the truck. "Sophia?"

Sophia didn't wait this time. She hurried out of the vehicle and did as Adan had done and stayed behind the cover of her door. "David, are you all right?"

Before she could run toward her friend, Adan hurried around the back of the SUV and tugged her close then put himself between her and David.

"Are you alone?" he asked David, his weapon centered on the other man.

David glanced to the right. "Uh…yessir."

"Are you telling the truth?" Adan asked as he advanced a step.

David nodded. "Is Karen all right?"

"She's fine," Adan called out. "We found her."

David didn't speak for a minute, then he stepped closer and dropped down. "He's hiding in the woods. Get down! He has a gun!"

Sophia ran toward David to help him, but Adan jumped in front of her, their bodies falling together toward the ground. Then she heard another gunshot and saw Adan's upper body jerk backward. He groaned and went still, then fell over her.

Sophia screamed as a dark liquid covered her jacket.

David crawled toward them, calling her name.

"Sophia, run," David shouted, still crawling toward her. "He wants you. Don't let him take you!"

"Adan?" she said, willing him to do something. But her hands were wet with his blood. "Adan?"

"Run," Adan said, a grimace of pain on his face. "Sophia, do as he says. Take your gun and get out of here."

Sophia sank down close to him then heard a crashing through the trees. Footsteps.

"I'm not leaving you," she said to Adan.

David shimmied up next to her. "Is he shot?"

She bobbed her head. "Yes. Get Adan inside

the car," she shouted as she went down on her stomach.

Adan tried to stand and she saw the blood rushing down his jacket. Leaning against the vehicle, he slid up. "Sophia, don't do this! I'm okay. Get out of here."

David grabbed at Adan. "You're injured. I'll get her out of the way but you need to do as she asked."

Another shot rang out. Adan grunted as he stood up and then turned toward where Sophia stood behind the front of the vehicle, her rifle trained on the woods across the way.

"C'mon," he said to her on a weak breath. "Get inside the car."

"No," she replied, her boots planted against the front fender. "He's after me. Well, here I am."

David tugged at her coat. "Sophia, please. You know what he'll do."

Sophia refused to listen. She'd known coming down the mountain that Joe would be waiting for her. He'd done exactly what she'd predicted. And she'd brought Adan right to him.

Adan put his hand around her waist and lifted her, his strained voice seeping out one question. "Do you want to get killed?"

"I don't want either of you to die," she retorted, tears in her eyes. "Let me go, Adan."

"Not a chance."

Another round of shots filled the cold, dark night.

Adan grabbed her rifle and tossed it to David, then he pushed Sophia to the ground. "Cover us, David."

She watched as Adan fell beside her and passed out.

CHAPTER THIRTEEN

SOPHIA'S HEART PUMPED with a mad dash through her body. She didn't know whether to shoot into the woods or try to get away. She'd gladly face Joe and try to shoot him, but that would only make David and Adan go all hero on her. She couldn't risk either or both of them getting killed.

David nodded toward her. "See to him. I'll cover you."

He fired off a round of shots for good measure and then hurried to kneel with her beside Adan.

Sophia tugged at Adan's coat. "Adan? Adan, wake up."

"He's bleeding pretty bad," David said. "Best thing to do now is get him home."

"And you, too," Sophia replied, biting back tears while she held her fingers to Adan's wound to stop the bleeding. The relief of finding David alive warred with the horror of seeing Adan shot and unconscious. He'd jumped in front of her and now he was bleeding.

She chanced a glance toward the woods. "But Pritchard will keep coming. He has a weapon now and he'll come back up the mountain." Shaking her head, she added, "He wants me. He won't give up." Because she had something else he wanted, too.

"Then we'll be ready for him," David said, his salt-and-pepper hair flashing in the moonlight. "He's not as scary as he seems. He didn't leave like he said because he wants to take you with him." He shrugged. "'Course he stole one of my finest hunting rifles, and he's using it now."

Sophia swallowed the fear of hearing those words. "Why didn't y'all go on down into the valley?"

David lowered his head and whispered. "My old truck was low on gas and it ran out about a half mile down the way. He made me wait in the cold for y'all. Said you'd come looking and you'd stop to help me."

He gave her a grizzly but apologetic glance. "He actually said running out of gas would work because you'd come looking and he would get your car and take you with him. So now I wish I'd thought that through more." He glanced toward the woods. "But he threatened to hurt Karen and the rest of y'all, too."

"It doesn't matter. He used y'all as a means of getting to me. You're right, though. He knew we'd come after you."

"Now we're trapped here with a shot Ranger,"

David pointed out. "And a crazy man gunning for us."

Sophia glanced over the now quiet woods. Joe Pritchard wouldn't let go so easily, but she was through putting her well-meaning friends in danger. And she refused to let him take her off this mountain. She'd have to find a way out of this without getting anyone else involved.

She moved toward Adan. "We're not trapped, but we have to avoid being shot ourselves. Let's get Adan back to my place and you can tell me all about it."

David nodded and after duck walking around the vehicle so he could put the guns inside, he helped her lift Adan onto the backseat. Not an easy task since they had to stay low and Adan was six feet of solid muscle.

She got him settled then stroked the hair off his forehead. "Adan, we'll get you somewhere safe, I promise."

Another shot rang out but Sophia hurried and got the door shut, her mind whirling with turmoil when she heard Adan grunt and fall over the seat.

Then she heard a voice that still haunted her dreams echoing eerily over the now still woods.

"Sophia? Why don't you just give up and come with me, sweet thing. Took me a while to find you, but now that I have, you know I'll never let you go."

Sophia jumped out of the SUV and answered

with a volley of rifle shot. "David, can you get us back up the mountain?"

"Sure." He stayed low and inched his way toward the driver's side while Sophia trained her rifle on the woods across the way and covered him.

"Sophia, don't make me hurt any more of your friends," Pritchard called. "I'll take them out, one by one."

"You'll regret ever coming to Crescent Mountain," she called. "Go away, Joe."

"Not without you," he called. "I've had about enough of this mountain. I want off and I'm taking you with me, one way or another." Then he let out a hoot. "We got us some unfinished business to take care of, don't we, sweetheart?"

When Sophia heard him stomping through the woods, she jumped in the back of the SUV and cradled Adan's head in her lap. "Drive, David."

The sound of gunshots chased them up the hill, hitting metal and chrome and shattering glass all over the back of the already dented SUV.

David didn't waste any time getting the vehicle turned around. He spun in the mud and ice but managed to head back over the ruts left from earlier. The engine groaned its way up the curving, treacherous road but David held steady.

"You okay?" he called to Sophia.

"Yes, how 'bout you?"

"I'm a tough old bird," he said on a chuckle.

"Now that I'm headed home I'll be right as rain." Then he turned solemn. "Is my Karen all right? Really all right?"

"She is now," Sophia replied. "She was scared and worried about you, though."

"I was sure worried about her, too." He glanced over his shoulder. "Remember, Karen was a nurse. She'll know what to do with that gunshot wound."

"I hope so."

Sophia felt for Adan's pulse and found a weak thread stringing together each soft beat of his heart. She took off her scarf and held it against his wound. Then she leaned her head down to hold on to that thin thread pulsing through his body and hoped they'd get him home before it was too late.

And all the while, they listened as gunshots chased after them, pinging against the SUV like pebbles falling off the mountain.

"GET ME SOME water and clean cloths," Karen said, her hand touching her husband's arm while he and Jacob helped Adan into Sophia's cabin. "Put him there on the couch."

"No," Sophia said, thankful that Karen had taken charge. "Put him in my room. He'll be more comfortable."

Bettye and Karen shot each other a knowing

womanly glance. "Okay, suga'," Bettye replied. "David, can you take him back there?"

David indicated yes with a quick nod. Jacob helped him lift and drag Adan to the bedroom.

"Open his shirt," Karen called. "I'll get water boiling so I can at least clean the wound."

Melissa stood with her hands to her mouth, her brown eyes on Adan. "Is he gonna die?"

"Not if we can help it," Karen replied. "Melissa, are you scared of the sight of blood?"

Melissa shook her head, but Sophia saw a deep fear in the girl's eyes. "No, I... I just don't want Adan to die."

Bettye gave her granddaughter a worried glance. "C'mon, honey. Let 'em take care of him. We can help."

Bettye dragged Melissa into action and then pushed Karen and Sophia behind the men. "We'll take care of the water. You go on and check on him."

Sophia followed Karen into the little bedroom. "He's been unconscious since we started back up the mountain. I tried to stop the bleeding but I'm really worried."

Karen helped the men place him on the bed. "Honey, he's got a messy hole in his left shoulder but from what I can tell, he should be okay. The bullet hit the fleshy part, thankfully. I'm pretty sure it's a through and through. The main problem now is to debride the wound and let him rest, then we need to keep an eye on him until we can get him to a doctor."

She looked from Adan's ashen face back to Sophia. "We don't want infection to set in."

"Can you get the wound cleaned out?" Jacob asked, his smile gone.

"I'll try," Karen replied, one hand pushing at her short hair. "It's a blessing that madman was still a good ways out in the woods when he started shooting. If he'd been in closer using that particular gun, your Ranger would be missing a shoulder." She turned to David and hugged him close. "I'm so glad you're okay."

"I'm just fine," David replied. "That Pritchard idiot would be wise to keep going downhill."

"He'll be back," Sophia said. "I shouldn't have gotten any of you involved."

"Honey, we became involved the day you showed up in his car," Bettye retorted. "You were in no shape to handle this alone." She gave one of her eloquent shrugs. "We knew what we were getting into and we all made a pact to keep what we knew to ourselves. We didn't know you only *thought* you'd killed the fool. But we can deal with that, too."

"If we can keep the Ranger alive to help," Jacob said with a bob of his half-bald head.

Sophia pushed back the tears burning in her eyes. "I thought I was done with Joe. I never dreamed he'd find me here."

"You thought you'd killed the sorry—"

A groan from the bed brought them all around. Adan's eyes opened wide. "You tried to kill Joe Pritchard?"

Sophia stared into Adan's feverish gaze. "You need to rest, just rest."

"What's going on?" he asked, glancing around.

Sophia gave Karen a helpless look.

Karen leaned over and held her hand on Adan's midsection to keep him still. "You've been shot, but I'm a retired nurse. I have my medical bag and we're boiling water. I'll need to see if it's a for-sure through and through." She gave him a pat on the arm. "You're mighty lucky it wasn't worse or lower, near your heart."

Adan lay back down. "Am I gonna live?"

"Yes," Karen said, now applying pressure to the wound with a clean towel. "If I have anything to do with it, you'll be up and around soon."

But Adan tried to get up. "I'm fine. As long as I'm still alive, might as well go after him."

"No, Adan." Sophia leaned over him, her hand touching on his brow. "No. Karen has to check you over. You got hit in your left shoulder, so you need to rest."

"I've had worse wounds." He blinked then stared straight into her eyes. "Did you…kill him?"

"Not this time," she replied, wondering how much he'd remember later.

"Nor before either, if I'm hearing right."

Then he passed out again.

ADAN WOKE UP in the middle of the night, a white-hot fever making him toss off the covers and grunt out words his mama wouldn't appreciate. At first, he couldn't remember where he was or why he was here.

He tried to lift up off the big bed, but a soft hand on his arm and a sweet whisper in his ear held him back. "Just rest, Adan."

"Where am I? What's going on?"

"Adan, it's Sophia. You're with me. I mean, you're back in my cabin. You…you were shot."

He remembered being on the road. And the cold. So cold. Gunshot. Had to save her. "Chasing someone."

"Joe Pritchard," she said. "He…he shot at us."

Adan closed his eyes, images of darkness curling and hissing along his frayed nerve endings. If he hadn't been so run down and sleep deprived, he could have handled this better. "Hurts like all get-out."

"I know. Karen checked you over and dressed the wound. She's afraid to probe inside the wound, so we have to wait until we can get you to a doctor."

He blinked again, the scent of flowers flowing around him like fresh air on a spring day. "Karen?"

"Yes. She's a nurse. Joe…he took her husband, David, hostage. But they ran out of gas and Joe made David wait until he saw us."

"Joe's not so dumb after all. Setup."

He remembered most of it but now he wanted to sleep, just sleep. But so many shadows pushed at his mind. He had to stand watch over Sophia. He needed to be somewhere. Somewhere important…

He watched as she fussed with the bedding, trying to get his to-do list back in sharp focus. "Water?"

"Yes, but just a sip."

She brought him a glass with a straw. "You have a big bandage and tape over your wound and your left arm is in a sling, so be careful."

He nodded and allowed her to help him up just enough to sip a few swallows of the cool water. He lay back against the cushioned pillows, his strength sapped. "Be better by morning."

"I hope so."

She moved away, but he reached out his hand to her arm. Adan knew he needed to watch over her. "Stay."

Sophia's hair fell around her face, that flowery scent teasing at his nostrils again. "I'll be right here."

He had to make sure. "Right here by me?"

She hesitated, her fingers touching on his forehead. "Right here watching out for you."

He wondered when she'd decided to become his protector. He feared she'd go out there alone. "Where's your rifle?"

"Right here by my side."

"Good girl."

He didn't want to let go of her hand. He wanted her near so he could take care of her. "I should be the one on watch."

"No. You need to rest that shoulder. You lost a lot of blood."

He tried to smile. "No rest for the weary."

She smiled back at him. "I sure know that feeling."

Adan closed his eyes but he held back from a dead-tired fatigue that tried to tug him into darkness. "Sleep here, with me. Keep me warm."

He heard a sharp intake of breath, but he was too sleepy to tell her he'd be a perfect gentleman. He only wanted someone near, someone to hold. He wanted Sophia.

And yet, she didn't make a move toward him.

But just before he drifted off, he felt the bed shift and heard a feminine sigh. Then a small hand curled in his and squeezed his fingers.

"Go to sleep, Adan. I'll be right here, I promise."

Adan smiled, his hand still in hers. As long as he kept her near, she'd be safe.

Then he slept.

SOPHIA DIDN'T SLEEP at all.

She was in her bed with a man who treated her differently than any other man she'd ever known. A man who hadn't made any moves on her except to protect her.

I only thought I knew love.

She closed her eyes to hold back the tears, memories of being at Joe's brutal mercy coloring the darkness with slippery shadows. That had not been love.

Possession. Control. Cruelty. A forced confinement. But never love, no matter how much he'd tried to convince her. No matter that she'd tried to convince herself.

I should have left him that first night.

Bettye always said everything happened for a reason. She had reasoned that Sophia came to Crescent Mountain to heal. And they'd taken her in without question and helped her hide the evidence of her own dirty deeds for a reason. Bettye promised one day Sophia would see that reason as clear as day.

But Sophia only saw her mistakes.

She'd tried to kill her ex-husband. She'd thought she had killed him. But maybe Joe was just too mean to kill. She'd taken his car and the cash he'd stolen from some very nasty people.

He'd forced her to go to the bank where she'd saved up part of her meager earnings and the few dollars he'd toss her way. She'd opened a secret account so she could finally get away from him, but he'd found one of her statements and he'd made her get her money out from the bank. Exactly to the penny.

Joe was precise in that way.

And then he'd gone by a big house on the edge of town and he'd disconnected the security system and gone in while she waited in the car. Then he'd come out with a big bag and told her to drive away. Fast.

After that, things had happened in a way that had no rhyme or reason.

But how could any of them reason this? That Joe Pritchard had lived to return and torment all of them? That this tall, strong lawman would be here in her room, shot and feverish because of her?

Or that this wonderful, good man could be here inside her heart even when she'd tried to hide the truth from him?

Where was the reasoning in that?

"I can't like you," she whispered to the night. "I refuse to love you."

She told herself she'd only known Adan a couple of days but it seemed as if she'd been waiting for him all of her life.

Is this my reason then, Bettye? Did I go through so much pain and humiliation from both my

*mother and then Joe just so I'd find Adan one
day? So I'd appreciate him all the more?*

Adan slept, quiet and still, his breathing even
and almost content. Probably the painkillers
kicking in. Possibly that he'd finally been forced
to rest. Just rest.

Karen had warned her to watch for his fever
to spike, had told her to give him pain pills and
keep him still.

"We'll have to get him down the mountain if
he gets worse with fever or if his wound starts to
redden and pucker," Karen had said before leaving to be with her husband. "I've done everything
I can for now."

They'd all done everything they could for
Sophia.

*I have to leave. I have to get up and get my
things and leave. Now.*

She'd always known this day might come, but
she didn't want to think about that now. She'd
have to leave, to somehow get away to save all
of them. She'd find a way to lure Joe out into the
open and then…she'd finish the job, one way or
another.

Because she'd never have any peace as long as
he stalked her. And she'd never forgive herself if
someone else she cared about got hurt. Or worse.

She turned to stare over at Adan. She never
would have met him if not for Joe. At least she
could call that something positive. She would

leave knowing that one amazing thing had come out of all of this—she'd fallen for a good man.

There's a reason for everything, honey.

She could hear Bettye saying that.

But she couldn't accept that Adan was meant to come here to catch a killer only to get shot while trying to protect her and then possibly die right here in her bed.

Where is the justice in that? she wondered.

And why would this man show up here and steal my heart after I've committed crimes myself?

Sophia lay still for a while longer, debating whether to leave tonight or to wait, and then she turned and snuggled close to Adan. Just for now. Just for tonight.

Tomorrow, she'd figure out how to get away.

From Joe's hate.

And from Adan's love.

CHAPTER FOURTEEN

ADAN WOKE WITH a start and stared up at the unfamiliar ceiling. A ceiling that had shimmering stars painted on it.

When he heard a soft feminine sigh, he turned to see Sophia asleep on top of the colorful quilt with a light chenille blanket over her body. She still wore her clothes from yesterday.

What had happened?

He lifted up and several jackhammers went off inside his brain. Then his left arm started throbbing in a cadence that kept right up with the jackhammers. His pulse was screaming at him to settle back on the pillow.

Adan said several colorful things on a low whisper while his memory returned reel by reel. His left shoulder burned and hissed like a mad rattlesnake, and his mouth felt as parched as a West Texas prairie. He remembered jumping in front of Sophia and then a searing pain and waking up in this bed.

Her bed.

He needed to get back out there and find

Pritchard. He wanted this particular criminal to see the inside of a prison cell for a long time. But mainly, Adan wanted out of this bed and away from this particular woman.

Sophia had way too many facets to suit him. Or maybe all of her facets suited him way too much. Either way, he'd been seriously distracted since arriving on Crescent Mountain. Time to get back to work so he could finish this and get home to Gaylen.

But when he tried to sit up, the room wobbled and danced like a drunken quarter horse and the woman beside him shot up out of the bed like a rusty cannonball.

"You can't get up," she said, one hand moving through her lush hair while the other one wiped at her bleary eyes. "Adan, you need to take it easy for at least the rest of the day."

"And what about Pritchard?" he asked, his tone deliberately full of mean. "What about your charming ex-husband?"

"The others went down the old back road to search for him. They didn't find anyone. They took a can of gas to get David's truck back up here."

"You planned this, right? Planned for him to have a way out yet again?"

Hurt shot through her eyes. "How can you even think that?"

"Because you drugged me. I could have gone after him. I've been wounded before."

She put her hands on her hips. "Really, Ranger? Really? You think you could have just gotten up last night and gone out in the cold and snow to track a man who's managed to somehow fool all of us?" She shook her head. "Maybe he's long gone by now. I sure hope so."

Adan still wanted to fight about it even if he was all wrong. He needed a reason to leave her once he'd captured Pritchard.

"How?" he asked. "On foot? Or did one of your well-meaning friends see to it that he's gone for good? Or did you take matters into your own hands and finish the job this time?" He grunted as he managed to sit up against the headboard. "Which one, Sophia?"

"You need coffee." She whirled to leave.

"Oh, no. No, ma'am. *You* need to come right back here and tell me the rest of the story between you and this man."

Sophia held her left hand on the doorjamb then tapped against the wood. Finally, she pivoted. "I need coffee and you need breakfast. I'll tell you everything after I get some caffeine in me."

"I'm not hungry," he said, gritting his teeth against his growling shoulder.

"Do you remember what really happened last night?" she asked, her tone going soft toward the end of the question.

He remembered a lot of things this morning. His daughter, Sophia's lies and that kiss. He also remembered how David and Sophia had risked their lives to get him back to safety.

Now he felt like a real jerk. "Sophia—"

"I'll bring toast anyway."

With that she strutted up the short hallway and a few seconds later, he heard pots and pans slamming around in the kitchen. Good, so she was as aggravated as he was.

Adan wanted to feel triumphant about that, but he was just too worn down to care at the moment.

SOPHIA BRACED HERSELF for what might come next. She'd been hiding out from the law for years now, so she guessed she'd get her due. Adan was a man who went by the letter of the law, no room for any gray areas.

Swallowing back the sweet hurt of being by his side all night, she slapped butter to bread and toasted it, then poured two mugs of coffee and placed it all on a tray with some of Bettye's homemade mayhaw jelly. But before she got back to the bedroom, she heard him slowly making his way into the living room.

Sophia hurried to place the tray on the coffee table, thinking he was also stubborn. Very stubborn. When she turned to face him, she saw the ashen color in his face and the grimace of pain growing with each step. She also noticed his open shirt and his bronzed skin.

Sophia hurried to help him, but he pushed her away. "I'm fine. I've had worse pain from a cactus thorn in my toe."

"Right," she said, watching him with her arms crossed while she tried to put the tempting image he presented out of her mind.

He leveled her with a glare. "You enjoying this?"

Sophia shook her head. "Not really. I could have saved you the trouble." She pointed to the tray. "But now that you've made it this far, sit down and have some breakfast."

He grunted himself down onto the old sofa. "Coffee." Then he squinted up at her. "Please."

She started to tell him to get it himself but decided she couldn't really be mad at him. While he had every right to be mad at her.

"Please," he added again, his scowl cracking a fraction. Then he said, "I'm sorry I got all ornery on you. I don't like getting shot."

"And you don't like to lose, either," she retorted. "You'd already worn yourself ragged before you ever came here."

He didn't bother arguing with that. "It's my job."

After she handed him coffee in his right hand, she placed a plate of toast next to him on the side table. But she refused to tell him how scared she'd been last night or that she didn't want him to die. Or that he'd asked her to stay there with him last night.

Instead she said, "Let me know if you need anything else."

He downed about half the mug of coffee and then cleared his throat and stared at her with his ever-changing gold-brown eyes. Reminding her of a big cat getting ready to tear into something.

In this case, that something was her.

"I need you to tell me the truth, Sophia. I need you to help me do my job so I can go back to Texas and check on my little girl."

Sophia saw exactly how serious he was, so she nodded and took a sip of her own coffee. But it left a sour burning inside her stomach. "I wanted to tell you last night, but then we saw David—"

Realization colored Adan's scowl. "David? How is he?"

"He's fine, thankfully. He knew his truck didn't have enough gas to make it down the mountain. He thought that would buy him some time. But Joe used that same time to wait for us to come searching, just as I figured. He thought he'd take me with him by carjacking us."

"Almost worked, too."

Sophia put down her coffee. "Yes, it did. He shot at me and you jumped in front of me and took that bullet."

"I think he was trying to distract us so he could

take you. Why would he kill you on the spot after all this trouble?"

"I don't know. I never know what to expect with Joe. He has a mercurial temper and he's impulsive."

"And yet you stayed with him for years."

Why did it hurt that he had to remind her of that? "Yes, I did. I'm not proud of that, but... I was broken, Adan. Beaten down and broken."

"Men like him tend to do that to women." He finished his coffee, his eyes softening on her. "Yet you seem to have overcome being scared of him."

"Oh, I'm still scared," she said, a warm glow at his compliment casting out her fears. "I've just learned how to deal with my fears in a more aggressive way."

"By trying to kill him?"

"Yes. When he came after me the last time, I thought I was ready. I'd tried divorce, a restraining order, talking to the police, enlisting friends, hiding out in a women's shelter and changing my phone number and address several times. He always found me."

"So he came after you again and what happened?"

Sophia pushed at her disheveled hair. "He took me hostage at gunpoint, right out of my driveway, and he made me take some money out of the bank. And later that night, he robbed a house."

"Were you with him when he robbed this house?"

Sophia dreaded telling Adan the truth. And even now, she couldn't bring herself to tell him the whole story.

"Sophia?"

"I was driving the getaway car."

Adan put down his coffee mug so fast it sloshed out onto the table. "You aided and abetted a criminal?"

"No. I was forced to do as he asked since he told me he'd shoot anyone inside the house and then shoot me."

"You didn't think to call for help?"

"I didn't have a cell phone. No money for luxuries like that. I was terrified and I panicked. Besides, it happened so fast I didn't know what to do. I just knew I'd go to jail with him if we got caught."

"Where did this home robbery take place?"

"Back in Texas. Near Waco."

He didn't ask what all had been taken, and she didn't volunteer that information.

"Y'all traveled around?"

"We'd settled there and I had a pretty good job at a local craft store but he didn't like me working at night." She put her coffee mug down on the nearby tray. "I tried to save up a little money but I put it in a secret bank account. I always cashed my check each week and gave it over to him, but I managed to skim a few twenties off the top."

She looked down at her hands, the shame of that time making a cold sweat break out along her backbone. "He followed me home from the store one morning and told me he'd seen me go to the bank."

"The bank where you squirreled away the money?"

"Yes. He confronted me and asked me how much money I'd hidden from him." She shook her head, trying to find the courage to explain. "I blurted it out—close to five thousand dollars."

"Over six years?"

She nodded. "In bits and pieces, through friends and any way I could think of. I always used a bank that had branches in several towns. I'd used this same one for years and he never knew. Never. I was careful to have my statements sent to a friend or a PO box."

Adan gave her a look that bordered on amazed. "And let me guess? He made you give over that money?"

"Yes." She blinked back tears and gritted her teeth. "He held a gun on me and made me go in the bank and withdraw all the money. Said he'd come in and start shooting if I tried anything."

"Did you also take up target practice—secretly?"

She nodded. "Another friend had a husband who was a cop. He agreed to show both of us how to shoot. We told him we wanted to learn for our protection. That was true at least."

Adan grimaced as he shifted on the sofa. "So he robbed this home and took from you what he considered his money and he forced you to help him get away?"

"Yes. We traveled the back roads at night and slept in the car during the day. He tied my hands to his wrist so if I moved he'd wake up." She looked down at her lap. "He fancied us a modern-day Bonnie and Clyde."

"But you wanted no part of that, right?"

She could see the distrust again in Adan's eyes and that was her undoing. "Of course I didn't want to be a part of it. How can you even doubt me on that?"

"Because you've been lying to me for days now. Because you knocked me out and held me tied up when you could have saved yourself a lot of trouble. Because you enlisted your neighbors in hiding the truth from me and now you're telling me that you drove the car away after he robbed some big house. Let's see, did I leave anything out?"

"My friends were trying to protect me and keep me from going to jail, Adan. I thought I'd killed him. I—" She stopped and pushed at her hair. "I wanted him dead and I don't care that you know that now."

"I want to kill him, too," Adan replied. "But the law demands that I take him back to Texas to stand trial for armed robbery and murder."

"I want that, too, but Joe will just keep coming until something bad happens." She got up and went to stare out the window. "It's close to Christmas, but I can't celebrate this year. I always used to get queasy around the holidays since he always got drunk and had his own brand of celebrating. And that meant taking things out on me."

She whirled and gave Adan a direct glare. "I want him either dead or in prison for the rest of his life. I thought I'd killed him and I knew no one would believe I did it in self-defense. So I ran away and I didn't look back."

Adan glanced around and then settled his gaze on her. "You found this mountain of misfits and you fit right in. An artist who likes being secluded and isolated. A woman who makes her own Christmas ornaments and helps her neighbors. You even make soup. On the surface, you seem like the real deal."

"But to you, I'm just as guilty as Joe Pritchard, right?"

His gaze drifted to her lips. "I didn't say that."

"You didn't have to. That look on your face—I've seen that over and over on other faces. Friends, family, even the police. You all think I brought this on myself because I stayed so long."

"I don't think that," he replied. "I know what you went through was real but—"

"But I shouldn't have taken the law into my own hands, right?"

"Right." He leaned back, his expression full of pain. "What did you do to him that made you think you'd killed him?"

She glanced back out the window, not sure how to explain what had happened on that night so long ago. "He got really drunk one night while we were stopped in some woods. I… I had some strong pain pills in my purse from having dental work done the day before he kidnapped me."

"You had your purse with you?"

"Yes. He took me right out of my driveway but nobody was around to see or to worry. He came up when I got out of my car and I tried to get away, but he grabbed me."

"So Pritchard was waiting and got to you when you exited your car?"

"Yes. I was so shocked I didn't even realize I still had my purse across my lap." She shrugged. "I guess I was still clutching it when he shoved me in his car and took off."

"And you had medicine in that purse?"

"Yes." She braced her arms across her midsection. "I waited until he passed out and with one hand I lifted my purse inch by inch. When he didn't move or wake up, I slipped my hand into the purse and found the pill bottle. Took me about fifteen minutes to open it without rousing him. Then I dropped a handful of them in the open whiskey bottle he'd left in the cup holder."

"But you said he was passed out."

"He was. I let him sleep awhile and then I kind of moved on purpose to rile him."

"And he woke up?"

Sophia closed her eyes. "He did but he was still kind of disoriented. He was angry, thinking I was trying to escape. But I told him I'd fallen asleep and accidentally turned away. I told him to have another drink."

"And…he did?"

"He never turned down a drink, and he was out of it enough to swig on that bottle again."

"So you deliberately tried to kill him?"

"No." She had to make Adan believe her. "No. I only wanted him to be so passed out that I could figure out how to untie myself. He had a certain knot he used that was almost impossible to untie with him just sleeping."

"So you gave him too many pills?"

"I don't know how many pills I put in that bottle. I got untied and when he didn't wake up, I thought I'd killed him. I'm not proud of what I did, but I pushed him out the car door and threw his whiskey bottle after him and I took off."

She got up and roamed in front of the fire-place. "I put Joe Pritchard out of my mind and I tried to live a good life once I settled here. I tried to ignore the guilt I felt about possibly killing him since he'd threatened to kill me so many times."

Adan let out a long sigh. "Seems to me he still wants you dead. He'll take you with him and he could still kill you once he has you."

She nodded. "And that's why I got so upset when I saw that poster inside my screen door that night. I knew he'd come for me."

Adan grunted but managed to stand. Then he walked over to her and took one of her hands in his. "Lucky for you I showed up that night, huh?"

"That depends," she said, "on whether or not you make me pay for what I did." Then she looked up at him and steeled herself for what might come. "Because I also took back what was left of my money when I stole his car and left him for dead."

CHAPTER FIFTEEN

ADAN DECIDED RIGHT then and there that he would never haul this woman in for anything. She'd obviously thought she'd done something wrong, but from what she'd told him, she'd only been trying to protect herself. Self-defense. From a man who was a coward and a bully, a man who picked on women and tried to take a whole community hostage. A murderer who'd spent most of his life on the run.

Adan couldn't understand how Sophia had wound up with a man like Pritchard, but he'd have to figure that out some other time. He wanted to get back to doing his job. Even though his folks were used to him being gone for days at a time, he worried about Gaylen and his promise to her that he'd be home for Christmas.

He had a few more days left before he had to honor that promise.

"Relax," he said to Sophia, his grimace more from pain than anger. "I tell you what—since you've leveled with me I'll level with you. I'm only on this mountain to apprehend Joe Pritchard.

He's wanted for robbery and murder and half a dozen other crimes and now I have an eyewitness to a few of his other escapades, too."

Sophia let out a gasp. "You mean me?"

"Yes, ma'am. He's here because of you."

Sophia starting pacing around, one hand moving like a garden rake through her hair. "He'll kill me for sure if he thinks I'll testify against him. And if I do get to live, he'll swear I stole his car and the money."

Adan didn't want to play mean with her emotions, but he needed her to give a statement about what had happened when Pritchard took her hostage. "Look, the man took you against your will after repeated attempts to keep him away and then he forced you to help him get away. You have a solid case and you can redeem yourself by testifying against him."

"Redeem myself?" She stopped pacing to stare up at him. "That's blackmail, Adan."

"Blackmail?" He grabbed her hand and held her there in front of the fire. "I don't call doing your duty blackmail. I call it seeking justice against a man who's wronged you. A man who's still coming after you."

"And what about my part in this? Will that just magically go away?" Her expression filled with a dread that spoke of all she'd suffered through. "I left him for dead and stole his car and a wad of money that he'll claim was his. I could go to jail right along with him. Can you keep that from happening?"

"If you agree to my terms, yes." He wouldn't string her along. "Look, what you did isn't that bad, all things considered. We can make it work."

"But you can't promise that. I know how it works with domestic violence. It's hard to prove."

"But you have proof. He took you."

"No one saw him take me, though. It's been almost five years and it's my word against his. He's been looking for me for all that time. What if no one believes he took me? What if no one believes I didn't want to drive that getaway car?"

"If you turn on him, you should be safe. And you have documented history of his actions—from verbal and physical abuse calls to a restraining order and death threats. You also have friends who might be willing to vouch for you. And now he's tracked you down and threatened you and me and everyone else in this community. We'll all be glad to testify in your defense."

"Should," she said as she pulled away. "I *should* be safe. But you can't promise that even after all that you just said about what he's done. No one can."

"I think I can safely say that you won't be prosecuted."

"Even if he tells everyone I poisoned him and took his car then left him for dead?"

"He was drunk and he might not remember anything. He didn't actually see you put the pills in the whiskey bottle, right?"

She shook her head. "No, but I don't like this. I don't like this one bit. He always wins one way or another."

Adan hated the defeat in her words. "He won't win this time, I promise."

"You shouldn't make that promise. I can't rely on a promise."

"It's a good solution," Adan pointed out, hoping she'd listen to reason. "I believe you and I believe you went through a lot with Pritchard. Too much for one woman to endure. You'll probably be applauded for pushing him out of that car and taking off."

"I'm not proud of it," she said on an almost whisper. "But I have to admit it felt good to be the one in control for once."

Adan wanted to pull her close and hold her tight, but he had to stay in professional mode. "I can't argue with that point."

She gazed up at him, her eyes moving over his face as if she were looking for signs of deception. "Do you really think this will work? All I have to do is tell the truth in a court of law?"

"I do believe it will work, yes. If you agree to testify against him, I think we can settle for a plea bargain that puts you on probation, but that will just be a formality."

"I guess it's the only way."

He finally did reach out to her. Pulling her close, he said, "Sophia, it's the best way. You've been hiding out here, thinking you'd killed a man. Now that man has come seeking some sort of justification or revenge. He's the kind that thinks if he can't have you, no one will."

He put one finger on her cheek and stroked her soft skin. "We have to end this, one way or another, so you can get on with your life. So you can feel safe again."

Her eyes went smoky before she closed them. "I want it to end, one way or another. I don't want anyone else to get hurt. I'll do whatever it takes to get him out of my life for good."

Adan lowered his head, his mind whirling with kissing her again. He remembered her sweet lips, remembered having her so close. He wanted that again. He'd wanted it last night even in a medicated fog. He just wanted her near. He wanted a lot of things but mostly, he needed to get Pritchard and get back home. He'd have to figure out the rest later.

He didn't kiss her because if he did, he'd never want to stop. "If you'll agree to let me help you, we can do this. We can bring Joe Pritchard to justice."

"And I can get my life back?"

"You will get your life back," he replied.

And he wanted to add that maybe he could be in her life once this was over.

LATER THAT DAY, Sophia glanced around the group of people in her cabin and wished she could go back and start over so she could prevent them all from being involved in this horrible mess.

Bettye with Melissa. She wanted to hear the rest of the story on those two, but she'd have to wait for a much quieter time for one of them to explain. Melissa seemed subdued and afraid. Maybe she was worried about her grandmother or that Adan would force her to go back to whatever horrors she'd run away from. Sophia knew that feeling.

How could she ever leave all of these caring people?

Karen and David—now happily reunited after their earlier ordeal with Pritchard, but willing to help her because they were that kind of people. The kind who cared for other human beings.

Jacob, sitting close to Bettye as always, but keeping his distance because he was a gentleman. A lost soul, but still a gentleman who believed in chivalry and honor.

Maggie and Arnie Burton, lovebirds who only came up here at certain times of the year. Strong and sure and sturdy, they'd helped Sophia hide the car and had been in on the whole secret from the beginning.

And Adan. A good strong man who was on the right side of the law. New and different and exciting and willing to help her get the albatross that was Joe Pritchard out of her life.

For good.

Even old Bandit stared up at her with expectant, knowing eyes. Did the dog sense that something was about to change?

They were all here for good. And they all believed in her. Sophia knew she didn't deserve their loyalty or their trust, but she loved all of them because they'd treated her like family. Like how a real family would treat someone.

But Sophia had withheld things from all of them, and now they were all suffering because of her lack of good judgment.

She glanced up at Adan, tears pricking her eyes.

"Go ahead," she said, giving him a weak smile.

"Are we in trouble again?" Bettye asked with a rebellious roll of her eyes, one hand rubbing Bandit's head. "I don't want to be on Santa's bad list."

Adan actually grinned at that. "I think you're good to go as far as Santa's concerned, Bettye."

Melissa's big eyes widened in worry. "Why are we here?"

Adan stared the girl down until she dropped her gaze, a look of guilt coloring her skin.

He stood like a drill sergeant in front of the roaring fire, his left arm in a sling and his whole demeanor wrapped in fatigue. "I asked Sophia to get everyone together so we could talk about our options."

"You mean how to deal with this Pritchard fellow?" David asked. "I shoulda pushed him off into a gulley when I had the chance."

"I say we hog-tie him and put him over a spit," Jacob suggested with a straight face. "He's aggravating all of us something terrible and well, he's ruining my Christmas spirit."

Bandit woofed at that suggestion.

Melissa shook her head. "That's cruel. We should just tie him up and ask him why he can't get a life. Why he has to try and hurt people."

"He's a cruel man," Jacob pointed out. "Not worth a dime."

Sophia hoped Adan would just get on with it. "What's the plan?" she asked, giving him his cue.

"I plan to do what I came here to do—find him and take him back to Texas, hog-tied and all."

Jacob grinned and clapped. "Okay, then. What can we do to help?"

Adan did a small pace, pain etched deep in his expression like a rock face. "I've thought about this. A lot." He glanced back at Sophia. "According to Sophia, this man has harassed her and bullied her...and abused her for a long time."

"But it stopped once she came here," Bettye

pointed out. "'Cause we all thought for sure he was dead."

"And we hid the car," Jacob said. "Probably covered in vines and saplings by now."

"I'll get to the car later," Adan replied. "I want you all to understand one thing—this man is very dangerous. So we have a dangerous man attacking us on all fronts because he wants to get at Sophia. He's already stalked her, broken into cabins to watch for her, held two people hostage and kidnapped one man to help him lure her down the mountain."

"Nothing he does makes any sense," Maggie said. "He could have gone away easily, but he decided to hang around. Why did he hold Karen and David hostage and make David drive him away if he doesn't want to get away?"

"He thought he could capture me and take me with him," Sophia reminded her. "He figured we'd come after him for taking David. And we did."

"We all fell for that one," Bettye said on a snort. "But we had to save David."

"And I'm thankful you came for me," David replied. Then he motioned toward Adan's shoulder. "Just sorry you got in the line of fire, Adan."

"I'm okay," Adan said, his gaze sweeping over Sophia. "I've been shot before."

"Well, isn't it against the law to shoot a Texas Ranger?" Melissa asked, her tone low and cautious.

"It's against the law to shoot anyone," Karen said, her hand in her husband's.

"Maybe he's gone for good now," Bettye said. "If y'all left him halfway down the mountain, he's either frozen to death or he's gone on down to the main highway."

"But he's a wanted man," Sophia said. "He can't be seen in any town down the mountain and no one will get to him on Crescent Mountain. I think he'll keep on coming until he gets what he wants. Me. That's why he did these things. He's trying to figure out how to get around Adan to come after me."

She didn't say anything about her alternative plan. She would simply wait for Adan to fall asleep tonight and she'd take Jacob's SUV and leave Crescent Mountain. What else could she do?

Karen looked frustrated and confused, her lips pursing in disapproval. "He could have demanded we find you, but instead he tried to trick us so he could take you when only David would be a witness." She put a hand on David's arm. "I'm terrified to think he probably would have killed you."

"Maybe he decided he should leave since we have a lawman guarding us now," Melissa said, her teenage eyes hitting on Adan with a sort of awe. "I mean, he would have hurt someone plenty more if Adan hadn't been here."

David shook his head. "I think his plan was to wait—maybe he thought Sophia would come to visit us at the house. But then Adan showed up, looking for him. He panicked. So he made me get him out of the house, but not off the mountain.

"He planned to wait for y'all even before I ran out of gas. He badly wanted to take Sophia, but he rambled a lot about finding a way to get her. If we'd been closer to civilization and y'all had followed us, he'd have been able to take her right away and make a getaway. But we foiled that plan when I ran out of gas. He'll be back, trust me. He talked about Sophia nonstop and swore he'd get her."

He glanced at Sophia. "Sorry, honey, but you're in real danger here."

"I know," Sophia replied. "And I don't like putting anyone else in danger again. I'm so sorry."

"Hush," Maggie said, her voice full of emotion. "When you showed up here you were so scared you could barely talk. I'm glad we were all here having our Fourth of July cookout. I'm glad Bettye rented you the cabin next to hers. If you had kept going, he would have found you. This is a safe haven and we're going to help you and Adan get this man off the streets."

She smiled over at Sophia and then grabbed her husband's hand. "Right, honey?"

"Right," Arnie replied. "I'm scared silly, I'll admit, but we all love Sophia and we don't want anything to happen to her."

Maggie bobbed her head but didn't speak again.

Sophia couldn't speak, either. Didn't these people see she wasn't worth them risking their lives?

Bettye touched a hand to her arm. "We're all in this together, darlin'. Don't go thinking bad thoughts. You know we want to help and we're bound to each other—have been since you rolled up that hill and got out of the car and started crying."

Sophia remembered that day and how Bettye had taken her into her arms and comforted her. "I… I don't know what I'd do without all of you," she said. "I don't deserve this but—"

"But we're going to help you," Adan said.

Sophia's surprise had to have shown on her face. Bettye winked at her with a knowing smile. "See there. You've got one more in your corner now."

Sophia laughed through her tears. "What can we do?"

"A lot," Adan replied, his eyes holding hers and giving her strength. "But you all have to follow my instructions and do exactly as I say, okay?" He went on to explain. "We wait and we prepare but I don't need any hotshots out there trying to bring him in. He'll come to us, and if he decides not to, well, soon every lawman in this state is looking for him. They probably are already, since the state of Texas put out a BOLO on him."

"Got it," Jacob retorted, his head bobbing. "No heroes and let the lawmen do their jobs."

"I'm in," Bettye said, her hands on her gingham apron.

"I'll help," Melissa said, suddenly very interested.

"We're all willing to help," David said. "Just tell us the plan so we can get on with things. We still have a Christmas feast to prepare."

Adan nodded. "First, we aren't going to do anything. You all need to go about your business."

"That ain't no plan," Jacob said with a huff. He crossed his arms over his chest in agitation.

"It's the best plan," Adan explained. "If we act like nothing is going on, he'll slip up and we'll trap him."

Bettye chuckled. "So you want us to pretend everything is fine but in reality, you want us to be watchful and alert."

"That's right," Adan replied. "Watch and wait. It takes time and patience to trap a raccoon, but sooner or later this one will take the bait."

"Humph, more like a skunk to me," Jacob shot back. He shrugged. "At least we done set some traps around certain areas that seem to attract mangy varmints. He'll trip up sooner or later."

"Is Sophia the bait?" Melissa asked, her eyes wide.

"She's not bait," Adan said, shaking his head. "We're not going to put her in danger. But if a wild animal wants something bad enough, it'll usually find a way to get it."

"We won't let that happen," Maggie replied, her determined gaze reassuring Sophia.

"No, we won't," Adan said. "But we'll let him think he can get to Sophia."

Bettye sat up straight. "Then we'll take him out?"

"No," Adan replied. "We'll take him to jail and he'll stand trial and with testimonies from Sophia and most of you, hopefully he'll be convicted and then he'll be in prison for the rest of his days."

"Or we could just shoot him and call it a day," Jacob replied with his arms crossed again.

"Only as a last resort," Adan said. "Remember that. I don't need any vigilantes around here. I want all of us to come out of this unscathed." He glanced down at Sophia. "Especially you."

She couldn't speak. So she just nodded.

How would she ever be able to sneak away from all of these people so she could give Joe what he'd really come here for—something that was much more valuable to him than she'd ever been? How would she ever find the courage to leave Adan?

CHAPTER SIXTEEN

THE SNOW BEGAN to melt.

Adan once again tried his cell phone and pumped his fist when he had two puny bars. Checking his watch, he saw it was only eight o'clock. Gaylen wouldn't be in bed yet.

He hit the number for his parents' home, waited and hoped he'd at least get to tell one of them that he planned to be home by Christmas. He couldn't miss yet another holiday.

His mother answered on the first ring.

"Mama, it's Adan."

"Adan, where in the world are you? You know we worry when you don't check in."

"I know. Look, I'm in Arkansas on a mountain and a snowstorm knocked out the power to the landlines and made cell phone calls sketchy for a while. It's hard to find service on a good day around here, but this storm was bad."

"We know. We've been watching the weather."

Their favorite pastime, Adan thought with a smile. "It's getting better," he said. "I wanted to let y'all know I'm going to be home by Christmas."

His mother's sigh told him she didn't believe him. "Gaylen has been asking for you."

"Is she still up?"

"Yes. Reading a Christmas story with Grandpa. Do you want to talk to her?"

The emotion choking Adan made it hard to form the one word. "Yes."

He heard his mother call out and then the sound of little feet padding across the room almost brought him to his knees.

"Daddy!"

Adan swallowed the lump in his throat. "Sweetheart, how you doing?"

"Miss wou."

"I miss you, too, honey. I told you I'd be there by Christmas, remember?"

"I know, but come home now. We're weading a story about wain-deers."

"Reindeers? That sounds like a good story for Christmas."

"Can a rain-deer bring you home?"

"No, honey. We have to let the reindeer help get Santa where he needs to go with all those toys. So I can't get there right now, but I'll be there before you know it."

"Before Santa comes?"

"Way before Santa comes, I promise."

Gaylen launched into the world of a child—going to the mall to talk to Santa again, reading Christmas stories with Grandpa in the big, comfy chair. His father's recliner. Making cookies with Grandma with "spinkalls." All the things he'd missed out on so many times.

No wonder his wife had left him.

No wonder his parents had raised his daughter in more hours and more ways than he could ever make up.

"I made wou a special cookie, Daddy."

Adan pinched two fingers against his nose. "What kind of cookie did you make me, sweetie?"

"A star one—like your badge, 'cept we put red spinkalls on it. It's weally big."

Adan glanced down at the badge on his jacket. Sometimes he wondered about that badge and what it had cost him. But a man had to do his job, he had to support his family, and that meant helping his parents and taking care of Gaylen's future.

But for now, he just wanted to get to his truck and get home. The tear in his gut tugged and pulled from both ways.

He glanced around, glad Sophia wasn't nearby.

"That sounds wonderful," he said, blinking away his homesick silliness. "You save me that cookie, okay? Don't give that one to Santa."

Gaylen's giggle sounded like little bells jingling. "Silly, we made some for Santa, too." Then, "Daddy, come home, okay?"

"I will, pumpkin. I love you."

"I wuv wou, too, Daddy."

He heard rustling while he cleared his throat.

"She's still smiling," his mother said. "Will you be okay, Adan? Are you safe?"

"I'm okay, Mama. I'll make it home in time."

"Okay. You take care. Daddy sends his love."

"I love you both," Adan said before he ended the call. "Thanks so much for being such good grandparents."

"No thanks needed," his mother said. "We love having Gaylen with us. She keeps us young. You stay safe and hurry home."

Adan put his phone back in his pocket and turned to find Sophia leaning against the door-jamb from the hallway, tears in her eyes.

Sophia had never seen such tenderness in a man. She'd never seen that kind of tenderness in anyone until she'd stumbled across the people on Crescent Mountain.

But in a man that she was attracted to—never.

This big giant of a man who commanded respect and attention each time he entered a room had been reduced to a puddle of mush by his little girl's charm.

Something inside Sophia's heart shifted and broke open to reveal such a fierce longing that it almost hurt to breathe. Tugging all that emotion back into a safe place, she stood there and tried to get herself together.

"I didn't see you there," he said, his right hand automatically going to the sling on his other arm.

"I wasn't listening," she replied, aware of the many currents that ran through them like the waters from the mountain stream. "I mean, yes, I heard. I was listening, but… I couldn't help but hear." She let out a frustrated breath. "I mean, I wasn't deliberately eavesdropping."

"I get it," he said, his tone resigned. "It's a small cabin and growing smaller by the minute."

Sophia advanced into the den, trying to imagine this place through the eyes of such a wide-open-spaces kind of man. Adan probably felt a stifling and too close intimacy that made him want to get out of here right away. He wanted to be with his little girl, not stuck here trying to capture a crazy criminal.

And yet he'd stayed. He could have taken off to find Joe, but he had made a decision to stay here to protect Sophia and her friends in case Joe came back.

And he would come back. They all knew that. Adan could fuss and fume and accuse her all he wanted, but he'd stayed because he was that kind of man. He wouldn't leave anyone in danger.

Everyone on this mountain, including Adan, had become twisted up in her messy past. A past that had come back to haunt her in a big way. She wished with all her heart she could have met Adan in a different way. But Sophia had also learned that she could only control the here and now.

And here in this moment, she was glad Adan was standing across from her.

"I like small," she admitted to disperse these random feelings, one hand touching on the tiny spruce tree she'd found in the woods and asked Bettye to help her decorate one rainy night. "I told you I grew up moving from home to home and sometimes... I got scared, especially in big foster homes where lots of kids crowded around and bullied me. I went for weeks at a time wondering if my mother was still alive or if I'd ever see anyone from my family again."

Adan turned then, his eyes full of compassion. "Since things have settled down for now, why don't you tell me about your life?"

"Trying to take the heat off yourself, Ranger?"

"Maybe." He walked over and sat down on the sofa, but his gaze held hers. "C'mon. Let's enjoy the quiet for tonight. First thing tomorrow I'll write up my report and then check in at headquarters, but for now let's just talk."

A man wanting to talk? Adan would never quit surprising her. But then, he probably hoped to interrogate her more instead of actually talking to her.

"Sophia?"

His eyes had gone a rich burning gold that reminded her of the sunset hitting the mountain hills and valleys. That color also reminded her of his determination, too.

"What?"

He lowered his head but kept his eyes on her. "We're done with the hard part. At least now I understand why you thought you couldn't tell me the truth."

A trace of guilt nagged at her, but she was still unsure and afraid to admit the one glaring mistake she'd made. A mistake of omission, but still…

Sophia swallowed that trace of guilt. "So what are you expecting me to tell you now?"

He motioned to her in a way that made her heart turn all warm and trusting. Sophia couldn't resist that commanding gesture, couldn't resist him.

When she reached the sofa, he tugged her down, his good arm pulling her close. "That fire feels pretty good."

"Yes. Do you want anything? Food? Pain pills?"

"No." His eyes said yes.

Sophia swallowed again and tried to stop the tremors of need moving through her body. "I have hot chocolate. With marshmallows. Freshly made hot chocolate—I can make it from scratch. Bettye won't let me use the boxed kind anymore."

He chuckled. "Bettye is a woman of principles."

Sophia smiled at that. "She's taught me so

much about unconditional love. About being true to myself and being real. I admire her honesty and wisdom."

"She seems like she's the real deal," he said, his breath tickling her earlobe. "What's her story, anyway?"

Sophia accepted the closeness and savored the warmth of the fire and the warmth of his hand on her arm. "We don't ask each other too much around here, but when she does volunteer things it seems she had a family. A husband who loved her and a daughter who gave her a hard time. I know she and her daughter were on the outs for a long time and that when her daughter died, something inside Bettye died with her. From what she's told me, it caused a break between her husband and her. Their marriage never recovered. After he died, too, she came here. And stayed."

"And Melissa?" he asked, his lips now hovering near her temple. "I should alert someone about her, but she seems to like it here and for the time being, I can't focus on getting her back to where she belongs." Then he frowned. "I'm pretty sure she's got some big secrets, too."

"I haven't heard the whole story," Sophia replied, wondering what he meant by that. "Too much else going on. But I get the impression that Melissa's mother was a lot like mine. I think she died of an overdose. Hard to believe Bettye had no idea where her granddaughter wound up."

"I can't imagine not being close to my folks," he said. "I'm in my mid-thirties and my mama still wants to hear from me."

"She loves you."

He pulled her closer then. "Some people get to have that experience and…take it for granted. I never will again."

"I'm sorry you're not there with your little girl."

"I'll be there soon enough. I promised her I'd be back by Christmas Eve."

She smiled up at him. "If we'd all just let you go, right?"

He turned to her then and lifted her chin so she had to look into his eyes. "A few minutes ago, I was ready to rush out that door and find my way home. Right now, I don't want to be anywhere else."

"You mean, not even chasing Joe Pritchard or tucking in Gaylen?"

"I'd like to do both of those things, but since I can't be two places at once, I can be in the moment. I also really like this. I haven't sat in front of a fire holding a pretty woman in a very long time."

Sophia didn't want to be anywhere else, either. "Do you think we're safe for a while?"

He shook his head, but his eyes held a certain

strength. "Pritchard didn't get what he wanted. He'll try again, but he'll get careless and we'll nab him once and for all."

Sophia wanted to shout out that Joe wasn't just here for her. That he needed her as a means to an end.

And it wouldn't be a good end.

Deciding she could at least be honest about Joe, she gazed up at Adan. "I fell for him because I thought I was worthless, because I got kicked out of my house one time too many. When I turned eighteen, I went back home hoping my mother would let me stay with her again until I could get things together."

Adan's hand moved from her chin to her cheek. "Why would you do that, knowing she wasn't good to you?"

"Because any mother is better than no mother— or so I thought." She'd also thought the same thing about her husband, too.

"I'm guessing that didn't work out so great."

"No. She wouldn't let me stay there since her boyfriend and his friends all flirted with me—I told you that's how I met Joe—so I stayed with friends for a few days and then one night I went to a bar and I ran into Joe again. He made me feel special and safe until I realized I'd exchanged one form of abuse for another."

She shrugged. "I never knew what real love was like until I came to this mountain. So yes,

I fought against telling you the truth. I couldn't face being dragged back into that world again."

Adan moved his hand through her hair and tugged her close. "You don't have to go back into that world—I won't let him take you there. He's not getting his hands on you, ever again."

"You can't—"

"I can," he said, his mouth moving over hers to silence her. He kissed her in a deep, intimate way that made Sophia feel like the only woman on the planet, in a way that should have scared her with its intensity.

But Sophia wasn't scared. She returned the kiss over and over, her heart growing stronger with each touch of their lips. Her hope emerging out from behind a wall of protection to allow him into her world.

He finally pulled away and held her head with one hand. "I can and I will. It's not only my job, but now it's something I have to do. For you, Sophia."

"You're a good man, Adan."

He chuckled. "But I'm thinking very bad thoughts. But in a good way."

She grinned at that. "I guess your shoulder is better."

"Getting better every minute. I think kissing you is helping a lot."

"Then kiss me again," she said. And this time she pulled his head down to meet hers.

Sophia had never experienced such a feminine power, either. She hadn't learned that a woman could kiss a man and still be respected. Adan wouldn't push her, wouldn't expect anything more of her than what she was willing to give.

There would be no force here, no punishment from an immature coward of a bully. This man was strong enough to be gentle, man enough to be tender and noble enough to show restraint and self-control.

So instead of stealing away in the night as she'd planned, Sophia later got up and made hot chocolate with marshmallows and shared Christmas cookies with Adan between kisses. And she also made the sweet mistake of falling asleep in his arms.

Too late to get away when she woke up the next morning and instead, found Adan gone.

CHAPTER SEVENTEEN

ADAN STARED AT his stranded truck and let out a grunt.

Jacob and David grunted with him.

"That there is a mess," Jacob said, shaking his head.

"Yep." David glanced at Adan, then looked back at the truck.

"Now that the roads are passable, we can take you and your tires into town to a gas station to get air in 'em again and we can help you mount 'em back on your truck, too."

"At least he didn't set it on fire," Adan said, still not sure why Pritchard would deliberately deflate the tires. "I don't get it. Why didn't he just steal my truck and go?"

"Me, either," Jacob said as they held their rifles up and advanced toward the truck. "He coulda used your vehicle to get away." He scratched his head. "If you want my opinion, I think the man is running scared and kind of doing a scattershot plan of action."

"I can't argue with that," Adan replied. "He

seems to have a knee-jerk reaction to things. I guess he did this out of a fit of anger."

"It was me."

Adan and the others whirled around, guns raised, to find Melissa trailing behind them. In one of Bettye's big coats and with a wool hat covering her hair, she looked like a lost hobbit.

"Come out from behind that tree and explain yourself," Adan said in a gruff voice. "What do you mean, it was you?"

Melissa pushed through the dirty slush left over from the snow. "He…he wanted me to… distract you…but I hit him over the head and ran. I just ran."

"Who?" Adan asked. "Who wanted you to do that, Melissa?"

She wiped at her eyes. "That man. The one you're chasing."

"Pritchard?" Jacob's blurry eyes widened. "Girl, are you saying you came here with that man?"

Melissa took another step and then jumped over a deep puddle of icy water. "I was…hitch-hiking and he saw me at a truck stop and asked me where I was headed. Once I told him Crescent Mountain, he offered me a ride. Told me he knew how to get here."

She glanced down and then lifted her gaze to the trees. Adan figured she wasn't telling them the whole story. Maybe Pritchard had tried something with her and she was too humiliated and embarrassed to explain.

"I'll just bet he was glad to give you a ride," David said.

She nodded. "He told me he was coming here, too. At first, I was relieved. But then he turned weird and creepy. Told me his wife had run off and he thought she was on this mountain. Offered me money to help him…get to her."

Adan stomped toward Melissa, causing her to step back. "I'm not gonna hurt you," he said, realizing the girl had her own issues. "If you hitched a ride with Pritchard, where is his car and why did you mess with my truck tires?"

Melissa started crying. "He hid the car when the roads got so bad and he couldn't drive. It's down the way on an overlook. We walked about a half a mile to get up the mountain road. When he saw this truck, he tried to find a way in. He knocked at the window with a big rock but it didn't break the glass so he went through your toolbox and found a screwdriver. I guess he pried the glass somehow. It shattered and scared me. I told him I didn't want to hurt anyone. But he said he was taking me with him as collateral."

Adan couldn't believe this guy. "He took advantage of you and used you, Melissa. You could have been hurt…or killed."

"I know that now," the girl said on a wail. "He was nice to me and… I trusted him. I—"

She stopped, wiped at her eyes. "I'm sorry. That's all."

Her words echoed what Sophia had told Adan earlier about how Joe had charmed her into thinking he was a nice guy. He couldn't wait to find Pritchard and knock him silly.

"So what happened?" he asked Melissa.

"I... I got scared after he told me what he wanted me to do and while he was looking around in your truck, I picked up the rock he'd used to try to break the window. When we started walking up the road, I lifted the rock and hit him over the head."

"And what happened next?" Adan asked, his tone gentle now in spite of his growing aggravation.

"I ran away and he...he got up and he was so mad. He got in the truck and tried to crank it but I... I think he flooded it. He cussed and then he got out and took off up the road." She let out a shuddering sob. "He hollered at me and told me when he found me, he'd kill me."

"And what did you do?"

She pointed to the truck. "I figured out how to let the air out of the tires so he couldn't take the truck—so he wouldn't have a way to take me." Her eyes went dark. "I'm done with men using me. Done."

Adan nodded and let that remark slide for

now. "So you deflated the tires but you hid in the truck."

"Only after I was sure he'd gone on up the mountain," she replied. "I was cold and scared and tired. I figured somebody'd come back for the truck and then I'd be okay." Then she pointed toward the vehicle. "And I slept with a crowbar I found in the toolbox."

"Smart girl," David said.

"Even though you sabotaged the truck," Jacob added. "You made it where he couldn't take you or the vehicle but you hoped the real owner would come back."

She bobbed her head. "Yes, sir. But I didn't know it belonged to a Ranger." Looking at Adan with big brown eyes, she said, "I was so afraid of you I… I didn't tell you the truth. Then when I found out he was after Sophia, I thought I had to stay quiet. I wanted to see my grandma and I don't want to go back to juvie or go back to my aunt's house. Please, Adan, don't arrest me. I didn't do anything wrong. I was just with the wrong people." She glared at the truck. "And I hitched a ride with the wrong man."

"You might have saved all of us," Jacob said. "If he'd managed to get that truck outta that drift and up the mountain, he could have taken Sophia."

"But we all have cars," David replied. "He

managed to get me out on a cold night to drive him away."

Adan rubbed his temple. He felt a headache coming on. "Nothing about this makes any sense," he said. "But we're all in it for the duration." He pointed to Melissa. "Even you. No more withholding information, okay?"

"Yes, sir."

If he'd been more diligent, he might have pulled all of this and more out of the girl earlier. But his mind had been centered on Sophia and guarding her. In a perfect world, he would have gone after Pritchard that first night and let the rest of the village people take care of themselves.

But he'd been blindsided and stonewalled at every angle.

No more of that.

"What are you gonna do to me?" Melissa asked.

The fear in her words brought Adan back into focus. Thinking there was so much more to her story, he vowed to question her again soon.

He raised a hand and held it out to her. "Melissa, I won't send you back, but I have to check your record and see if anyone's reported you missing. Did you run away from juvie?"

"No. I served my six months and went into a foster home. Then my aunt took me in, but I ran away from her sorry boyfriend. She's my daddy's sister but she hates me and hates my daddy even more." She put her hands across her midsection in a firm stance. "I'm not going back."

Jacob and David gave each other a quick glance then both sent pleading gazes toward Adan.

"She should have a decent Christmas," Jacob said. "She deserves a Christmas with her loving grandmother."

Adan rolled his eyes. "I'm not so mean as to make her go back before Christmas," he said. "But I have to report her to the state authorities and soon. So everybody just relax."

He glanced at his truck then turned back to Melissa. "You did a brave thing, but it was dangerous to hitch a ride with a stranger." Adan repeated his concerns, hoping the girl would think before doing this again. "He could have killed you."

Melissa burst into tears again and ran into Adan's arms. "But he didn't. And now you won't let him hurt anyone, right?"

Adan held the girl and stared out into the dark, wet woods. "I'll do my best, honey."

He wasn't sure he was heroic enough to protect all of them, but he'd do it or die trying.

SOPHIA SHOULDN'T HAVE panicked when she woke up on the sofa by herself. Adan had wrapped her in a blanket and left her stretched out and all curled up like a content kitten.

He made her feel that way.

How could a man she'd only known for a few days do that to her when Joe hadn't treated her with any type of kindness in the six years they'd known each other? And how could she feel this way about Adan after she'd given up on trusting men at all and forever?

This one is different, she thought as she got up and walked around the cabin. Did she think she'd find him hiding in a closet? Or waiting to hit her and drag her into the bedroom?

No, that was more Joe's way of doing things.

But she had to wonder if Adan was out there searching for Joe Pritchard or if he was somewhere doing background checks on all of them. Did he trust her yet?

They'd kissed and cuddled last night in a very trusting way, so Sophia had to believe they'd moved a little closer toward that end.

But he was still on the right side of the law.

And she still didn't trust the law.

Pouring herself a cup of coffee, Sophia figured she'd find out the old-fashioned way where Adan had gone. She'd ask the one person who knew what was always happening on this remote mountain. Bettye.

When she was halfway up the path, Bandit met her with a woof and a whish of his tail. "What are you doing out here, boy?" Sophia asked, concern causing her to hurry.

"He's looking for Melissa," Bettye said, meeting her on the path. "I can't find her anywhere."

Sophia heard the fear in that admission. "Are you sure she's not visiting with Karen and David or maybe gone on a walk with Maggie and Arnie?"

"I've checked with Karen," Bettye said. "David left earlier with Jacob and your Ranger-Man. But no one's seen Melissa."

"Let's get inside and we'll figure out how to find her," Sophia replied.

The cold couldn't be good for Bettye's arthritis. With her bad knees, the old woman could barely walk even on a warm, sunny day. And even though Jacob swore eating raisins soaked in gin would cure any ache.

"What are you doing out so early?" Bettye asked when they were back by her fire.

"I was looking for Adan," Sophia replied. "But you explained where he's gone. Are they looking for Joe?"

Bettye shook her head, her long gray braid still loose from her everyday chignon. "No, honey. They went to check on getting Adan's tires fixed. Now that the roads are more passable, he wants to get his truck back up and running. Karen said he told David he needed to be home by Christmas."

"He has a little girl—Gaylen," Sophia explained. "He's worried he won't make it in time."

"Hmm. A child." Bettye let that tidbit soak in. "Is he a married man?"

"She left him," Sophia replied. "When his daughter was a baby. They divorced but I don't know if he's over her or not."

Bettye didn't say anything more. "What should we do about Melissa?"

Sophia checked the girl's room. "She left what little she had on her when she showed up—her other clothes and her purse. But I don't see her cell phone anywhere."

"She keeps that thing with her at all times," Bettye said, her eyes bright with concern. "She's waiting for her boyfriend to come. With that crazy Joe out there, I worry about her. I'm not used to having a teenager around."

"I'll go look for her," Sophia said, turning to head back to her place for her rifle.

"No, no." Bettye raised her hand in the air. "I was told to keep you out of the woods."

"And who told you that?" Sophia asked, her hand on her hip.

Bettye looked sheepish. "Ranger-Man." She shrugged. "I did find Melissa gone but I was on my way to check on you, too. I get antsy when people just up and disappear."

Sophia stepped back toward where Bettye sat in her big chair by the window. "Is that what your daughter did—just disappeared?"

Bettye nodded, her head held high. "We didn't get along on many fronts, so when she told us she was pregnant, things didn't go very well. So she ran away with her good-for-nothing boyfriend. I... I worried night and day but she called after a year or so and told me she was fine and the baby was fine but that I needed to stay out of her life." Bettye wiped at her left eye. "A few months later, we got a call that she'd died of an overdose. And her husband had taken off with... our granddaughter."

Sophia sensed Bettye finally wanted to talk. "And *your* husband?"

"He left, too. Blamed me for running her off and for him not being able to help his granddaughter. Daddy's little girl and all that." Bettye twisted her braid up onto her head and pulled a hairpin out from behind her ear to secure it. "He was one of those fine, upstanding types. Never approved of my creative nature. He seemed to forget that he didn't approve of his daughter being pregnant at seventeen, either. So I got the blame for a lot of things."

Sophia came to kneel down beside Bettye. "So when Melissa found you, I guess it was a shock."

"You can say that again," Bettye retorted, tears in her eyes. "She hasn't said much, but I think my daughter's wayward ways had to affect her, too. Not to mention her daddy dumping her with his hateful older sister all the time. All I know is that my granddaughter is afraid to go back home and I will not force her to do so. Not as long as I got a breath in me."

"You won't have to do anything much," Sophia said, patting Bettye's hand. "No one is going to force her to go back."

"Your man might," Bettye replied. "He's a good, solid man, kind of like the one who left me. He has to follow the law. I'd expect no less of him and I wouldn't hold it against him. But I'll fight him on it."

"I'm going to find her," Sophia said. "I'll get my gun and walk the road. Maybe she's afraid Adan will report her now that the weather is letting up."

Bettye put a hand to her mouth. "Or she's gone off with that Sean she keeps talking about. Says he's already here. She might have run off with him."

"Let's not assume anything until I check around," Sophia said. "I'll be right back."

But before she could get to the back door, it opened and in walked Melissa and Adan.

"Hi," he said to Sophia, his expression bordering on perplexed. "I found someone down near my truck."

"Melissa," Bettye said, pushing up out of her

chair with a breathy groan. "Honey, I was so worried—"

"I'm sorry, Granny," Melissa said.

Then she burst into tears and rushed into Bettye's waiting arms.

CHAPTER EIGHTEEN

"WHAT HAPPENED?" BETTYE ASKED, lifting Melissa away to give her a once-over, her bony fingers digging into the old coat Melissa wore. "Are you hurt?"

Melissa shook her head, tears rolling down her face. "I... I knew about him, Granny. I knew about Joe Pritchard and I didn't say anything."

Confusion creased Bettye's forehead. She whirled to Adan and Jacob. "What's she talking about?"

Adan sent Sophia a troubled glance then turned back to Bettye. "She hitchhiked to get here and ran into Pritchard along the way. Joe heard her talking at a truck stop on the interstate about coming to Crescent Mountain and he approached her and offered to give her a ride. She followed us down to my truck today and admitted that she'd let the air out of my truck tires so Pritchard couldn't take my truck."

"What?" Bettye and Sophia both asked at the same time.

Sophia felt sick to her stomach. "Melissa, you… you were with Joe?"

Melissa nodded and sniffed. "Yes. That first night here. I needed a ride and he said he was passing right by here. I didn't know until later what he'd done to you. Once we got here, he told me he knew someone on the mountain and he needed my help to find you." She wiped at her eyes. "But when he started talking about getting even and getting you back, I got scared. He's creepy."

"Did he hurt you?" Sophia asked, her tone rising with anger. If Joe hurt one more person she cared about, she'd find him and finish the job.

Melissa shook her head. "No. He wanted me to distract everyone so he could get at you. Only I didn't know it was *you* and he told me y'all were still married and that you'd been hiding from him and that all I needed to do was lure you out." She inhaled and gulped back a sob. "But he got all creepy and scared me. I was afraid for Granny, too."

"So how did you get away?" Sophia asked, afraid to hear it.

"I wanted to hide from him and warn y'all," Melissa said. Then she glanced at Adan, her expression unsure. "But I didn't know the truck belonged to a Texas Ranger. I got scared and… I lied. I didn't mention Joe Pritchard to anyone because I was so afraid I'd be in trouble."

"You were afraid you'd get sent back to juvenile jail?" Bettye asked, nodding.

Melissa bobbed her head. "Or my horrible aunt. I didn't know what to do. I was afraid of Adan and afraid that Joe would do something to one of you if I talked."

Sophia agreed with that assumption. "How did you get away?"

"She knocked him up against the head with a rock and then she hid in the woods," Jacob said on a proud note. "Mighta addled his brain a tad."

"I hope so," Bettye replied. "That man has gone too far."

"He went too far when he forced Sophia into a car with him a few years ago," Adan said, his irritated tone matching Sophia's. "But forcing a scared young girl to do his bidding takes things to another level. His crimes are multiplying and sooner or later, he'll make a wrong move."

"What if he comes after us?" Melissa asked, real fear in her eyes. "He won't like what I did."

"I don't think he even knows you're here," Sophia pointed out. "If he did, he'd make you pay."

Bettye gasped and wrapped her arms around Melissa. "Not if I can help it."

Guilt once again clouded Sophia's common sense. "I should have found a way to report him the day he took me. I've made so many mistakes regarding Joe. Melissa, I'm so sorry you got involved." Her gaze hit on Adan. He'd remained alert and quiet while Melissa told her story. "I'm sorry I allowed any of you to get involved."

"That's not your fault," Melissa said, shaking her head. "I was stupid to hitch rides with creepy old men anyway. But he seemed nice and safe and I never dreamed he would do this to you. He made me believe you'd run away from him." She started crying again. "Now I can see why."

Grabbing Bettye's arm, she added, "I'm sorry, Granny. Don't make me go back to Hot Springs. I want to stay here until Sean comes for me."

"You're not going anywhere, darling," Bettye said, her fierce glance daring anyone to dispute that. Then she threw down the gauntlet. "Right, Ranger-Man?"

Adan gave Melissa a stern glare. "For now, you don't have to worry about that. But sooner or later we have to talk about reporting your whereabouts." He ran a hand over his hair. "And Melissa, I'll need a complete report on the rest of the story."

Melissa looked shocked. "You mean—"

"Later," Adan said. "I mean you will be honest with me...or I'll be forced to deal with you in a less lenient way."

Melissa didn't speak, but she nodded her head.

Sophia was glad to see Adan didn't seem too worried about enforcing that right now. And she had a bad feeling the elusive Sean wasn't ever

going to set foot on Crescent Mountain. Melissa
didn't need any more reasons to run again.

"What can we do?" she asked after everyone
had settled down. "Joe probably heard Melissa
talking to her boyfriend on the phone about coming here and once again, he used that to his advantage by approaching her and convincing her
he could help her."

"We're doing what we can," Adan replied. "Jacob's gonna carry me back to town to get the
truck tires aired up and he and David will help
me mount them. Then I'll have my truck again."
He leaned close. "After that, my truck will be
parked at your cabin, but I don't think that'll
stop Pritchard. In fact, I hope he'll try to pay us
another visit."

"We just can't guess when he'll strike next,"
Sophia replied, her heart flipping over at the dan-
gerous dare in Adan's eyes. "I'm worried about
Bettye. This has been a lot for her to deal with."

Adan glanced into Bettye's kitchen, where she
stood with Melissa. She'd been fussing over the
girl since Melissa had come back with the men.
"I don't want to leave them alone, so I think it's
a good idea for you to stay here with them while
we take care of my tires."

Sophia saw the troubled look in his eyes and
her heart flipped again, this time for good reasons. "You don't want me to be alone, either,
do you?"

COWBOY WHO CAME FOR CHRISTMAS

Adan glanced around then lowered his voice. "No. I can't deny that. But it looks normal for you to be visiting your neighbor. Just don't leave until I get back, okay?"

Sophia nodded and smiled up at him. "Okay. I'm learning to follow your orders, you know."

"Really? I sure hope so. We can laugh, but this is serious business. Now tell me where you've set traps for Pritchard so I don't accidentally step in one."

Sophia told Adan exactly what she and her merry band of followers had done two days ago while he'd been traveling downstream to look for signs of Joe. "Are you upset with us for doing that?"

"Not any more than usual," he replied with a wry smile. "I only ask that y'all stop hiding things from me. That MO isn't working." He touched a hand to her hair. "We've got to work together. Me going it alone while y'all plot behind my back isn't going to work anymore. I have to know everything that goes on from here on out."

"Okay. No more secrets," she promised, her memories colored with their late-night kisses. "Adan, I do have to ask about one thing. What about the money I took back?"

"What about it?"

"Will that be part of my deal? I won't be prosecuted for taking stolen money?"

"I think I can make it part of the deal. Since Pritchard thought in his twisted way that he was only taking *your* money."

"He claimed it was his money," she retorted, anger making her feel sick to her stomach again. "He said since I'd hidden it from him, it only made sense for him to take it. I've made such a mess of things."

Adan gave her a forgiving stare. "Well, now it's all about to end. You can make it up to the citizens of Texas by cooperating with the law. And right now, darling, the law is me."

Sophia wanted this nightmare over, but she didn't want her time with Adan to end. What did it matter now that she believed Joe had come here for reasons besides just taking her? She wouldn't keep Adan from his little girl, but how would she handle having to tell him goodbye?

If she just left—

Maybe her idea of leaving so Joe could get what he wanted was the best one after all. That way she could give Joe the prize he wanted so badly and then she wouldn't have to tell Adan goodbye.

ADAN SAT IN the Crescent Café, nursing a cup of rich, dark coffee and a big slab of pecan pie. Jacob and David were next to him, talking to some of the locals and asking questions about any Pritchard sightings while Adan checked in with his parents and with his fellow Rangers back in Austin. He'd found a garage that was now airing up the four tires off his truck. Then he'd gone by the tiny police station to give a report to the locals and he'd put in a request to Ranger headquarters in Austin for background checks on Joe Pritchard and Melissa Curtis so he'd have all his ducks in a row when he got back home.

And he'd asked for a check on Sophia Mitchell, too.

He wanted to follow the rules on this one so… so what? So he might have a chance with Sophia?

Did he want a chance with her? Did he trust her enough to take that next step?

Sure, they'd been forced together for days now but after getting off that mountain for a couple of hours, Adan's head had cleared about as fast as the snow melted. He couldn't believe he'd only been here a few days. He was running out of excuses to stick around, but he still had to do his job and bring in Pritchard. For more reasons than one now.

Only Adan couldn't wrap his head around how he'd be able to carry on a long-distance relationship with Sophia with him working in Austin and her wanting to stay on the mountain.

Or did she want to stay on the mountain?

"What's got you frowning like an old bull?" Jacob asked, his gaze centered on Adan. "We're getting air in your tires again and you talked to Sheriff Demont about helping us out with Pritchard."

Adan grunted and took a bite of pie. "And I've still got a conniving criminal on the loose and other things to deal with."

Like getting home to see Gaylen and having to leave Sophia when he did go home.

David poked Jacob and grinned. "I think he's sweet on Sophia."

Jacob jabbed at David's flannel shirt. "I think you might be right there, my friend."

Adan rolled his eyes. "Did you both just step out of a Larry McMurtry novel? All this cowboy talk is rattling my brain." He took a sip of coffee and tried to be nonchalant. "I'm not sweet on anybody."

"Right," David said with a snort. "You and Sophia got eyes for each other. No denying that. No, sir."

Jacob bobbed his head. "I concur on that."

"And you two are like 'Dear Abby' or something, always offering such sage advice and spot-on observations?"

"We're better than any dear anybody," Jacob retorted. "We got eyes in our head and we got sensitive souls. Sophia has changed since she tied you to her bedposts. She's worried about that stupid, sorry you-know-who messing around, but she's also—" He glanced at David. "Help me with the right word."

"Softened," David said with a nod. "She's softened. Smiles a little more. Laughs some. Seems downright content at times."

Adan liked her smile, but he didn't dare tell that to these two. "And in between hiding things from me and setting traps for Pritchard, you two have noticed this?"

"Sure have," David said with a scratch to his head. "We are romantic at heart, you know."

Adan couldn't hide his grin. "Romantic, my foot. More like two old busybodies."

David looked affronted. "Hey, we saw how broken that girl was when she got here and we know how she hates that man who done this to her. It's not a coincidence that you and Pritchard showed up at the same time. It was meant to be."

Adan couldn't deny that his timing had been almost perfect, but he also couldn't deny who had brought him here. "I followed Pritchard," he said, reminding them why he was here. "That's not coincidence. That's just the order of things. Criminal high-tails it from Texas to Arkansas. Ranger follows in pursuit."

"Right," Jacob said with a bob of his head. "Worked out pretty good all things considered."

"'Cause you following that idiot here caused a lot of things to take place," David said. "One being he brought Melissa here, and after giving up on her daughter, Bettye needed to see her granddaughter. Two, he brought you here and you've helped Sophia. Even though she's strong and stubborn, she needs a good man in her life. And three, he's messing with all of us and we can take him and end all of these shenanigans so we can get on with Christmas and so Sophia can finally have a happy life."

Adan grunted. "Uh-huh. You've summarized things nicely, but you both need to understand I have a young daughter waiting for me back in Austin. And I promised her I'd be home on Christmas Eve. I can't break that promise."

David and Jacob glanced at each other then back to Adan. "But you know the way back here now. And we'd like to see more of you. Got it?"

Adan nodded. "Got it." Then his phone dinged. "Let me take care of the one glaring thing that did bring me here and then we'll see how the rest goes."

The two men didn't look happy, but they backed off and went on with gossiping with the locals. Adan listened while his fellow Ranger told him he was sending the information Adan had requested in an email. Now Adan would have the facts to back up his pursuit of Joe Pritchard. And he had all the background checks he needed on the principals involved in things. He still found it mighty interesting that Melissa had just happened upon Joe Pritchard at a truck stop. Hoping the background information would help seal some of the holes, he put his phone away until he could find a time to study the files in private.

But he'd deal with Melissa and Sophia once Pritchard was safely behind bars. Because he had a gut feeling that if he tried to take either of them off this mountain to atone for their minor indiscretions, he'd have a riot on his hands.

CHAPTER NINETEEN

"I DON'T LIKE WAITING."

Sophia heard Adan's grunt on the other end of the phone after she made that remark. He'd called to tell her they'd be late getting back home since the gas station people were working on country time, according to Jacob. The garage attendant wasn't in any hurry with airing up tires.

"Waiting is part of my job," he said, "but I know how you feel. It's been a long day."

She chuckled into the phone. "The odd couple driving you nuts?"

His groan changed to a laugh. "You could say that. But those two are good at unearthing information. I think their constant badgering wears people down."

Sophia was used to that badgering, but she hoped David and Jacob hadn't dug too deeply. "Did they find out anything we can use?"

"Just stuff to confirm that Pritchard is in the area."

"Such as?"

"Several people reported seeing an abandoned

car at the foot of the mountain. The sheriff had already impounded it but he let me take a look at it. Surprise—it's stolen."

"I can believe that," Sophia said, unease making her stare out the windows at the front of Bettye's house for about the tenth time. "Joe's never owned a car in his life—except the one I stole from him."

"Consider that poetic justice," Adan retorted. "We're waiting to identify the prints they found but we're pretty sure they'll be Pritchard's. Just takes longer here to get them back from the lab. The sheriff said he'd update me on that one when he hears."

"Anything else?" she asked, hoping they'd find enough evidence to put Joe away for good. Hoping she wouldn't have to tell anyone anything else and that Joe would find what he was looking for and then just leave.

"Some receipts that prove he was at the same truck stop as Melissa. They show the time and how much gas he bought, along with the fast food he purchased, too."

"That's good. Melissa can vouch that he was there and brought her here."

"Yep. These things take a lot of tedious footwork but when we put it all together, it's called evidence. We're building a case."

Then he sighed. "I'd better go. Jacob and

David are getting in a heated discussion about football with the garage mechanic."

"Okay," Sophia said. "I'll be right here with Bettye and Melissa. They're making Christmas cookies."

"Save me one," Adan said. "And, Sophia?"

"Yes?"

"Maybe you can make us a batch of that good hot chocolate when I get home."

Sophia hung up but held Bettye's old phone to her heart and had to swallow back the awareness that grabbed at her throat. He'd called her place home. But she had to remember they'd been confined in a too-small space together during an extreme event in both of their lives. Would things between them cool off once Pritchard was out of the way and they could relax?

Did she really know Adan? And would he like the real her once he got to know her more? Would he forgive her for not being completely honest with him about things? She could be temperamental and hard to deal with at times. But if she had someone like Adan around, her mood would probably improve drastically.

Over the last few days, Sophia had learned not to interrupt Adan when he scribbled notes on his notepad or typed things into his phone app. But she loved watching him doing his job. She was intrigued by the way his brow creased when he stewed over some new grain of information regarding Joe Pritchard and the way his eyes changed colors depending on his mood.

Since they'd become more intimate, she'd look up and find him watching her, too. Not that she'd had much of a chance to get back to her art. He mostly watched her while she moved around the kitchen preparing meals or trying to look busy.

But she was anxious to get her life back. Taking buttons and hot gluing them onto an old mirror made her feel less alone and less of a failure. Her button- and jewelry-encased mirrors were popular with what Bettye called the festival folks who attended any art fair or bazaar in Arkansas.

Art had saved her and made her less lonely. How would she deal with the loneliness after Adan left?

Her place had been special to her from the day Bettye had offered it to her. They'd cleaned it and decorated it piece by piece and Sophia had given Bettye rent money after her first big art sale down in the village.

Bettye had never told her how much the rent would be.

Her friend had just said, "Whenever you get ahead and whatever you can give, honey."

Sophia checked on Bettye and Melissa, her thoughts on her own solitary life. Did she have anything left to give in a relationship? What could she offer someone like Adan?

"You're mighty quiet over there," Bettye

called from the kitchen. "What did your Ranger-Man say?"

Sophia pushed away from the windows and joined Bettye and Melissa, the sweet smell of cinnamon filling her senses. "They found a car they think Joe was driving—a stolen car."

Melissa's eyes widened. "He told me he'd bought that car. Said it was practically new." She shrugged. "That explains why it quit working when he tried to get up the mountain road."

"He lies a lot," Sophia retorted. "You can't trust anything Joe Pritchard tells you."

Bettye gave her a sympathetic stare. "You look tired, honey. Why don't you go take a nap in Melissa's room?"

"I can't rest," Sophia admitted. "I'm worried about…everyone. We should call Karen. She's probably getting concerned about David being away."

"I'll go get her," Melissa said, whirling to head to the back door. "She'll want to try some of our awesome cookies."

"Take Bandit with you," Bettye called after her. "Tell Karen we're having a girls' night in. Safety in numbers."

Sophia agreed with that logic. After Melissa was gone, she turned back to Bettye. "She seems to love being with you."

"I sure love having her here," Bettye admitted.

"But I wonder if she'll want to stay here even if she could. Teenagers get so bored these days."

Sophia hadn't considered Melissa sticking around. She hadn't considered Adan sticking around, either. They'd both kind of wandered in underneath the shadow of Joe's crimes.

"Has she told you anything about her time with Joe? I mean, are you sure he didn't try something with her?"

Bettye's expression was serene in spite of the flare of fear in her eyes. "She has assured me that he was in a big hurry to get here so he didn't bother her much. I think once they got going from the truck stop they mostly compared notes on the map and who they both knew here. Besides, she also said she would have decked him if he did try anything."

"Well, she did just that after she realized how crazy he is," Sophia said. "Thank goodness."

"I'm so thankful she found me," Bettye replied. "I shouldn't have let her mother go, should have loved her through everything, but I didn't know how to handle things back then. I had a nervous condition and stayed doped up on anti-depressants."

Bettye was now adamant about not taking any prescription drugs. She preferred natural remedies—most of which she could find in the woods if she looked long enough.

"Did you ever try to find Martha?"

Bettye nodded. "After Walter died, yes. But it was too late." She took the spatula and lifted up the cooling cookies to place them on a big platter. "We didn't do right by our daughter and…we didn't forgive her or each other. I had to get away."

"But you've made a life here."

Bettye put down the spatula and glanced toward the door. "When I first came here, I was so lonely at times, I wanted to die. I'd failed my only child and I'd ruined my marriage." She reached out to touch Sophia's hand. "The day you came, honey, I was close to just throwing myself off the side of the mountain. You…you saved me."

"Oh, Bettye." Sophia hugged the older woman close. "You're like a mother to me. The best kind of mother."

"Maybe we're both getting a second chance," Bettye replied. "I'm sure trying with Melissa."

"If she could stay, would you want that?" Sophia asked while they finished cutting the last batch of cookies.

Bettye stood still, her gaze lost in the past. Finally, she nodded. "I think I'd like that. But I doubt she'll stay. She's waiting for her *one true love* to come and get her."

"Sean?"

Bettye nodded. "I fear he got lost somewhere. On purpose."

"I fear the same," Sophia replied. "Has she heard from him?"

"No, and she checked her phone an hour ago." Bettye glanced toward the door again. "She should have been back by now."

"I'll go out on the porch and see if I can find her," Sophia said. They'd always been watchful around here, but now it seemed they had to stay in groups in order to make it through the day. She hated Joe Pritchard all over again for causing this.

She eyed her rifle and decided to take it out the door with her. But when she got out on the porch, she saw Karen coming up the path by herself.

"Hi," Karen called. "Melissa said y'all were having a good time making Christmas cookies. Thought I'd join y'all. I'm working on Christmas cards so I brought them with me to address." She patted a floral tote bag.

"C'mon on over," Sophia said. "Hey, where are Melissa and Bandit, anyway?"

Karen nodded toward the road. "She saw a car pulling up and jumped for joy. Something about her boyfriend finally finding her."

ADAN AND THE other men pulled up to his truck just as the sun was starting to make its descent over the mountains to the west. In an hour, dusk would hit and they'd have to use flashlights to get the tires remounted onto the truck.

"Best get right to it," Jacob said, eyeing the sun. "Dark comes early these days."

David lifted the collar of his heavy barn jacket. "And when that sun goes down, it gets cold out here."

Adan glanced at the sky and then back to the vehicle. "At least the snow's melted enough that we can get it out of this mud hole." The front end of the truck was sitting in the mire.

David's SUV had a winch to help pull the truck back onto the road once they had the tires back on... "Let's get going."

After using the jack to painstakingly lift the truck to put each tire back on, with Adan at the wheel of the truck to gas it out of the bog, David worked the pulley cable attached to the winch into tugging Adan's truck onto the road. That accomplished, they checked each tire to make sure they were secure.

"Ready?" David asked while Adan stood there stewing.

He glanced at the sun then back at the messy road ahead. "I'll get the window fixed once I get home... We need to hurry and get back to the cabins."

The men had spent their time together talking about fishing and hunting and having a big Christmas dinner. Now, they were covered in mud and dirt, but Adan had enjoyed the comradery at least. David and Jacob had insisted Adan stand back and let them take care of the tires since his gunshot wound was still painful.

"Hey, we need to throw you a party before you head back to Austin," Jacob told Adan when they were about to leave.

"I'd like that," Adan said. "I have to admit, you've all been real good to me."

"Why wouldn't we?" Jacob asked, his white hair sticking out around his face. "You can't help what brung you here."

"I came in here ready to do battle," Adan retorted. "I didn't want to be here. The weather was lousy and so was my mood."

"Why?"

Adan glanced at Jacob's ever-hopeful features. Giving that one-word question a lot of thought, he said, "I guess I wanted to be home with my little girl."

"That's understandable," David said. "Me and Karen will head out after our celebration here to see our grandkids in Tennessee." He shook his head. "My wife can't go over two months without seeing her grandbabies."

Jacob grew quiet. "I never had any children. We just couldn't bear fruit. But since I lost my wife, I'm learning to take my family where I can get it. Bettye and me, we understand each other and we respect each other." He winked at Adan. "You could have a good mama for that little girl."

Adan grunted and started putting away tools. "I told y'all to stop with the matchmaking. It takes more than three days together to decide about a lifetime commitment."

"Maybe you ain't into committing to anyone," Jacob suggested. "I believe in love at first sight but maybe you can't see what's right in front of you."

"Maybe you're correct there," Adan retorted. "I do have blinders on for a reason, though. My wife didn't stick around long enough to work things out, so I'm kind of gun-shy about ever marrying again."

"Sophia wouldn't run off on you," David said on a pragmatic note.

Adan didn't bother pointing out that she'd been forced to run from her first husband. She had good reasons for that.

"I like Sophia," he admitted. "But... I can't do anything about that right now. Pritchard won't give up now that he knows where she's living. I've seen his kind before. He'll be back."

"And you need to be here when he does come back," David said. "Let's get up the mountain. The sun'll be gone by the time we get home."

Adan looked at the bright golden glow coloring the trees. It was good to see sunshine and warmer temperatures even if it was still in the forties during the day.

I'll be home soon, he thought. He missed Gaylen so much it hurt him to breathe, but he'd talked to her and his parents this morning. They were all okay but he'd taken advantage of his parents time and time again. While he knew they didn't mind, he feared if Helena ever did come back she'd try to win custody based on how much time he spent away from home.

Was he any better than his ex? He'd left his daughter with other people way too much lately. Thankful for his accommodating parents, he got back to business so he could see them again soon. He did a check of the surroundings to make sure he'd cleared out everything and that his bruised vehicle was intact.

The men kicked the caked mud off their boots and tried to clean their hands with some old grease rags from the toolbox on the back of the truck. Adan searched the toolbox for his prized Bowie knife but couldn't find it. Had Pritchard taken it? Or Melissa, maybe? He made a note on his phone pad. Just another puzzling variable to deal with.

Jacob hopped in the truck with him and they waited for David to get in his vehicle and lead the way back up Crescent Mountain.

"I'm gonna ask Bettye to marry me," Jacob said out of the blue once they were on their way home.

Adan was impressed with the honesty of that sentiment. "Well, then, I'm happy for you. You two make a good couple."

"She'll say no." Jacob stared straight ahead, his hands across his chest. "But I won't give up."

"Okay," Adan replied. "I'm wishing you luck anyway."

"You might have to ask Sophia more than once, too."

Adan hit a hand against the console and winced when his arm and wound started throbbing. "Jacob, I'm not gonna ask Sophia to marry me. You need to stop hoping that will happen. And don't you dare mention it to her or Bettye."

"Oh, Bettye knows it'll happen. We've already talked about it."

Adan didn't know what to say to that kind of optimism. "Well, don't spread that tale to Sophia. She's already been through a lot. I won't be part of hurting her again."

"Then don't give up on her so fast," Jacob said on a stubborn note. "Just 'cause you been through one bad experience don't mean you have to give up on love."

Adan had to admit he'd like to get to know Sophia more, after Joe Pritchard was behind bars and once the holidays were over and he could catch his breath. But he wasn't ready to go whole hog and marry her. Then why did the thought of leaving her hurt as much as his bum shoulder?

He'd have to figure that out later.

Now, he'd settle for saving her from her killer ex-husband.

CHAPTER TWENTY

DARKNESS COLORED THE mountain in deep purples mixed with rich burnished oranges and shimmering silvers. The last of the sun's rays shot in dappled yellow through the oval circle of cabins and pierced through the bare-limbed trees.

"Perfect timing," David said on a sigh as he came over from his yard after parking his truck to greet Adan and Jacob in Sophia's yard. "I think my wife is in there with Bettye and Sophia. No telling what kind of world-domination plans they're cooking up."

Adan leaned against his truck, glad to have his vehicle close by once again. He couldn't stay here much longer. The weekend was coming up and then Christmas Eve. He had to find Pritchard. But with the last light of day fading to the west, he wished he could see that sunset view every day for the rest of his life.

With Sophia by his side. But he had to put that image out of his mind.

Determined to ignore this new and disturbing mind-set, he looked at Jacob and David. "Maybe

I should just keep going north so I can find that idiot and get this over with."

The two men glanced at each other and then back to Adan. "You think he's given up? Or are you just tired?"

"I don't know what to think," Adan replied to David's pointed question. "He knows I'm after him. He's harassed just about everybody on this mountain and he shot me. He'd be a real fool to strike again, but then, he's after someone he believes to be his property." Then he added, "And yes, I'm tired. Real tired. But I did come here for a reason. I don't like failure."

"Then you need to stay right here and wait him out," Jacob said, nodding his head. "You can't quit on us now."

Adan had to agree, but he'd have to reel in his feelings for Sophia. "I'll give him a couple more days and then I'm either going after him or I'm going home. I might have to hand this off to the locals and the state."

"You saw how they reacted," David pointed out. "Seemed relieved to have a Ranger on the case."

"They're shorthanded," Adan said in defense of the substation down in town. "But we did make sure the state police and the locals were on the lookout for Pritchard. It could turn into a statewide manhunt before this thing is over. They've already alerted everyone else."

If the weather hadn't sabotaged things, Adan would have had Pritchard and been long gone for home by now.

But then he might not have met Sophia.

"Are you sure you want to just up and leave, after all of this? After everything that's happened this week?"

Jacob again. His tone indicated he couldn't let things go so easily. Adan realized this had gone from him doing his job to him becoming a bridegroom.

How could he explain that he wasn't ready to go down that road again? He glanced around, thinking he'd have to make Sophia understand. Not that she'd made any moves except returning those sweet kisses they'd shared.

No, Adan had made all the moves. The wrong moves. He had no business kissing a woman connected with the criminal he was chasing. As soon as he got cleaned up, he'd read over those files he'd received from Ranger headquarters.

Then he noticed a new vehicle sitting off to the side of the yard and his heart betrayed him with a fierce need to get to Sophia. "Someone's here," he said to the men.

He drew his gun and hurried into the house.

SOPHIA GLANCED OUT the window. "They're back."

She hadn't realized how worried she was until she saw Adan standing out front with Jacob and

David. She wanted to rush out the door and ask what took so long, but she turned back toward the pot of chili they'd cooked for dinner tonight.

"I'll check on the corn bread," she said to anyone who might be listening. "We can eat now that everyone is here."

She glanced over to where Melissa sat cuddled on the sofa with a lean, blond-haired boy who looked way too old for her.

Sean Martino had found his way to the mountain.

Bettye had frowned once upon meeting Sean and then made the boy so welcome he'd probably go running for the hills. There wasn't any cool here except the air outside. Bettye was wise to hover and stifle the two with her unconditional acceptance, but Sophia hoped it didn't backfire on her. Melissa might have stalled out here, waiting for Sean, and she could easily sneak away with the boy, never to be heard from again.

That would break Bettye's heart.

Bettye and Karen went about getting bowls and pouring tea. "Has anyone checked on Maggie and Arnie?" Karen called out.

"They were going on one of their hikes this afternoon," Melissa said, obviously aware enough to take time away from staring into Sean's blue eyes to report in. "Said not to count on them for dinner."

Sophia wondered about the young couple. They were quiet and liked to keep to themselves, and her only complaint had stemmed from the way Arnie glanced at her every now and then. Maggie didn't seem to like him noticing other women. Nothing wrong with that before. But now she'd become suspicious of everyone, thanks to Joe's antics.

When the front door opened, she glanced up and right into Adan's eyes. He took a quick survey of the room, but she noticed his right hand hovered near his gun belt. He had his gun out.

"Adan, this is Sean Martino," Bettye said in a cheerful warning. "Melissa's *boyfriend*."

Adan relaxed, tension draining from his face while he slowly hid his gun inside the holster. "How you doing?" he asked the boy by way of a greeting.

"Whatssup." The boy never even looked Adan's way but at least he'd made a halfhearted attempt at a greeting.

Adan grunted something and then he lowered his head. He dropped his hat onto Bettye's hall tree and made his way toward Sophia. "One extra for dinner?"

"Yes. He showed up this afternoon." She shrugged. "I can't say how I feel about him. He's only been talking to Melissa."

"So that's his car outside?"

"Yes. I'm sorry. I guess that was a surprise."

"Not one I needed." He glanced around. "Is everyone accounted for?"

"Yes, but Maggie and Arnie went on a hike."

"But I told them—"

"They kind of do their own thing," she said in defense of her friends. "They were going to stay close to home, so they should be back any time now."

"I hope so," he said through a grunt. "It's getting dark, so I don't want to have to go search for them out there."

"How are you?" she said, acutely aware that something had changed with him. He didn't seem to want to look at her.

"All right. Sorry we're late." He motioned toward his feet. "My boots are caked with mud. Thought I'd try to freshen up at your place before we eat."

"Sure," she said, ignoring the stab of regret centered in her chest. Regret followed by worry. Had Joe done something else? Or had Adan found out something more in town? "We washed your extra clothes and put them back in your duffel bag."

"Thank you," he said, giving her a hesitant smile. "I'll hurry up and get right back. That chili smells good."

"Bettye's recipe," she replied, her gaze moving around the room. "Adan?"

He turned in a whirl of what looked like dread. "Yep?"

"Did you find out anything else while you were in town?"

"No, not much more than I told you over the phone."

She nodded and he turned to go. Had he found something that bothered him too much to share? Did he think she'd lied to him yet again?

"What's going on with you two?" Karen asked. She took a bread knife and starting slicing the cornbread.

"Nothing," Sophia replied. "I think we're just all tired of...thinking about Joe coming back. Maybe he's gone for good."

And maybe tonight would be her best chance to go after him on her own and end this constant tension that shimmered through the air. Every time she thought about leaving, Adan pulled her back in, at first with his injury and later with those all-seeing golden gazes and his delicious kisses. He'd hinted at more when he'd called and reminded her of hot chocolate.

She'd need lots of chocolate after he left.

Karen gave her a concerned glance and then headed for the door when she saw David coming in. He'd already gotten cleaned up over at their house. He gave his wife a quick hug and a soft smile. Jacob had washed up in the bathroom here and was now entertaining Melissa and Sean. And probably sizing up the boy, too.

No one made a big deal out of seeing Sean, not even Adan. Or maybe Adan hadn't even noticed the boy after he'd walked through the door and assessed the situation as safe. He'd left in such a hurry, she wondered if he'd even come back for dinner.

Sophia wished she could have gotten more out of Adan, but it wasn't as if he owed her any explanations. She had to keep reminding herself that he'd be gone as soon as this was over and Joe was out of the picture. Adan had a daughter and parents who loved him and wanted him in their lives.

And she had a good life here. A life she'd missed lately in spite of being lonely at times. The solitude of this remote mountain had helped her to heal. That solitude had been shattered when Adan and Joe had arrived, however.

They both needed to go back to their own worlds. That would be for the best, after all. Tonight, she had people to feed.

Soon, Bettye's little cabin was full of people. Used to these impromptu gatherings, Sophia helped Bettye gather chairs and stools so everyone could crowd around her dining table.

"Where's Adan?" Bettye asked, glancing around.

"He went to my cabin to get cleaned up," Sophia replied. "He should be back any minute now."

ADAN STARED DOWN at the reports on his phone, his gaze scanning over the words again. He knew everything about Joe Pritchard but he skimmed over the long rap sheet anyway. One thing stuck out that he had seen before but forgotten.

Joe had been involved with some nasty people back in Waco, including a major drug dealer. The dealer's last known address was listed as one of the places Joe hung out. A note stated, *last seen at this location on the night of...*blah, blah. Adan skipped the details since he hadn't seen anything new.

Melissa's information was sealed so he couldn't take things any further there without a court order.

Then he came to Sophia's information. Why was he afraid to read hers? Would he find something else she'd forgotten to tell him about? When he saw a note from one of his fellow Rangers, he breathed a sigh of relief.

"Clean as a whistle," the note read. "No known criminal records. But she did fall off the radar a few years back."

Adan stopped reading and let out a sigh. Sophia was clean in spite of being associated with Pritchard. Probably because Pritchard had lied to her so many times. He wondered if anyone had even noticed she'd gone missing. It didn't sound that way.

But as he headed back over to Bettye's cabin, something nagged at Adan's mind. Thinking a lot of things were nagging him these days, he let it go and headed in to get a bowl of chili.

Adan came back in and nodded to everyone but Sophia noticed he still seemed a bit cool and detached. "I'm a little cleaner now. The snow's melting but the mud might be here awhile. My truck was buried in it."

Maybe now that he had his truck back, he'd become even more impatient to get this over with and done.

"That slush is messy," David said, smiling at Karen. "I thought we'd left the snow for good when we moved here from Illinois."

"It'll pass," Bettye said. "We're all safe and warm and that counts for something." She waved everyone through the receiving line. Smiling at Adan, she said, "We never go hungry around here."

Sophia glanced at him, her smile hopeful. He did lift his head but the twisted smile he had pasted on his face looked more pained than happy. What was he hiding from her?

Sophia didn't press him. Too many people in here for them to get into an intimate conversation. But she knew something had changed with Adan while he'd been down the mountain.

And she intended to find out what when she got him alone again.

ADAN DID A visual sweep of Sophia's cabin and then motioned for her. "All clear." He intended to get her settled for the night and then he'd keep watch and go back over his notes.

He had to think about something besides being here with her. Alone.

"Not too many places to hide in here," she said from behind him, her tone tinged with a nervousness that caused him to wonder what was wrong with her. "I don't have a root cellar like the Harpers. We all usually go into theirs whenever a tornado warning sounds."

He rattled door locks and closed curtains. "That's good to hear."

"We don't get many tornadoes, but you never know."

Adan tried to ignore the image of her being tossed about by a tornado. "Yep. Could be right."

"What am I so right about, Adan?"

He whirled to find her staring at him with those big blue eyes. "Uh… I don't know. Tornadoes?"

"Why are you ignoring me?"

Adan wanted to deny that, but he couldn't lie

to her. "I'm…trying to stay on track. We don't have much time left and I need to stay focused."

"You mean, Joe needs to hurry up and come for me so we can get this over with and done?"

"Yeah, that's what I mean," he admitted. Then he shook his head. "I mean, I don't want Joe to come for you, but I want Joe to make a move so I can capture him."

"So you're tired of this? Well, so am I. Nobody wants this over more than I do."

"I understand that," he said in a gentle tone. "I talked to my parents this morning. They're worried about me and… Gaylen is upset because I'm not home yet."

He saw the compassion in her eyes. And the acceptance. "Of course, you need to get back to her. You don't have to stay. We're very capable of taking care of ourselves around here."

"I can't leave you."

The words were out before he could hold them back. "I mean, I have a job—"

"To do," she finished. "We all know that."

"What does that mean?" he asked, spoiling for a fight. Or a kiss, maybe.

"It means you don't have to sit around waiting for him to return. It means now that the roads are passable, you can call in reinforcements and let the state of Arkansas take things from here."

"I've already alerted the proper authorities," he blurted. "The state police have put out an APB on Pritchard and we could have a manhunt on our hands before this thing ends."

Fear flittered through her eyes. "So…you can leave."

"I should leave," he replied, peeling out of his jacket while he favored his left arm.

"Where's your sling?"

"I ditched that thing this afternoon. Had to get those tires back on the truck."

"And of course, you had to prove you could do it with only one good arm."

"I had help, thank you."

She looked skeptical but didn't have a comeback. "David used to work at a big-box store. I'm sure he knows all about changing tires."

"He told me that, and he helped me get the mechanic to hurry on up this morning."

"Sounds like you three had a great day away."

"I've had better." Hoping to clear the air, he asked, "What's got a bee in your bonnet, anyway?"

"You," she said, her hands on her hips in full warrior mode.

"Me, what have I done?"

"You seem… I don't know…different."

Adan lowered his head and wished he could get in his truck and leave. But he couldn't do that. Then he wished he could sweep her up and take her with him. But he couldn't do that, either. So he decided to be honest.

"I'm tired. I had a long day of waiting around a garage and going over details with the local sheriff. Then I had to get those tires back on my truck. Or at least, I tried. Jacob and David did most of the work."

"So your manhood is threatened because your shoulder hurts?"

He turned then, full of mad. "Excuse me? This has nothing to do with my manhood. But it has a lot to do with you."

"Me?" She stepped closer. "Explain that comment."

"I had a background check done on you," he blurted. "And you're clean."

Shock clouded her face. Followed by relief. "All you had to do was ask."

"I did," he retorted. "Several times."

"So now that you know…you can hunt down Joe and get on with things. You certainly don't have to protect me, especially since you still don't trust me."

Adan could tell she was hurt and upset. "I had to be sure. It's what I do. I need honesty, Sophia. Complete honesty."

She nodded and lowered her head. "I can accept that, but I don't have to like the way you go about things." With a shrug, she added, "I told you a long time ago you could leave any time you want."

Adan dropped his hands to his side. "Yeah,

and I keep telling you that I can't abandon you. Not if Joe comes back."

"Then I can make it easy for you," she said, advancing even closer. "I'll leave. I've been trying since the first night you arrived, but—"

"But the first night, you had to find out why I'd come here," he interrupted. "And then we were both too tired to fight about it. Then I got shot and...you had to watch over me all night."

"And don't forget last night and all that hot chocolate," she retorted.

"And those kisses."

"Can't seem to find a time to run," she said, her voice going soft. "Maybe I'm still a coward after all."

Adan couldn't stop himself then. He rushed to her and gathered her close. "Do not go out there and try to be a martyr, Sophia. If you do that, you'll be letting down all the people who love you. You don't have to put yourself in harm's way."

She gazed up at him as if she had a lot more to say. "But I—"

He lifted her chin up. "But nothing. If I have to put guards on the doors around the clock, I won't let you sneak away in some misguided effort to find Joe. He's dangerous. You know how these things can end. If he takes you, you might not make it out alive."

"I don't have any other choice," she said against

his throat. "I don't want the people who've been so good to me to get hurt or worse, killed."

"You do have a choice," he whispered, hoping he could convince her. "You do. Always."

Her eyes went a deep blue. "But you don't need to stick around. It would be better if you leave."

"Yes, I do have to stick around," he finally admitted. "I…have a choice, too. And this time, I'm choosing you."

"What about Gaylen?"

"I'll be home by Christmas Eve," he said. "But tonight, I'm here with you."

He leaned in to kiss her, to show her that he wouldn't abandon her.

But a knock at the back door pulled them apart.

Sophia rushed around, Adan on her heels.

"Who's there?" she asked, her words full of apprehension.

"It's David."

Adan opened the door and David pushed inside. "Maggie just showed up at our door without Arnie. He fell down a ravine. She says Joe Pritchard pushed him."

CHAPTER TWENTY-ONE

ADAN AND SOPHIA grabbed coats, flashlights and guns and rushed out the door.

Sophia shook her head and put a hand to her mouth. "I can't believe this. Do we need to post more guards all over this mountain?"

"Guards can't cover every inch of this place." Adan grunted, his hand guiding her as they hurried behind David. "The Burtons chose to ignore the warnings, but we can't worry about that now. I'm calling the sheriff and a rescue team. Pritchard is a menace and he's running amok on this mountain." He pulled out his phone and made the necessary calls and then turned back to Sophia. "I should have gotten the locals involved from the beginning, but I had him cornered."

"You thought you'd be long gone from here." Sophia stopped and glared up at him. "And then I came into the picture and you had to change your tactics."

"I had to protect you, yes," he countered. "But I can't do that by myself anymore."

"And I can't keep putting people in danger,

Adan. It's the same argument we've had since you got here."

"It ends now," he said when they started toward where David and Jacob were standing with Maggie and Bettye.

Sophia took one look at Maggie and rushed to her side. "Maggie, I'm so sorry—"

"You both need to get this man out of our lives," Maggie said, tears streaming down her face. She was dirty and disheveled, her hair matted with leaves. "He came at us when we were almost home and terrorized us. This isn't a game anymore, Sophia."

Adan stepped between Sophia and Maggie. "Maggie, tell me what happened."

"No." Maggie pushed at him. "Not until we call a search party and an ambulance. My husband is hurt and he could die if we don't get him help. I don't even know how bad he is, but I do know he's in a lot of pain. He was able to talk to me a little but he…he passed out and I… I couldn't get him to wake up and answer me."

Adan held a hand on her arm. "I've called the authorities and the paramedics are on the way. We're going to start an extensive manhunt for Pritchard and I need your help since you were the last person to see him on the mountain." Lowering his voice, he asked again, "What happened?"

Sophia wanted to curl up in a ball and hide away. The look on Maggie's face said everything.

Maggie and Arnie had chosen to go on a hike even though Adan had warned them all to stick close to home, but it was Sophia's fault they'd all gotten involved in this. If she'd left Adan alone that first night instead of holding a gun on him and tying him up because of her own fears, she could have told him the truth immediately and he might have been able to capture Joe that night.

"I messed up, Bettye," she said to her friend. "I should have told Adan everything right up front."

Bettye gave her a frown. "Let's don't dwell on that, honey. You've had a long, hard road and you were scared. I'm the one who hit the Ranger-Man over the head with a frying pan."

"But you did it for me," Sophia said. "I don't want to dwell in self-pity, but this is my fault."

"You can whine all you want later," Bettye said in a harsh voice. "You need to go with them to see about Arnie. Karen and I will get Maggie calmed down and we'll both have our guns with us."

Sophia pulled herself together and decided Bettye was right. Nothing to be done now but get this over with. "Where's Melissa?"

"Inside with Romeo," Bettye said on a more cheerful breath. "Those two are lost in their own little world."

Sophia wished she could be lost in that kiss Adan had been about to plant on her, but that kind of distraction had contributed to this mess.

She had to get her head back in the place where she stayed safe and made sure everyone else on Crescent Mountain did, too. "Okay. I'll go with the men and I'll report in to you and Maggie."

"Good idea," Bettye said, relief obvious in her words.

Sophia decided her friend wanted to keep her away from Maggie for now. So Sophia listened while Maggie explained what had happened. What else could she do at this point?

ADAN TOOK IN Maggie's breathless explanation, a throbbing beat echoing in his aching head and wounded shoulder. Something wasn't right here, but he couldn't put his finger on it. Maybe he was still caught up in how he'd wanted to kiss Sophia back before they'd been interrupted. Pushing aside that aching need, he focused on what Maggie was telling him.

"We were tired of being cooped up in our cabin," Maggie said. "We decided to take a short hike right before sunset, to one of our favorite spots near the stream. We'd had a good walk and enjoyed the sunset when this man came out of nowhere and blocked our way."

"Pritchard," Adan said, nodding. "What happened next?"

"He held a gun on us and demanded we bring him back here so he could...find Sophia." She glared at Sophia, anger in her moist eyes.

Adan gave Sophia a reassuring glance but wondered why Pritchard hadn't just tried to get to Sophia on his own. He sure knew which cabin belonged to her. "And did you comply with his demand?"

Maggie bobbed her head and wiped at her eyes. "We started walking back toward home with him right behind us, holding the gun on us. When it got dark it was hard to see, but Arnie decided to be a hero. He turned at a curve in the path and tried to wrestle the gun away. They fought and Arnie had the shotgun in his hands, but Joe Pritchard charged at him and Arnie fell. He fell down into that ravine and I heard him calling out. We need to hurry." She started at a run but Adan followed and halted her.

"What did Pritchard do then?" Adan asked, his tone demanding since Maggie glared up at him.

"He wanted to take me with him, but he didn't have a weapon. The gun fell with Arnie." She glanced over her shoulder. "I took off running as fast as I could and here I am. Now can we please go and check on my husband?"

"You should probably stay here," Sophia said before she could stop herself.

Maggie turned and stalked back to her. "No, you need to stay here. This is your fault, so don't even try to help me now. I have to show them where Arnie fell." She pointed a finger at Sophia. "If she goes with us, I'll demand she's arrested for what she's done to all of us and I'll make sure everyone knows she helped Pritchard get away from the law."

Sophia swallowed back a retort. Maggie was right. This was her fault and she had to accept that. She was tired of running from the truth.

She gave Adan a quick nod. "Okay, I'll stay behind but…be careful." Then she turned back to Maggie. "I'm really sorry."

"Save it," Maggie retorted. "I have to go and find my husband. And you'd better hope he's not dead."

Adan stepped around Maggie and got inches away from Sophia, forcing her to look at him. "Stay with Bettye. Keep the gun nearby. Jacob will watch out for all of you, too." Turning to Jacob, he said, "Show the authorities the path. The first responders will have to go down on foot, so you can guide them to the path, but don't leave the women alone, okay?"

"Got it," Jacob said, his eyes bright with determination. He handed David an extra flashlight.

"We'll be back soon," Adan said to Sophia.

Sophia couldn't speak, so she just nodded. Then she watched Adan walk away and prayed he'd stay safe.

ADAN FOLLOWED MAGGIE down the path toward the stream, his mind whirling with this latest turn of events. Something didn't add up. Why had it taken Maggie so long to reach the cabins if they'd started back at sunset? That had been over two hours ago.

Even Pritchard could walk faster than that. And how had Pritchard managed to survive out in these woods for days now while somehow eluding the authorities and the only people on this mountain? Deep inside the trees, snow still stood in places. It grew cold here each night. Yet they hadn't seen a campfire or any other signs of him being around. Other than the poster he'd left for Sophia that first night and him taking David hostage down the mountain, Pritchard had somehow managed to avoid being seen or caught.

Now he was back again. Sure, Adan had wanted this, but not in this way. Arnie was badly hurt in a ravine while his wife had managed to get away and run for help?

Why hadn't Maggie called the authorities herself?

Too many unanswered questions nagged at him like the shadows chasing them back down toward the creek. So he held his gun close beneath his flashlight and half expected Pritchard to jump out of the shadows and attack them.

Maggie didn't speak. She moved swiftly down the familiar path, David and Adan on her heels. The high beam of the powerful flashlights danced ahead of them in an eerie yellow stream while she hopped like a nimble gazelle across the treacherous tree roots and rocky curves.

"Are you sure you can remember where Arnie fell?" David asked breathlessly.

"Of course," Maggie said over her shoulder. "I know every ridge and path on this mountain." She hurried ahead, her focus on getting to her hurt husband. "I just hope Sophia's ex-husband is long gone."

"He could be hiding out, waiting for us," David said. "I don't want him to take me with him this time."

"The local sheriff's office will send someone soon." Adan pressed on, his boots hitting the dirt path with skidding urgency while he tried to watch the moonlight-dappled woods. "Did you try to call an ambulance before you found us?" he asked as he caught up with Maggie.

"I was too busy trying to get away," she retorted. "I had to save myself so I could help Arnie."

But she could have called for help while she was on the run. Any woman alone in these cold woods would have pulled out her phone and tried to get help. Maggie had found the way home without a flashlight, so she was obviously capable and strong.

And she'd called the gun a shotgun. Pritchard had taken David's high-powered rifle. Had she just misspoken? Or maybe Pritchard had stolen another weapon.

Adan grabbed her by the arm. "Maggie, what really happened today? It took you two hours to get back to us. Why did it take you so long?"

Maggie pushed at her hair and pulled away. "I told you, that man kept messing with us."

"But you also told us he wanted you to bring him to Sophia."

"He did. He…he kept saying that over and over."

"And what did he do when you ran away?"

"He tried to follow."

"He didn't catch up with you?"

She shook her head. "I don't know. I didn't look back, but I could hear him on the path. I don't know where he went. He could have been injured from the fight with Arnie." Pushing at her bangs, she kept glancing around. "Why all the questions? You're wasting time. Why don't you believe me?"

Adan refused to bulge. Her voice shook and her story was beginning to unravel. "We can't do much for Arnie until the paramedics arrive," he pointed out. "And I never said I didn't believe you. I just want to know what happened."

They heard a siren coming up the winding country road. Maggie's eyes widened. "They're here already!"

Had he heard panic in her voice? Or just relief?

David swung his flashlight back. "New roads make getting here quicker. Thank goodness the snow and ice melted enough for them to get through." He let out a sigh. "Don't worry, Maggie. We'll have Arnie out and in good hands before you know it."

Maggie glanced at Adan then turned back. "Good, because if he's dead it'll be Sophia's fault."

"And what about Joe Pritchard?" Adan asked. "Won't it be his fault, too?"

Maggie didn't bother to respond. She took off toward the ridge where she'd left her husband.

But Adan didn't believe a word of her story.

CHAPTER TWENTY-TWO

SOPHIA COULDN'T STOP staring out the window toward the back hills of Crescent Mountain. She wanted to run after Adan and help him or maybe protect him. Not that the man needed protecting.

"I hope they've found Arnie by now," she said to Bettye.

Bettye sat at her small kitchen table with a cup of hot tea in her hand, her gaze moving from Sophia to where Melissa and Sean sat tapping away on their smartphones. Jacob was outside patrolling around the cabin. He checked in every ten minutes so they wouldn't worry about him.

"They know what they're doing, honey," Bettye finally said. "Maggie is an outdoorswoman. She'll take them right to Arnie."

Sophia's heart did a little lurch each time she remembered Maggie's harsh words to her. She'd become too complacent here in this safe environment. Too complacent and too dependent on the help of her hapless neighbors. Somehow, she'd managed to forget the things she'd hidden away here on this mountain.

She glanced over at Bettye again. "It shouldn't have gone this far."

Bettye didn't respond, so Sophia gave up on staring into the dark, grabbed her rifle and came to sit down across from her. "Maggie's right. I am to blame for this."

Bettye seemed distracted, her gaze switching back to Melissa. When she didn't offer any sage advice, Sophia became alarmed. "Bettye, are you all right?"

Bettye gave Sophia a blank stare, her old eyes dark with worry. After checking on Melissa again, she said, "I did something really bad, honey."

"What?" Sophia couldn't imagine Bettye ever doing anything bad. She was the moral compass for everyone on this mountain.

Bettye leaned close and whispered, "I got a hold of Melissa's phone and…scrolled through her private information."

Sophia absorbed that tidbit without too much shock. "That's not that horrible. You have reason to check up on her. She's a runaway, after all."

Bettye shook her head. "From what I was able to read before she came out of the bathroom this morning, she just turned eighteen and she's aged out of the foster care program."

"How do you know that?" Sophia asked on a low whisper.

"I read some of her emails—mostly to him." She sent a covert glance toward the sofa. "She went on and on about finally being able to get away from her mean aunt, about how being eighteen would change her life." Bettye shrugged. "She wants to be free to roam the world with… our Romeo over there."

"So she's legal," Sophia said. "That's a relief at least."

Bettye didn't say anything but when she started twirling her shimmering gray braid, Sophia saw the frown on her face. And she saw disappointment, too.

"What's wrong?" Sophia asked, her hand on Bettye's arm.

"I've been here a mite over fifteen years," Bettye replied. "My daughter had her baby a year before that. There's no way that young girl can be my granddaughter if she's really eighteen. She's two years older than my granddaughter would be."

Sophia glanced to where Melissa sat with her legs curled over Sean's lap. He leaned over the girl, whispering and snickering, his hand on her hair. "Oh, I think she's your granddaughter all right," she said to Bettye. "But it could be that she's lying about her age. She and Sean must have cooked up a way for her to get a fake ID before she came here and that's what they were talking about in their emails."

Bettye let out a gasp, but the two kids didn't

even look up. "So that means she did leave the foster care program…or the mean aunt…or both?"

"I think so," Sophia replied. "I kind of know how the system works and…if you know the right people, it's easy to get a fake ID and just leave. But it's still considered running away. Her aunt could have applied to be her legal guardian, for all we know. Happens more than people realize." She patted Bettye's hand. "She might be using a fake name, too. She could have found your granddaughter's name in a file, or maybe she even knew your real granddaughter."

Bettye's brown eyes grew misty. "I want to find out the truth. I had my daughter a little later in life than most and…she was the love of my life. I wanted so much for her, but when she got pregnant at such a young age, all of *my* dreams went out the window. I never considered *her* dreams. I failed my only child and lost my husband because of it. I don't want to lose my granddaughter, too."

Sophia wished for a mother like Bettye. She wondered how Bettye's husband could have left her and considered there might be more to the story there, too. Bettye's life had fallen apart like so many of the others. Just like her own, Sophia thought.

Right now, the distraction of what Bettye had found was front and center in her mind. "Then we need to pin her down and get the truth out of her. If she can prove you're her grandmother, then you should be able to petition to become her guardian. That is, if she wants to stay here with you."

"I want her to so bad," Bettye said, wiping at her eyes. "I need a second chance. But what if she runs away again?"

Sophia didn't know how to answer that except to be honest. "We can't stop her if she does leave, but getting everything out in the open is the only way to deal with this. Adan gave us a few days before he reports her, but he's already got one crisis to handle. We don't need another one."

"Can I wait a while longer?" Bettye asked. "She seems to like it here."

Sophia glanced toward the young couple on the couch. "She and Sean seem to be infatuated with each other right now, so she might leave with him no matter how much she loves you. You need to be prepared for that. This could just be a stopping-off place for her."

Bettye nodded and wiped at her eyes again. "Let's see what happens with Maggie and Arnie and then I'll talk to her later."

Sophia nodded. Then they heard sirens coming up the curve in the road. "They're here," she said, jumping up to go out onto the front porch.

Bettye followed and together they watched as

Jacob told the first responders how to find the footpath down to the stream.

"I hope Arnie's okay," Bettye said on a hopeful breath.

"So do I," Sophia replied. If Arnie Burton had died from that fall, she'd certainly be the one to blame.

ADAN STARED DOWN into the shadows below. The ravine wasn't too deep, thankfully. Arnie had fallen into what looked like a copse of mountain laurels and shrub brush. But with the dry winter branches and limbs, the fall would have done some damage.

David got down on his belly and held his flashlight straight into the bushes below. "Arnie? You there, buddy? Can you hear me?"

Adan watched as Maggie leaned over and stared down. "Arnie?" she called, her tone low and gravelly. Did she expect her husband to respond, or did she fear he was dead?

When a low moan echoed up to them, David grinned and slid back to sit up. "He's alive."

Adan ventured a glance toward where Maggie still stood. She didn't say a word for a full moment. Then she called again, "Arnie? Help is coming. Hear those sirens? You hang on now."

Adan knew a good bluff when he saw one. She seemed more surprised to find her husband alive than dead. And her voice was shaky, but it sounded a lot more like fear than the relief a wife would exhibit at hearing her husband's moans.

What had happened on this path today?

THE PARAMEDIC TEAM headed down the mountain with whatever equipment they'd need to bring Arnie up out of the ravine. The ambulance sat with lights flashing behind Bettye's cabin, a constant reminder of the urgency of the situation.

Jacob went back to keeping watch while Bettye piddled in the kitchen, her gaze returning to Melissa and Sean over and over.

Sophia went into the tiny living area and sat down across from Melissa and her boyfriend. "You two hungry?"

Melissa shook her head, a steady frown creasing her porcelain face. "I'm not hungry. We just had chili."

"I guess pizza delivery is out," Sean interjected with a shrug.

"No pizza delivery here," Sophia retorted. "But there might be some homemade pizzas in the freezer. Bettye makes up a batch every time we bring in supplies."

Melissa's face lit up. "Granny makes pizza from scratch?"

Grasping at a way to make conversation, Sophia nodded. "We all do. We have a pizza day where we make sauce from fresh tomatoes and herbs and we put it in jars and preserve it for winter days like this one. Then we just buy the cheese and any other toppings we want and whenever we get a chance, we make our dough and start preparing the pizzas to cook. We put the toppings on and cook them and let them cool. Then we eat some and freeze the rest."

"Is that even possible?" Sean asked with a hint of disdain.

Melissa gave him an eye roll. "She just told you how it's done. Don't you believe her?"

A trace of anger glinted in the boy's eyes before he laughed. "Yeah, just, this place is straight out of a slasher movie or something."

Sophia saw Melissa's hurt expression. So there might be some trouble in paradise after all.

"How did you two meet?" she asked in a casual tone.

Sean gave Melissa a quick glance. "Uh…at a coffee shop in Hot Springs."

"I had a part-time job there," Melissa replied, her tone nervous. "He was a regular customer."

"And I worked at the bar, the restaurant not far from there," Sean added.

Old enough to work at a bar. That concerned Sophia. Melissa might be on the cusp of being an adult, but even at sixteen or so, she was still underage. And Sean obviously knew that.

"So…you started dating?"

Sean gave Sophia an impatient shrug while Melissa looked around the room. "Where's Mr. Jacob?"

"Okay, I get it," Sophia replied. "I'm being too nosy." She motioned toward where Bettye stood peeling apples for a pie. "But if you two are hiding anything from your grandmother, you might reconsider and come clean now. She's willing to let you stay here, but sooner or later Adan—that big Texas Ranger you met earlier, Sean—will want to alert the authorities and let the proper people know you're okay." She gave Melissa an encouraging smile. "You can trust your grandmother, and you can trust me, too."

Melissa's eyes misted over, but Sean gave Sophia a cold, harsh stare. "We'll keep that in mind," he said to Sophia.

Sophia planted a serene smile on her face and stared him down. "I was talking to Melissa, since that will be her decision to make."

Melissa looked surprised, but she gave Sophia a grateful smile, at least. Sophia waited for the girl to say something but Melissa stayed quiet, her gaze downcast. Sean lifted the girl's chin and whispered something in her ear. Then he laughed.

But to Sophia, it sounded more like a smirk.

WHILE THE PARAMEDICS worked on getting Arnie up with a pulley and a stretcher, Adan tried to get Maggie to talk to him.

"Did you really see Joe Pritchard?" he asked her when they were out of hearing of the others.

"What do you mean?" she asked, her tone lifting, her back to the people trying to save her husband. "You've doubted me all night, Ranger Harrison. It's insulting."

"You've been acting strange since you came running to report Arnie's fall," Adan countered. "It's confusing."

"Now you're just messing with my head," she replied before taking off toward the ravine. "I need to see what's going on down there."

Adan followed her, his instincts telling him something was off. Maybe something had been off with these two all along, since they stayed apart from the others and seemed to like to hike at the oddest times.

He'd missed it, obviously, but that didn't surprise Adan. Since he'd arrived here, he'd been preoccupied with getting his man and getting home. But the added distraction of a pretty, intriguing woman who just happened to be the ex-wife of his suspect had certainly thrown Adan off kilter.

Tonight, he was back on high alert and back on the mission.

Starting with Maggie Burton's odd behavior.

"Tell me again where Pritchard assaulted you two," he said to Maggie's back.

She let out a sigh and waved her left hand toward the gurgling stream. "Somewhere down there."

"In the same spot where y'all camp a lot?"

"Yes, nearby."

"And he held you both at gunpoint and started back up toward the cabins with you."

"I told you that, yes."

"What was he wearing?"

She whirled then, panic twisting in the shadows on her face. "I don't remember."

"A hat? A beard? Boots or sneakers? Jeans and a jacket?"

"What does that matter? He terrorized us both and then when we were almost home, Arnie played the hero and they struggled."

Adan let her finish then said, "So it took you a while to get from the campsite back to this spot."

Maggie's eyes widened. Adan saw a lot in the halo of moonlight that played over her face. "Yes. We kept stopping. I think Arnie was trying to figure out a way to overtake him."

"You mean, to stop Pritchard from forcing y'all back to the cabins. Back to Sophia."

"Yes. Yes, that's it. Arnie's always had a soft spot for Sophia."

A break in her armor at last. "Did that bother you?"

"No!" She whirled and put her hands to her face. "That was the least of our problems."

"I see."

She twisted back around, shock at her own confession causing her to grasp for words. "You don't understand at all. Joe Pritchard pushed my husband off the side of this mountain and all you want to do is protect Sophia. It's her fault that terrible man came here. And it's her fault that Arnie and I had a fight today."

"What do you mean?" Adan asked. "Maggie?"

But before Maggie could answer, David called out. "Adan, Maggie, they're bringing him up. Hurry on over here."

CHAPTER TWENTY-THREE

"I DON'T THINK Sean appreciated my conversation with Melissa and him," Sophia whispered to Bettye while they cut dough for the pie crust.

"Do we care what he thinks?" Bettye replied on a wry smile.

"No. I only care about her and the truth," Sophia said. "I think she's about ready to talk." She eyed the two on the couch. "I'm sorry, Bettye. I'm really doing this for you. *You* need to know the truth."

"I agree." Bettye patted butter over the freshly peeled apple slices in the deep-dish pie plate then sprinkled sugar, cinnamon and nutmeg over them. "I want to know if she truly is my kin and if I can keep her here with me."

"We'll get to the truth," Sophia said, glad for the distraction. "I've cracked worse targets than these two."

They hadn't heard anything from the first responders or Adan in over an hour. Jacob had checked in, mostly because he smelled apples and spices and wanted to see if there was a pie being assembled in the kitchen, even at this late hour.

Karen was back and forth, checking on them and watching for her husband and Adan, worry evident on her face since David had already had an eventful week. She refused to stay here and insisted she needed to be out there in case they needed her. Jacob was watching out for her, too.

Sophia glanced over at Melissa and Sean. They were watching an old movie on the ancient DVD player connected to the even more ancient television set. Sean had already complained rather loudly that this movie was boring.

Melissa seemed to get more aggravated at him with each complaint.

Sophia decided to make a move. "Hey, Melissa, could you give me a hand over here?"

The girl glanced around and almost looked relieved. But when Sean placed his hand around her neck and tried to keep her by his side, she tugged away and glared at him.

"I'm coming," she said, giving her boyfriend a warning glance.

"Hurry back, babe," he called, his head lobbing back against the old couch as if he was in agony. "I don't like being alone, you know."

He would be alone and in a lot of agony if he hurt Melissa, Sophia decided.

"What do you need?" Melissa asked, her kohl-lined eyes looking like a dramatic clown's.

Bettye didn't waste any time. "We need to know if you're only sixteen and if you're really my granddaughter," she said into Melissa's ear.

"What are you talking about?" Melissa said, her voice rising. "Of course I'm your grand-daughter. And I just turned sixteen." She looked completely guilty since she'd left out the part about possibly having a fake ID. "How can you not believe me? You said I looked just like my mama."

"You do," Bettye replied. "You do. Just had to be sure."

"I can prove it," Melissa said. "I have my birth certificate."

"Now she tells us." Bettye shrugged. "I guess I should have demanded that proof from the be-ginning." She crimped the bottom of the pie crust and went about cutting strips for the top crust. "Now, did you escape to here with a fake ID?"

"How did you know that?" Melissa didn't even bother to keep her voice down. When she real-ized she'd confirmed their suspicions, she low-ered her voice again. "Did you go through my things?"

"Shh," Sophia said, a hand on Melissa's arm. "We're worried that Sean might be too old for you since he said he worked in a bar."

"And since he seems too stupid for words," Bettye said on a practical huff.

Melissa glanced back to make sure he hadn't heard. "Granny! You don't even know him. He's sweet and he's good to me." The girl watched as her grandmother finished making the pie. "I mean, he was when I first met him."

Sophia heard the echo of her own excuses in those words. If she could save this girl from what she'd gone through, she might be able to find some redemption.

"I'm sorry," Bettye said. She spread strips of pie dough across the apples to form a lattice. "I don't like him. His hair is too long and his eyes are shifty."

"Did you talk like this to my mother?" Melissa asked, tears in her eyes. "Is that why she ran away?"

Bettye stopped her busy work and stared at Melissa. "Probably," she said. "But I loved her all the same. Same as you, if you're even my granddaughter." Bettye's eyes watered but she took a deep breath. "I think I'd love you even if you ain't my granddaughter."

Melissa looked properly chastised but she didn't confirm anything else. "Can we talk about this later?"

"Now's a good time for me," Bettye retorted. She opened the oven door and shoved her masterpiece inside. Then she turned and put her hands on Melissa's arms. "I want you to stay here where you're safe. If you level with me, we can make that happen."

Melissa didn't speak for a moment but a single tear fell down her left cheek. "I hope I can stay, Granny. Sean wants me to leave with him, but that's not how we planned this."

"Then tell us what the plan is—now," Sophia said.

But before Melissa could come clean, the back door burst open and Karen rushed in and shut it behind her. "Jacob's missing. I came out to give him some coffee and he wasn't there. I can't find him anywhere."

ADAN WATCHED MAGGIE for any reactions to her husband being found alive. She paced back and forth, waiting for the paramedics to bring Arnie up from the treacherous ledge, her hands constantly shoving through her hair, her face ashen and her expression anxious. Since it was a slow process, her pacing became more frantic with each minute that ticked by. Was she worried about her husband or worried about what he would say?

Adan approached her again. "I'll give you one last chance to tell me the truth, Maggie," he said. "Once your husband is taken to the hospital, he should hopefully be able to fill in the blanks for me himself. You can end this right now and let me get on with my job."

Maggie stopped pacing and pushed a hand through her dark hair. "I… I don't want to talk to you. I'm worried about Arnie."

"Did Pritchard really push him?"

She held three fingers over her mouth as if to stop herself from saying anything else. "It happened so fast."

"What? The fight between Arnie and Pritchard? Or the fight you had with your husband?"

That comment tugged her around in an angry whirl. "What are you talking about? Arnie and I didn't have a fight."

"But you said he had a soft spot for Sophia and you told me that she was the reason you two got in a fight today."

Maggie let out a gasp. "I don't know anymore. I just want Arnie to be okay."

Adan wasn't satisfied. He doubted all over again that Joe Pritchard had been anywhere near this area of the mountain today. In fact, he was pretty sure Pritchard had moved on by now. He was a wanted man and he was on the run. Why would he risk lurking about here when he could go into hiding and come back later?

Adan again wondered if one of Sophia's so-called friends was helping Pritchard. With a massive manhunt now activated and more and more questions about this whole thing, Adan wondered how he didn't have an even worse headache to go along with the throbbing pain in his injured shoulder.

And he wondered if Sophia was all right.

"WE HAVE TO find Jacob," Bettye said on a raw plea. When she slumped against the counter, Melissa gathered her close.

"I'm so sorry, Granny. So sorry."

Sophia didn't have time to question that apology.

"Y'all turn around slowly now," Sean said in a long, smug drawl.

Karen and Sophia whirled to stare at the young man holding a handgun on them. Bettye gasped again and clutched Melissa's jacket. "I knew he was no good."

Sophia's gaze hit on Melissa's ruddy blush. "What have you done?"

The girl burst into tears. "I didn't want to do it. They made me. They both made me."

Sean advanced toward the women. "Shut up, Melissa."

Bettye raised herself to her full five feet height, her eyes piercing. "Do not tell my grand-daughter to shut up, young man."

Bandit growled and stood up to stare at Sean. Bettye called the old dog to her side and ordered Bandit to sit.

Sean laughed and waved his gun. "This place

is like something out of a bad movie, dude. But hey, if we can just find that cash—"

"What cash?" Sophia asked, her mind roiling with the implications of that statement. "What do you want?"

Sean rolled his eyes and reached for Melissa. "C'mon, baby. Help me out here. We get the cash and we get off this creepy mountain. Remember?"

Melissa's sobbing echoed out over the room. "I can't do it, Sean. I love my grandmother and I won't do this to her."

Sean leaned in and pointed the gun toward Sophia. "We ain't doing it to your granny, babe." He shot Sophia a nasty glare. "We're doing it to her—for leaving my daddy there to take the rap."

Sophia gulped in air, a dizzy horror causing her to feel weak at the knees. "What are you talking about?"

Sean brought the gun to her stomach and yanked her by the arm. "Don't play dumb with me, lady. My daddy told me all about what you did to him. Helped him rob a drug dealer's house and then tried to kill him, left him for dead and took off with his car and his money. He's here on this mountain and he's gonna kill you for what you did."

Sophia tried to get away, but Sean's grip was strong. She knew how to defend herself, but she couldn't leave her friends.

"You're Joe's son?" she asked to stall, her stomach clinching at the thought of this slime bag touching Melissa.

Sean nodded. "Yeah, that's right, sweetcakes. Guess the old man neglected to tell you he'd been married before. Left us just like he always leaves everybody."

Sophia let the shock of this new revelation roll off her shoulders. She had to keep him talking until she could figure out what to do next. "So how did you find him? I mean, he's a wanted man and...you came here looking for him, right?"

Sean's angry expression reminded her of Joe. She could see it there in his cruel frown. "He'd call me now and then and...sometimes send my mom money. Told me he was gonna find you 'cause you'd double-crossed him."

Bettye held tight to Melissa. "If you belong to that man, you won't touch my granddaughter again."

Sophia sent Bettye a warning glance then looked up at Sean. "So...he told you he was coming here?"

Sean laughed and pushed the gun into her ribs. "No, stupid. He never said stuff like that. But he did tell me that if I'd help him out, he'd make sure I got some cash."

Melissa started crying all over again. "They both found me at the truck stop. Sean promised he'd come and get me after…after his daddy had taken care of his business."

Sophia didn't know who to believe. "But you told us Joe brought you here."

"He did," Sean interjected. "He brought her with him and I followed. But she's too dumb to do what she's told."

Melissa's hurt expression told Sophia the girl had been played big-time. "What did they promise you?"

Melissa held onto Bettye, her dark eyes full of tears. "I don't know. I just wanted to see my grandmother, but they cornered me at the truck stop and convinced me I'd be helping them capture a wanted criminal. They said you'd stolen a car and their money. Said if I pretended to be Sean's girlfriend I'd get a cut." She gave Bettye an apologetic glance. "I only wanted some extra cash to help out around here, Granny. I thought it was their money."

"My money," Sophia said. "Your dad made me give him the money I'd saved up." She faced Bettye and finally blurted out the secret she'd held for so long. "I didn't know about the drug money until…until I found it in the car—after I got here. I left it there, Bettye. I left it and I haven't touched it."

"I believe you," Bettye said. "I believe you."

"And you took it from him," Sean said, tugging her arm around. "Now enough small talk, ladies. My daddy is waiting for you. We can't find that car or that money. But you're gonna take us right to it."

"No," Sophia said. "No, I won't do that."

Sean glanced at Melissa. "You will. My dad's on his way here to make sure you do."

Sophia couldn't believe this. "Did your dad push my friend down at that ravine today?"

Sean looked confused. "Don't know what you mean."

"The Burtons," Bettye said. "Arnie? Did your daddy hurt Arnie Burton?"

Sean shook his head. "My dad has been hiding in the woods in an old shack for days. I've been taking him food and blankets. We tried to find the car while Melissa was supposed to keep y'all busy, but no luck yet."

He nudged Sophia closer. "I don't know any Burtons. But I can vouch for my old man. He's got that old geezer Jacob out of the way and he's been waiting for me to signal that I have you. He should be here any minute and then you and he are going for a long walk in the woods." He grinned over at Melissa. "While I stay here with the other ladies."

CHAPTER TWENTY-FOUR

THEY HAD ARNIE on the stretcher but he was in so much pain he kept going in and out of consciousness.

Adan walked close. "Arnie, you hang in there, okay?"

Arnie opened his eyes, blinking with a slow awareness. "Maggie?"

"She's right here." Adan motioned for Maggie since she seemed to be afraid to look at her husband. Maybe he'd find out what happened if he let her talk to Arnie.

Giving him a defeated frown, she hurried to Arnie's side. Adan stood nearby, deliberately eavesdropping.

"Sorry," Arnie said, tears in his eyes. "So sorry. Love you."

Maggie started crying. "I love you, too. I never meant for this to happen. Arnie, don't die on me, okay? I don't care about the money."

Arnie's grimace of pain served as a grin. "Never mind that. Doesn't matter anymore."

Money? What in the world were they talking

about? Maybe they'd had some sort of argument about money and he'd tripped and fell? Or had he been pushed?

"How is he?" Adan asked one of the paramedics working on Arnie. He cataloged what he'd just heard, memorizing the conversation until he could question Maggie or Arnie later. He also noted that Arnie hadn't mentioned Joe Pritchard, but he could just be scared and anxious to see his wife.

"Hard to say right now," the young man replied. "Broken right leg, possible internal bleeding and slight concussion, several lacerations and abrasions and a sprained left arm. He's lucky to be alive. Those bushes and shrubs cushioned the fall and kept him from going over the next ledge, which looks like a long way down there."

"Did he say what happened?" Adan asked, his gaze on Maggie.

"An accident," the man replied before he went back to his work. "That's what he kept telling us." He pointed toward where a sheriff's deputy stood. "The deputy questioned him several times when we were working on him and that's all he'd say."

Adan absorbed that information and then took out his phone to call Sophia. He'd been so busy trying to get to the bottom of this latest event he hadn't been able to get a free minute. When she didn't answer, his pulse moved in a jumpy warning. She'd promised to keep her phone nearby.

Turning to David, he said, "Sophia's not answering. Can you try Karen?"

"Sure," David said. "She'll be worried anyway."

Adan waited while he watched Maggie's every move. Right now, she was holding Arnie's hand. "Are you going with him to the hospital?"

She glanced up at Adan, her eyes red rimmed and frightened in the glowing lights from the ambulance and the flashlights.

"Can I?" she asked, more demure now.

"Do you want to go with him?"

She bobbed her head. "I know you have lots of questions and I'm willing to tell you the truth. But…after I make sure he's going to be all right."

Adan nodded. "Okay. I'll get to the hospital as soon as I can." Then he added, "I'm trusting you to be honest with me, Maggie. I've had enough of people keeping secrets around here."

"Me, too," Maggie said. "But if you want the truth, maybe you'd better start with Sophia."

Then she turned and hurried toward the ambulance.

David came up next to Adan. "Karen's not answering her phone, either. I think we'd better get back up there."

"I agree," Adan said, worrying nagging at him all the way around. "I'm gonna figure this out, one way or another."

"YOU CAN'T BE SERIOUS."

Sophia shook her head at Sean. "I'm not going anywhere with Joe Pritchard."

A knock at the door halted any retort, so Sean dragged her to the door with him. "Open it."

Dreading whatever waited for her behind that door, Sophia shook her head. "No. I won't leave you here with them."

"Open the door," Sean repeated. Then he moved the gun from her to the three women in the corner. "Or I'll have to shoot one of them."

Sophia did as he told her, her mind still trying to absorb that this scrawny kid was Joe's son and that he'd been married before. Did he even know this kid or had he grabbed another innocent victim to do his dirty work?

When she unlatched the door, Joe pushed his way inside and grinned at her, his brown eyes wild and darting, his stringy hair dark and matted. "Well, well, at long last." Then he let out a chilling laugh. "Honey, I'm home."

Sophia's knees went weak, but she refused to show fear with the man who'd tormented her for so long. "You won't get away with this. The mountain is covered with law enforcement people."

Joe kicked the door shut. "Don't I know it! Been playing cat and mouse with them for days now. If my boy here hadn't helped me, I'd probably be under the jail by now." Then he glared across the room. "That girl caused us a bushel of bad luck, but we'll take care of her soon enough."

Melissa started crying again. "You lied to me and tricked me—"

Joe whirled, his eyes turning to dangerous slits. "And you did the same to me, missy. Tried to kill me and ran away—just like this one right here." He grabbed Sophia and pulled her to him, a gun at her head. Then he shouted at Melissa again. "You were supposed to wait until Sean got here to help us. Messed up all of our plans."

"I didn't like you," Melissa retorted, still crying. She turned to Sean. "He…made a pass at me and promised me all kinds of things. He said we could ditch you. Sean, he's not a good man."

Sean's face blushed with hot anger. "He's doing what he has to do to get away. I told you that already. I told you people lie about him, but he's my dad. He found me after all these years."

"You only told me to act like we were together and then you'd let me go," Melissa shouted. "I didn't want to do this anymore but you showed up and so I tried all day to figure out a way to stop it. You both make me sick."

Sean bolted toward the girl, but Bettye and Karen got between him and Melissa.

"You try anything, sonny boy, and I'll kill you myself," Bettye told him.

Joe twisted Sophia against him, his hot breath on her neck. "Tell your guard dogs to back off,

Sophia. Or I will let my son kill them one by one."

Panic rocketed through her body, but Sophia had to do as he asked. Just until she could get him alone. "It's okay. I'll be all right. Bettye, please don't try to stop them. Just be careful, please. Soon this will all be over."

Bettye held Melissa and Karen close. "We'll be fine, honey. You don't let that animal hurt you."

"He won't," Sophia replied. She'd kill him before she let him touch her again. "I'll be back soon and this will all be over, I promise."

Joe grabbed her by her hair. "Don't make promises you can't keep, sweetheart." Then he forced her out into the cold night, his gun pushing into her backbone.

Sophia took one look back before he slammed the door behind them.

ADAN'S GUT CHURNED with the sure knowledge that something had gone wrong. He couldn't reach Jacob or anybody else. Running now, he and David made good time back up the rocky path.

When they came up on level ground, Adan halted David. "I don't see Jacob anywhere. Let's make sure we aren't about to be ambushed."

David complied for a moment. "We have to get to our women, Adan."

"I know." Adan stared toward Bettye's cabin. "Looks like the lights are on. Maybe they're busy and away from their phones."

"Or maybe we're wasting time speculating," David retorted.

Adan put a finger to his lips and motioned for David to follow him up toward the cabin. The two men hid in some heavy bushes while Adan scanned the area for signs of Jacob. Or anyone else. When he didn't see or hear anyone, he went into action.

"I'm gonna check through the window," Adan said. "You stay here in case I get caught."

David nodded and pulled out his gun. "I'll cover you."

Adan took off in a crouch and carefully stepped up onto the back porch. At first, he saw Bettye and Karen in the kitchen. Peering as far inside as he could without being seen, he stared toward the living room. Melissa was with Sean.

And Sean was holding a gun on her.

Adan strained to see where Sophia was. When he didn't see her anywhere in the tiny house, he turned and headed back to where David stood in the shadows.

"Are they all right?" David asked.

Adan shook his head. "I don't think so." He explained what he'd seen. "I think Sophia's either out here trying to figure out what to do...or she's gone looking for Jacob." Then another thought occurred and he bristled. "I hope she hasn't gone all heroic and decided to search for Pritchard."

David grunted. "If that kid is holding our women, what's that got to do with Pritchard?"

"I don't know," Adan admitted. "Maybe nothing. Maybe everything."

"So what's the plan?"

Adan did another visual of the moonlit woods. "First, we get in there and apprehend that idiot holding them. Then we find out where Sophia is."

David stood. "I'm ready. Had about enough of idiots messing with us."

"Me, too," Adan replied. "Let's get in there."

PRITCHARD PUSHED AT HER, his fingers and the gun barrel stabbing at her backbone and ribs. She wasn't sure where he was taking her, but Sophia knew this might be her last night on earth. He'd kill her this time. Of that she was sure.

She thought of Adan and pictured him getting back to little Gaylen by Christmas Eve. Would he grieve for Sophia? Or would he breathe a sigh of relief that this was finally over?

Stop that, she told herself. Adan cared about her. She'd felt it in his kisses, in his soft smiles, in his wry sense of humor and his serious sense of justice. Maybe they'd only known each other a few days, but each hour in those days had been a lifetime of…falling in love.

Tears pricked at her eyes.

I love him. How can that be?

Was she so caught up in dying that she finally wanted to live again?

Joe's poke brought her back to reality. "What you thinking up there, suga'?"

"Nothing that concerns you," she retorted. Her mouth was what usually got her in trouble with him, but she didn't care now. She'd tried to get away and for a while, just a while, she'd been content and almost happy and almost safe.

Now he'd come back alive and found her, and if she couldn't have Adan and a good life, then she didn't want to do this anymore.

Don't give up.

She could hear Bettye saying those words. Could hear Adan telling her to hang on. Should she fight one more time? Would it be worth the fight? Or should she just go away with Joe and find a way to survive so that her friends and the man she'd fallen in love with would stay safe?

"What's the deal with you and that infernal Ranger?" Joe asked, his hand snaking around her waist.

Sophia shivered, but the goose bumps came more from the revulsion she felt at Joe's cruel touch than the chilly night air. "What do you mean?"

"I mean, I saw y'all together on that first night."

Sophia felt sick to her stomach. How long had Joe been watching her? "Then you must have seen me hold a gun on him."

"I saw that," Joe said, chuckling. "That old lady laid him out. Funny, about that. I figure you had a lot of reasons not to get all tangled up with a Texas Ranger."

She nodded. "Yes, but I had one very good reason to get to know him. He and I had a really good discussion regarding you."

Joe whirled her around. "What did you tell that Ranger?"

"I told him everything," she said, glad to have it all out in the open. "I told him I thought I'd killed you and that I left you on that deserted road and I took off in your car."

"With my money," Joe said, his teeth grinding together with each word. "Did you tell him you took the money? All of the money?"

Sophia's fear disappeared. She had Adan to thank for that. "I did tell him I took back my money."

Joe snorted, his grip on her arm stinging. "Yeah, right. So that means you didn't let on about the real money hidden in that trunk and that's why I'm here, sweetheart."

Sophia's bravado slipped again. "What are you talking about?"

"I got my ways, but I got wind of a rumor that you were on this mountain and that you had some money hidden away somewhere. My money. And I aim to get it and get out of here—with you, of course. After all, we got a lotta catching up to do, don't we, sweetheart?"

CHAPTER TWENTY-FIVE

"On three."

Adan motioned to David as they both crouched on opposite sides of the back door to Bettye's cabin. "When we go inside, you head left for the women and get them behind the kitchen counter. I'll go right and take out the kid and make sure Melissa isn't caught in the crossfire."

"Are you sure we can do this?" David asked, doubt in the question. "I don't want anyone else to get hurt."

"I can take that stupid little twerp without firing a shot," Adan said, letting out some of his frustrations while he tried to shed his own fear over Sophia possibly being taken. "I knew he was trouble."

He couldn't think about his fears right now. He couldn't think about Sophia in her big flannel shirt and soft gray sweatpants. He wouldn't think about those kisses that had heated them up like the fire she kept stoked in the fireplace. And he sure couldn't think about her out there in the dark with a deranged ex-husband who just would not give up. Right now, he had to do this job one step at a time.

Because it was obvious Joe Pritchard had made his move. Now Adan wondered if the Burtons had something to do with this latest. Or one of them, at least. He'd deal with Maggie later, too.

Adan didn't have a choice. He had to find Sophia.

"Are you ready?" David gave him a confused stare.

"Yeah, just going back over everything."

Everything about Sophia. Was it possible he cared way more about her than he'd let on?

Not only possible. But a sure fact.

I'm falling in love.

That realization propelled Adan forward. He had to end this tonight, one way or another. He wanted Sophia in his life and he'd figure out how much that could complicate things when he was done with Joe Pritchard for good.

"Let's go," he said, nodding to David.

Adan counted to three then kicked the back door open and turned to the right with his rifle trained on Sean. "Drop the gun right now! Melissa, get on the floor."

David turned to the left and through a flutter of feminine comments and screams, hurried the women behind the kitchen cabinets and counter.

Melissa screamed and did as Adan told her— she dropped like a rock onto the floor beside the coffee table. Sean's shock was evident. His eyes went wide and the expression on his face turned him from smug to afraid in two seconds flat.

The boy laid the gun on the coffee table and held up both his hands. "He made me do it," he said on a long whine.

"Who?" Adan asked, advancing on the trembling man. "Who made you do it?"

"My daddy," the boy replied. "Joe Pritchard." Then he gave Adan a satisfied smirk. "But he should be long gone by now, with all that drug money and that woman who hid it from him."

"WHY DID WE STOP?"

Sophia tried to get her bearings, but she was afraid they were lost deep in the hills of Crescent Mountain. The man pushing her forward had been unusually quiet. Which agitated and scared her. "Joe, where are we going?"

Joe pushed at her then stopped so fast she fell back against him and smelled sweat and a woodsy, smoky odor. "You tell me. You know where that old car and the money are. I need you to take me there."

How did he know she'd hidden the car? Who had told Joe she was living on this mountain? Everything started making more sense in her mind, even Sean and Melissa's rants before Joe hadn't just stumbled upon Crescent Mountain on a hunch. He'd obviously known she was here.

Which meant someone on this mountain must have helped him.

"The car?" Sophia shook her head and tried to play dumb. "You think we can find a car in the dark? What car?"

His aggravation came to the surface. "Shut up and stop pretending you don't know what I'm talking about. I thought I knew where it was but I got some bad information. You're gonna fix that, though. Once we get the car and the money, I can leave this place. I never want to be on a mountain again."

"I can't help you," Sophia said, panic and fear rising with each step they took. If he got her to that car and it actually cranked, he'd take her with him. And she'd really be in serious trouble. "I... I can't remember where that old car is."

Joe stomped his dirty boots and shifted his rifle. Pointing a finger at her nose, he said, "You know this mountain and you hid the darn car, so yes, you do know where it is and yes, we will find it tonight."

Stalling, she said, "We can't find it in the dark without a flashlight."

"I got a flashlight right here," he said, waving the tiny pocket flashlight he held in one hand.

"That thing isn't worth the few bucks you paid for it," Sophia said, her mind whirling with possibilities. "We need a powerful flashlight to find the right path. I think we're lost. I don't recognize this path."

Joe let out a string of curse words. "Am I ever gonna get off this godforsaken mountain?"

Not alive, Sophia thought. "I don't know, Joe. You're the one with all the big plans."

He yanked her around with such force her teeth rattled, causing her to bite her cheek. The sting of that raw wound only reinforced her desire to get out of this alive.

"I don't need your smart mouth, Sophia. You'd better think hard about how we can get to that car…or you'll regret you ever messed with me." His sneer turned sinister, his eyes flashing with anger. "You love your mountain friends so much, don't you? Wouldn't want one of them to suffer the consequences of your actions, right?"

"What do you mean?" she asked on a weak breath, afraid of what this man was capable of doing.

Joe leaned close, his dirty fingers caressing her cheek. "I mean business. One of your buddies could die tonight, or maybe that cute little girl who scammed my son and me will be the first one to go. All I gotta do is call my boy and he'll put a bullet through her head."

Sophia gulped back a retort, fear and loathing making her sick inside. "I'm not sure I can find the car in the dark, Joe. I can try at first light." She swallowed the taste of blood where she'd bitten the inside of her mouth. "Don't hurt any-one. That'll just make things worse for us. Let's just wait until the morning."

"I can't wait to first light," he said, his whis-per wrapping around her like a boa constric-tor. "Your excuses are tiresome as always. Try again."

Sophia closed her eyes and hoped she could survive this night. Ashamed that just minutes ago she'd been about to give up, she decided she hadn't come this far to let Joe kill her now. Not when happiness was just out of her reach.

She thought of Adan and compared how he'd treated her to how this man had always treated her. There was no comparison. Adan had shown her what a true man could be like, how a real gentleman could act. Even if they could never be together, she'd always remember how Adan had changed her life.

So she came up with a plan that she hoped would work. "I think I can find the car, but we need to go back the way we came so I can start on the path near the road out in front of the cab-ins. There's a way toward the other side of the mountain that will lead us straight to the car... and the money."

Joe hissed and stomped but finally he nod-ded. "Okay. But I'm warning you, if you're up to your old tricks, it won't be pretty for you or your friends."

"Just call your son and let him know what we're doing," she said. "Melissa and my friends shouldn't have to pay for what I've done."

"No, they shouldn't," he retorted, "but you made this bed, sweetheart, so you gotta lie in it."

"You're right," Sophia replied, a chill settling in her bones, her face numb with cold, her hands frozen in clenched fists. "This is my fight and I'm tired. I just want it to end. I want you to take the money and get out of my life. Forever."

Joe chuckled and tugged her close, the echo of his laughter sounding eerie as it lifted out into the night. "I told you, you're going with me. 'Cause you know what they say—if I can't have you, no one will."

ADAN STARED DOWN at the sniveling young man in front of him, all of the pieces of the puzzle falling into place with a clicking clarity. The big house, the robbery, Sophia driving the getaway car and Maggie Burton telling him all of this was Sophia's fault. The house Pritchard had robbed had belonged to the drug dealer, and he'd taken a lot of money. Did Sophia know about that money? Was that what she'd tried so hard to hide from everyone? Maggie had told him to ask Sophia about the truth.

Now he knew everything. But he still had a job to do.

"Where did he take her?"

"I told you, I don't know," Sean said, diverting his eyes in what looked like a lying way to Adan. "Man, I just do what he tells me and he told me to get up here and keep the girl occupied."

"Because he knew Melissa wouldn't betray us," Bettye said on a disgusted breath. "She figured out you both were crooked and she tried to warn us."

Melissa sat with her grandmother, a sheepish expression puckering her face. She didn't say a word, but Adan guessed she regretted her part in all of this. The details were still murky but he'd pin her down once he could breathe again. Once he had Sophia back here and safe.

In spite of what she'd withheld from him, he still cared about her. But could he forgive her?

Adan pushed that thought out of the way and tried again with the boy. "Look, we know he's your long-lost daddy. So he came to Arkansas to find you and make up for lost time. That's a sweet story, but Joe Pritchard is a dangerous, out-of-control criminal who killed a woman back in Texas. So you'd better start talking or you'll soon be in a jail cell right beside him. And that won't be so sweet, trust me."

Sean looked up, his greasy hair swaying like aged straw against his skinny face. "He wants that money. That's all I know."

Adan's head came up. "The money that he stole from a drug dealer he'd been in cahoots with?"

Sean's sneer returned right along with a fist of attitude. "No, the money that *she* took after she tried to kill him. He told me it was his and that he'd taken it out of the bank so they could start over somewhere. She double-crossed my daddy, so he's doing what he has to do."

"He's lying to you," Adan said, his heart striking up a strange dance that moved between panic and desperation. "Do you know where this car is located?"

Sean shook his head. "I don't. Really, I don't. But he's gonna find it and then he's gonna take her with him. He's determined to make her see that…he still loves her."

Adan took one long breath and leaned over Sean. "I'm going out there to find them but before I leave, you need to understand a few things about your daddy. He won't get away this time. The kind of obsessive control he has over people, especially women, is not love. You need to understand that right now, son, or you'll wind up just like him."

Sean's eyes misted over. "I just wanted to meet my daddy. That's all. He left when I was a baby, so when he found me, I was willing to do anything he wanted. I only wanted to help him out."

And Pritchard had played on that in order to get his way and to get some help pulling this off.

They probably found an easy mark in Melissa and used her to help cover and carry out their plan. Joe Pritchard wasn't worth the dirt under their shoes, but these two kids didn't need to hear that lecture right now.

He gave Sean an understanding stare. "Sometimes we do the wrong things for what seems like the right reasons."

Sean shook his head and stared over at Melissa. "Yeah, I guess so. Whatever, man."

Adan wished he had time to stay here and talk some sense into the kid, but he had to go and find Joe and Sophia. He placed a gentle hand on Sean's shoulder. "I understand how you feel, and I know you love your father. But he's done some bad things and you don't need to be caught up in this, understand?"

Sean nodded and wiped at his nose. "I wish I'd never seen this mountain."

Adan could certainly agree with that, but this place was growing on him in spite of the urgency of his mission. He turned to David. "Will you make sure he doesn't go anywhere?"

David nodded. "I'll tie him to a chair if he tries to move." Then he winked at Adan. "And while I've got him and Melissa here, I'm gonna read both of them the riot act—just for good measure."

"Great idea," Adan said. Then he grabbed his gun and headed out the door. He'd been on this mountain for too many days now and he longed to get home and hold his daughter tight.

But he had to save Sophia first. After everything, if he couldn't do that, he would never forgive himself.

CHAPTER TWENTY-SIX

SOPHIA THOUGHT OVER and over that she should try to trip Joe so she could run away. Or she could find something to hit him with and hope she injured him enough to get away from him. But both of those options left things wide-open for Joe to call his son and tell him to shoot one or all of her friends.

Adan should have found out by now that she was missing, and he probably knew about the hidden money, too. That one thought gave her hope that he'd track them and come to her rescue. Adan might not forgive her for not telling him about the drug money—he'd want to confiscate that money and save her. But Sophia was used to saving herself. Maybe what she'd believed to be courage was actually her taking the coward's way out. If she'd called the police the night she'd left Joe for dead, she could have returned the money and taken a plea bargain.

But now she was back in the same spot with the same man in what felt like a never-ending carnival ride in a house of horror. She wanted to survive. She wanted to live. She wanted her life back, without Joe and his crimes hanging over her head.

You have one of the good guys on your side now.

Sophia held on to that thought while Joe pushed and shoved her back onto the path they'd taken. Determined to get off this horrible track, she pledged to do the right thing if she ever lived to see tomorrow. True courage could only mean being completely honest.

Why had it taken her so long to see that?

Joe's arm hitting her shoulder brought Sophia out of her musings. "You wouldn't be taking me on a merry chase now, would you, Sophia?"

"I'm taking you back to the only path I know to get to your car," she said, meaning it. "It's hard to see very much in the dark, even with the full moon. But if you're patient with me, I think I can find where I hid the car."

Or I can find a way to kill you and make it stick this time.

"No thinking about it," he said on a harsh breath. "We'll walk all night if that's what it takes. If you don't take me to that car, somebody's gonna get hurt."

Sophia found the nerve to pull away from him. She was cold and dirty and afraid, but a dark heat pulsed through her, giving her strength. "I told you I'll take you to the car and the money, Joe. So quit threatening me. My friends are smart and independent and they can take care of themselves. Not to mention, you have a Texas Ranger on your tail, in case you've forgotten. You can't make threats, so just stop it."

Joe grabbed her by her neck and yanked her back, his nose inches from hers. "You sound so brave and sure, honey. But if you keep messing with me, I'll put a bullet right between that Ranger's eyes. I don't like how you two have been shacked up together. It ain't right, know what I mean?"

Sophia willed the fear that shuddered through her body to settle. "We aren't shacking up," she said. "He's been protecting me—all of us—from you."

Joe's laughter cackled out over the woods. "That many people he has to protect—from little ol' me? I'm impressed with myself."

"Don't be," she replied. "If I know Adan Harrison, he's probably got your precious son tied up and under lock and key right now. How does that make you feel?"

Joe's hand came across her face in a hard slap that left her stunned and brought tears to her eyes. She bent over, a hand to her face, but Joe lifted her up, his eyes burning with a mad fire. "If he lays a hand on my boy, I'll kill him right in front of you."

ADAN DIDN'T KNOW which way to go. The sheriff's deputies posted at different roads and lanes across the mountain hadn't seen any sign of Joe Pritchard and they didn't want to send out any more search teams this late at night. First thing in the morning, the sheriff would bring in tracking dogs.

Adan couldn't wait till morning. Pritchard had Sophia now, so he'd try to get off this mountain as soon as he could. But greed would make him look for that lost money, which might give Adan the time he needed to find them.

He was beginning to think the man was a ghost.

But everything that hadn't made sense before was starting to fall into place now. Pritchard had help—Sean and Melissa—and maybe someone else. The Burtons?

His gut shouted that one of them had helped Pritchard and the other one hadn't. They'd argued and a fight had ensued or possibly Pritchard had argued with one of them and Arnie had fallen during that fight.

Maggie had mentioned money—could she have been talking about the money allegedly hidden in the car Sophia had brought here? Pritchard had stayed on the mountain because he wanted to find that car and now he needed Sophia to help him.

He'd kill her once he had the dirty money.

Adan's brain buzzed with all of the ins and outs of this case. Should have been an easy hunt. He had Pritchard cornered and all he had to do was nab him and take him back to Texas. But there were so many variables to this mess, he felt as if he were caught in a giant maze. And Sophia was with the madman at the end of that maze.

Adan trained his flashlight on the woods and called the sheriff for help one more time. If he could gather a few men, they could comb the nearby woods. After arguing back and forth, the sheriff finally agreed to send some men.

Adan hung up and glanced around. When he heard a moan coming from across the road, he hurried in that direction, thinking it might be Sophia.

And he was met with a shotgun in his face.

"Jacob?"

The old man moaned again. "I was gonna let you have it with both barrels."

"Who did this to you?" Adan asked, suspecting he knew the answer. He started feeling Jacob for any broken bones.

The ornery old man pushed him away. "Cut that out. I ain't dead, so help me up."

"Was it Pritchard?"

Jacob rubbed his head. "Don't rightly know since whoever it was came up behind me. Gave me a good wallop, I reckon, since my head is banging like a hammer hitting stone."

"He's taken Sophia," Adan said, his voice low. "Can you make it back to Bettye's place?"

Jacob steadied himself and checked his gun. "Of course I can." He wobbled and grabbed for Adan's arm. "Or maybe you can just get me to the door."

Adan pulled Jacob up and half carried, half dragged him across the road and up onto Bettye's porch. At their knock, David opened the door with his own weapon at the ready.

"Jacob!"

Bettye came running and soon they had Jacob inside.

"Take care of him," Adan said. "I've got some of the sheriff's men coming to help me do an immediate search."

"Good luck," David called. "Be careful."

Adan nodded and took off. Then he saw several cars coming up the mountain road. At least he had reinforcements. He only hoped it wasn't too late.

SOPHIA HEARD VEHICLES circling the winding road, several of them, from the flash of highlights she saw. Glancing back at Joe, she steeled herself for his reaction.

He stopped and jerked her around. "What have you done?"

"Me?" Her surprise was sincere. "How could I

have done anything? I've been traipsing around with you for over an hour."

"You deliberately brought me back here," he said. "That was a bad decision, sunshine." Grabbing her by the arm, Joe twisted her around so quickly pain shot through her body.

"I ought to beat the tar out of you right here," he said. "You never did know how to follow directions."

"No, I didn't," she said, trying with all her might to find something to hit him with. "But I'm telling you, the path to the car is that way."

She pointed to the one path she knew would get him what he wanted. And while they walked that path, she'd find a way to either kill him or run from him as fast as she could.

"Don't be playing with me," Joe warned on a low growl.

"I'm not," she said, her nerves shot with anger and frustration. "Let's get going before that search party gets here."

Joe poked her with the rifle. "Get on up that path. Now!"

Sophia looked back toward the approaching vehicles, her one prayer that they would follow Joe and her straight to the hidden car. Then it occurred to her that she could make things easy for Adan and the search party by leaving clues. While they talked, she broke dry twigs and scraped her boots over muddy earth to leave a definite print.

"Joe, what did you do when you woke up? After I left you?"

He grunted and coughed. "What do you think I did? I had to get to a hospital, but I was a wanted man."

"You've always been a wanted man," she said, her hand snagging a branch that had slapped at her light sweater.

"Shut up on that," he whispered. "If you had just stuck with the plan, we'd both be somewhere else right now."

Or she'd be dead.

"I didn't like the plan from the get-go," she retorted. "I didn't want to be a part of any robbery."

"But you sure liked being married to me."

Sophia dug her heel in the moist dirt left over from the snow. Dug it and pretended the soft earth was Joe Pritchard's head under her shoe. "I kind of got over that, too."

He knocked her off her feet. "You made a big mistake, leaving me for dead. I've had to hide out for years. I don't think I can just let you get away with something like that."

Sophia lay there, catching her breath, her hand around her neck, on the blue scarf Bettye had crocheted for her. She slowly pulled it into her right hand. With her other hand, she lifted up onto her

knees and then pushed up to stand. She left the
scarf lying there on the path for Adan to find.

ADAN GATHERED THE half dozen law enforcement
people and explained the situation. "We have
one man and one minor in custody." He went
over the details of Sean and Melissa's involvement and turned to the sheriff. "You can take the
boy in, but the girl came here to find her grandmother. I'll make sure she gets back to where
she belongs."

The sheriff looked skeptical but nodded. "We
got other fish to fry right now." He instructed
his men to spread out and stay near the perimeter of the small community. "In the morning,
we'll have hounds up here." He turned to Adan.
"We'll get your man, Ranger Harrison."

Adan nodded. "That's my intention, too, sir."

But he knew this would be like trying to find
a diamond in the rocks. He took off along one
of the beaten paths anyway, a deputy close behind him. While he walked, Adan wondered why
he couldn't just let go. He'd held back from any
kind of relationship for almost five years. Determined to raise his daughter, he'd finally had
to turn to his willing parents for help. This life
didn't work with raising children, especially if
you were single.

What had he been thinking? That always getting his man was more important than being a

good daddy? He thought about Joe Pritchard and the poor kid who was his son. Had Joe walked away from a young wife and left a toddler?

Adan closed his eyes for a moment, a scene of him laughing with Gaylen warming his insides. Then Sophia came into the picture, her smile beaming as she tugged at Gaylen's hand.

Adan opened his eyes and blinked. Could that be possible? Could he overlook how she'd withheld this last important detail from him because she was so afraid to trust anyone?

Later, he thought. *After this. After I finish this job and put Joe Pritchard in jail for good.*

After an hour of walking through leftover snowdrifts and crossing streams that left his feet and legs numb, Adan turned to the deputy helping him. "I think we need to give up on this path and try another one."

The deputy gave him a relieved nod. "I agree, sir."

Adan did one last sweep of the area, his eyes now adjusted to the gray moonlight. When he found a dark looming shape about fifty feet away, he started toward it. "I see something," he told the deputy.

They traipsed up a hillside to the odd-shaped mound. Winded and tired, Adan shined his light on what he hoped was that infernal car everyone wanted to find.

But it wasn't a car.

"It's a lean-to," the deputy said, surprise mixed with disappointment in his words.

"Let's search it." Adan pushed forward, his gun ready. "Hello. Anyone inside?"

When no one responded, he held up his light. Signs of a doused campfire and a few open cans and small boxes indicated someone had been living here.

"I think we just found Joe Pritchard's hideout," he said.

"Want me to call it in?"

Adan nodded. "We need to process this place, but I can't do that right now."

"I'll get it done," the deputy offered. "Not much to see or find, but I can take pictures at least."

"Good idea," Adan replied. "You stay safe, okay?"

The deputy nodded. "I'll be careful. We get this kind of work up here in the foothills all the time."

Adan didn't doubt that, but they had a desperate killer without any sense of conscience out here on the loose. With a desperate woman as his hostage. A woman who'd try to take matters into her own hands, no matter how scared she was.

"I'm gonna keep moving," he told the deputy after they'd radioed the sheriff.

Soon he was alone in the quiet forest. He'd always been a loner and doing his job his way, on his own time, had always defined him and made him a good Ranger. So he listened and worked his way across the many meandering paths through the hills and valleys of Crescent Mountain.

Another hour had gone by and with each minute, his heart rate accelerated. Pritchard wanted Sophia but he also wanted that stolen money, too. Adan knew if push came to shove, Pritchard would kill the woman and take the cash.

Gritting his teeth against the cold and his own stubborn determination, Adan tried not to lose hope. He shined his penlight on the root-filled, rocky path. When his light hit something blue, he stopped, his breath hitching. Adan bent down and lifted the soft crocheted scarf, his heart pulsing with relief and dread.

Sophia's favorite scarf. She'd told him Bettye had made it for her last Christmas. Adan held the scarf tightly coiled around his finger and inhaled the scents of almonds and oranges. Then he called in his location to the sheriff. Soon, he'd have backup to help him up the mountain.

And hopefully, he'd have Sophia in his arms again soon, too.

CHAPTER TWENTY-SEVEN

SOPHIA DIDN'T KNOW how much farther she could go. She'd left her scarf at least two miles back and she'd managed to drop a stretch bracelet she'd made for the art fair two years ago over a loose hanging branch.

Would anyone find her clues before she died?

Joe grunted for the umpteenth time. "Are you messing with me, Sophia?"

"How do you mean?"

"I mean, I'm tired and ready to get on flat ground again. You'd better find that car and soon. I've had enough of you holding out on me."

He pushed her again, but she managed to keep her balance this time. She already had skinned hands and torn jeans to show for trying to resist his shoves. She had a bruise on her left cheek for being sassy with him, too. Several times, she'd stumbled on broken limbs and huge rock, but she didn't dare try to attack him with either. He'd shoot her, no doubt about that. So she decided she'd bide her time until they got to the car. Then somehow she'd distract him and find a way to make her move.

She wanted to watch him die a slow death.

Tired and irritated, Sophia searched the moon-lit woods and hoped she had brought him along the right path. If he wanted the money so badly, she'd gladly let him have it. She'd pay any price to be free of his cruel shadow.

But she was so afraid she'd taken the wrong turn. She'd only been back to check on the car one time until the other day when she'd tried to hide it more and in the meantime, she'd tried to forget the bag of money she'd found in the trunk. Drug money, tainted money, sad money. That money couldn't buy her any happiness, so she'd hidden it right along with her guilt and her shock.

But all of her denial had finally come crashing down around her. Joe was back and it all had to end here, tonight, one way or another.

"I think we're almost there," she said, her voice raw, her words winded and weary. "Joe, you know that car might not start. How do you plan to get out of here with all that money?"

"I got me a plan," he said. "My son knows where to pick me up."

She almost reminded him that by now his son would surely be in custody, but she didn't want to anger him again. Sean would have to pay for Joe's sins, too. When would this end?

She didn't get to dwell on that final scenario. Joe poked her with the gun. "What's that up ahead?"

Sophia lifted her head and stared into the moonlight. She didn't know whether to be happy or to run for her life. "That's your precious car. And your bag of money is hidden in the compartment in the trunk."

Joe poked her hard with the gun. She was so cold and tired she could easily lie down and let him finish the job. Her lightweight sweater and thermal sweatshirt couldn't protect her from the biting wind. But in spite of the numbness stalling her every move, a white-hot desire to survive burned through her.

Because somewhere along this cold, dark, frightening path, she'd had the sweetest daydream. She'd dreamed of seeing Adan with his little girl, Gaylen, laughing and playing. Then she'd pictured herself in that dream.

A single tear fell warm and liquid down her cheek.

Sophia wanted that dream. Somehow.

So she ignored Joe's threats and headed toward the mound of bramble and branches and bushes that had grown over the car she'd stolen and hidden. The forest had tried to bury her sins, but the winter wind had brought them back to the surface again.

As she stood a foot from the car and watched

Joe trudge forward, Sophia felt a sense of relief. No one could ever hold this over her head again.

But that relief was short-lived when she heard Joe's screams and curses. Then he whirled on her and slapped her to the ground. "Where is the money, Sophia? What did you do with the money?"

A BRACELET.

Adan held the dainty, colorful circle of threads in his hand as if it were made of diamonds strung together by a delicate spiderweb. "It's Sophia's," he told Sheriff Demont. "She wears this all the time." He snuggled the bracelet into the inside pocket of his jacket to keep it safe.

"Keep walking," the sheriff said, the cold sending up puffs of his breath into the damp night air. "We got 'em on the run now." The stoic lawman had followed Adan up the path and caught up with him.

Adan stomped ahead over ruts and dips, determination heating his numb insides. He might hate winter forever after this week. Heck, he might retire after this week.

They climbed over broken limbs and ragged rocks while he searched for another clue, another sign of Sophia. But no other signs appeared and he was just about out of hope.

Until he heard a growl of a scream piercing

into the night, followed by a feminine cry that echoed like a lost plea toward him.

Sophia.

SOPHIA SCREAMED BACK at the man hitting her. She wouldn't die this way, out here, alone and beaten, cold and cowardly. Scooting away, she did a desperate feel of the ground around her. Now was her only chance to try and get away before Joe finally killed her. But every branch she tried to lift was only a protruding root that refused to let go. Every rock she cut her hands and arms on was so packed into the earth that she couldn't pry it loose. Out of her reach, the way all of her dreams were always just out of her reach.

Joe charged after her, raising the rifle to use as a whip. She cringed and screamed again, her only hope that someone would hear her and come to help her.

"You sorry good-for-nothing," Joe shouted, his boots stomping toward her. "The trunk's open and the money's gone. What did you do with it, Sophia?"

"I don't know where your money is," she cried. She scooted against an outcropping of jagged rock and shielded her face with her bleeding hands. "Joe, listen to me. It was there last time I checked. Someone must have found it. Someone else took your money."

But Joe was beyond listening now. He grabbed

her by her arms and wrestled her up against the rocks, causing her head to hit the unyielding wall behind her with a crack. She saw stars that weren't up in the sky, her hands gripping the rocks to steady herself. A baseball-size rock moved against her touch and somehow she managed to hold onto it and clasp her fingers around it. A wave of dizziness pulled her down into the darkness, but she took a breath and blinked only to see Joe's face inches from hers.

"I'm gonna kill you," he said. "But first, I want to finish something we didn't get to start." His wet mouth on hers brought Sophia out of her stupor. She groaned and twisted away, but his hand on her face held her there. "Gonna fight me to the end, aren't you?"

"Yes," she said on a hissing breath, gaining strength with each defiant word. "Yes, to the bitter end. You disgust me."

Joe dropped the rifle and pushed her back against the rocks, his hands moving over her body. Sophia knew what would come next and with every ounce of energy she had left, she allowed him to touch her long enough to give her time to raise her right hand and hurl the heavy rock down against his skull.

She hit her mark. Joe growled in pain and reached up for his head. She hit him again, this time on his temple and forehead. He went down in a slow motion that scared her because she was so afraid he'd rise up again, the way he had over and over.

When he fell at her feet, Sophia thought she was finally free. But Joe came back up with a raging howl, a knife in his hand. Sophia screamed and held her hands over her face and then moved down the wall, trying to escape.

"Stop!"

The one word, coming from a now familiar voice, gave her renewed energy and hope.

Adan!

But Joe didn't stop. He plunged toward her, his eyes like a dirty midnight river. He followed her and cornered her, the knife slashing at her. Sophia kept fighting, kicking and slapping. She could hear Adan screaming at Joe to stop, to halt.

Then she heard a shot ring out into the night. Joe's expression went from rage to shock as he jerked back in pain. He gave her one last hateful glare and then he plunged at her and fell at her feet.

Sophia breathed a gulping sigh of relief and stared down at the man on the ground. Then she glanced up, searching for Adan. He was running toward her. But a searing hot pain hit her in her right side. Sophia grabbed at her sweater and felt the blood running down her fingers.

Joe had stabbed her.

The blackness she'd been fighting overtook her. She started sliding down the rocks, landing in a sitting position. She stared over at Joe and wondered if Adan had killed him.

Then she heard another voice, the voice she'd dreamed about on this long trek to find her buried sins.

Adan's voice. He was calling her name, but she couldn't stay awake. She couldn't answer. So she drifted to sleep and hoped her dreams would stay sweet.

ADAN RAN TOWARD SOPHIA, her name stalling on his lips. He'd struggled to see into the darkness but when he'd seen Pritchard holding her against these rocks, he'd raised his handgun and fired—at exactly the same time Joe had plowed toward Sophia.

The bullet had hit its mark. Sophia was safe now.

Or so he'd thought. He watched in horror as she clutched her midsection and then slid down the wall. Had she been hit? Adan reached her and bent down to look at her.

"Sophia?"

She moaned, her eyes glassy. "Knife…"

Adan checked her wound and then glanced back at where Pritchard lay moaning, a bloody knife clutched in his right hand. Adan's missing Bowie knife.

Adan screamed to the sheriff, his hands covering the blood that filtered through her clothes,

"Call 911. She's been stabbed. He stabbed her. Hurry, call now!"

Grasping for anything to stanch the bleeding, he pulled out the blue scarf he'd found on the path, tears pricking at his eyes. After balling it up, he held the scarf over the tear in her sweater with one hand and felt her pulse with the other.

She was cold and probably going into shock, her pulse weak.

Adan didn't think about what he'd done...or what she'd done. He only thought about how to save her. "Sophia? Sophia, can you hear me?"

She didn't respond, so he tried again.

"Sophia? Listen, I'm here. We're getting help for you. I'm so sorry, do you hear me? I'm so sorry." He blinked and held tight to her wound, the lacy blue material turning a rich bluish-red now. With his other hand, he grabbed her fingers and tried to will some warmth into her body.

The sheriff hurried up. "Got help coming." He toed Pritchard. "Is he dead?"

"I don't know," Adan admitted. "And I don't care."

Sheriff Demont didn't say another word. He checked Pritchard's wound. "I think he'll live for now." Then he dragged a moaning Joe Pritchard out of the way and searched him for weapons before he stood up with his gun trained on Pritchard. "He ain't going anywhere."

When Joe woke up and started thrashing,

Adan didn't stop to think. He got up and charged on Pritchard, pounding on the man's face with his bloody hands.

"You happy now?" he shouted at Pritchard. "Are you satisfied? She's injured. She's bleeding!"

Pritchard rolled his head side to side. "Only got what she deserved. So…yeah… I guess I'm… pretty satisfied, all things considered."

Adan hit him again, knocking him out.

The sheriff turned a blind eye and helped Adan off him. "Go check on your lady, Ranger Harrison."

Adan came out of his anger-infused daze and hurried back to Sophia's side. She was still breathing so he sat down as close as he could get to her and held her tight.

"I'm so sorry," he said again. "So sorry. I tried to get here before he hurt you. I tried."

Her eyes fluttered open at the sound of a helicopter somewhere overhead. "Adan?"

"I'm right here."

She held his jacket. "I'm sorry, too. Didn't tell you—"

"Shh," he said, thinking how insignificant that was now. "It's okay. We'll talk about all of that later, okay?"

"But—" Then she gulped, her eyes going wide in fright as she struggled to get up. "Joe?"

"We got him," Adan said, gently pushing her back down. "You're safe now, Sophia."

She shot him a lopsided smile and closed her eyes.

CHAPTER TWENTY-EIGHT

THE MOUNTAIN WAS crawling with law enforcement agencies and first responders. And Adan's insides were crawling with a solid dread that wouldn't let go.

His phone rang and when he saw his mother's caller ID, he immediately answered. His mother never called unless it was an emergency. Hoping nothing had happened to Gaylen or either of his parents, he glanced at where two able-bodied men were strapping Sophia onto a stretcher to get her out to the old logging road near where they'd found the hidden car.

Walking behind the stretcher, he followed the men down the rocky curving path. "Mom?"

"Hi, honey. Everything's okay here, but we were just worried. Gaylen was asking about you."

Adan pinched two fingers across the bridge of his nose. "I'm okay. Just…tying up some loose ends. We got our man, but it sure wasn't easy."

He wanted to add that he'd found his woman, too. But he wasn't sure how to handle the myriad feelings rushing through him like a river. He had a lot to sort out.

First making sure Sophia was taken care of and, second, making sure Joe Pritchard never saw the light of day again.

After reassuring his mother and telling her to give Gaylen a hug first thing in the morning, Adan ended the call and stomped down the mile-long path to the ambulance parked down near the circle of cabins.

All of the neighbors were waiting for him, including a worried-looking Maggie Burton.

"Ranger Harrison, I need to tell you something important."

Adan had pretty much figured out what she wanted to confess. "Not now, Maggie," he said, his hand in the air.

"But…it's important," she said, tears forming in her eyes. "Arnie's going to be okay. A long haul to get well, what with a broken leg and his other injuries. But we feel blessed that he'll be okay. I just hope we can go on our long hikes again one day."

"Yeah, me, too," Adan replied. "And I just hope you're talking to me right now because you know where that drug money is and you intend to turn it in."

She nodded, tears running down her face. "I do and I will. But it's a long story."

"I'll take your statement, don't worry about

that," he replied. "Stay right here until I can do that."

"But I want to go back to the hospital with Arnie."

Adan couldn't fault her for that. "I'll have to put a guard on you, then. First thing tomorrow I'll want to take your statement, okay?"

"Okay. He's sleeping for now so David came and brought me home so I could talk to you."

Adan glanced at where the others stood talking. He'd have to explain all of this to them later. When Bettye came toward him with her arms opened wide, Adan accepted her embrace.

"Thank you for saving our girl," she said. Then she reached up and whispered in his ear, "Don't be so hard on her, Adan. She was so scared when she came here, and she never spent a dime of that money."

Sophia had tried to tell him. She'd mentioned she'd only taken back her own money. She'd tried to explain.

Adan couldn't speak at first. Swallowing back his guilt and fear, he looked down at Bettye. "I almost didn't make it. Just a second or two more and she'd be—"

"You did make it," Bettye replied. "She's alive and safe now. And she has a new champion." She poked two fingers against his badge. "She has you. You're the cowboy who came for Christmas. It's like a gift we all needed."

Adan didn't know what to say. "I have to go," he said but he turned before he took off to take care of business. "And, Bettye?"

Bettye whirled, her long gray braid dancing around. "Yes?"

"Thank you."

Bettye winked at him. "I didn't do anything. I didn't have to. I knew you two were meant for each other the night I hit you over the head with that frying pan."

That brought a smile to Adan's lips. He shook his head and hurried to catch up with the ambulance.

SHE WAS HAVING that dream again.

Sophia snuggled underneath the warm blanket, her sleep-laced brain registering that she was no longer cold or scared. She felt warm and safe because she could see Adan's face in her dream.

Then she opened her eyes and there he was.

Asleep by her bed.

Sophia glanced around and realized she was in a hospital bed, hooked up to an IV drip. But no handcuffs. At least not yet.

"Adan?"

His head came up in surprise but his hand on hers was warm and comforting. He laced his fingers in hers, cleared his throat and leaned close. "Hi."

"Hi," she said, her mind reeling with the horror

that had occurred in reality. Her nightmares had all come true.

But so had her dream of a hero.

"Where's Joe?" she asked, her voice shaky. Her hope even more shaky.

"In another hospital under lock and key," Adan said. "We transported him as far away from you as possible. He's being treated and guarded at another regional hospital closer to the Texas border. He'll be hauled over the line back to Texas as soon as the doctors clear him for travel."

"He's not dead." She closed her eyes, hating herself for wanting another human being to die. "He never really dies."

Adan's fingers tightened on her hand. "No, but he'll spend a long time in prison. The rest of his life, I'm sure. He'll probably wish he were dead."

She struggled with her blankets. "What if he escapes?"

Adan hand on her shoulder soothed her. "He won't. Trust me on that."

She did trust him on that. "Thank you," she said. "For so much."

Adan lowered his head. "I thought we'd lost you."

"I thought you'd never find me until spring, but you followed my clues?"

"Yes. Good thinking. Got there in time."

A new shyness engulfed her, making her wonder what they had in common now that Joe was out of the picture. "That's all that matters."

"Yep." He looked distressed and guilty. "Every second mattered last night."

But when she gazed into his eyes, she knew that a lot more than timing mattered between them. Afraid to voice her feelings, she shrank back on the bed. Did she deserve a man like Adan Harrison?

Deciding to worry about that later, she asked, "Where is the money? What happened? What about Joe's son?"

Adan clasped her hand. "We can talk about all that later. You need to rest. That stab wound was pretty deep, but luckily you didn't suffer any major damage. Doc got you stitched up good and proper, but you'll be sore for a few days."

"When can I go home?" She tried not to cry. "Or…am I going to jail?"

"No jail time," he said, smiling. "Home maybe tomorrow, if you behave. You'll have to take it easy for a while."

She swallowed back the tears clogging her eyes and throat. "What will happen to me now, Adan?"

"Only good things if I have my way," he said. Then he stood up and leaned down to place a sweet kiss on her forehead. "Let's worry about all of that later, okay. You need to rest and sleep.

Your wound was bad enough but you were close to hypothermia, too."

"Do I still have all my fingers and toes?" she asked, wiggling her feet just in case, the memory of being chilled to her bones still causing her to shudder.

He pulled her blanket up tight around her neck. "Yes, you sure do. But you need to get some rest. I think Bettye and Karen are coming to visit later so you can catch up on things with them."

"But what about everything else?"

What was he hiding from her?

"Don't worry about anything," he said, his smile lighting up the room while his manner bordered on awkward. "Hey, you just need to remember that…we all love you, okay?"

We all love you.

Not *I love you.*

She wanted to pin him down on that and ask him did *he* love her? But she didn't have the right to even ask that question. They needed more time, more chances to be together without the threat of danger around every corner. And she needed to know what her future held—going home or going to jail.

Would he love her now that he'd settled things? Now that he had Joe where he wanted him to be? Now that he had her where she needed to be and all of the money accounted for? Or would he make sure she was behind bars, too?

Adan looked as if he couldn't wait to be out of this room. And just like that, her sweet dream seemed to fizzle out like a dying ember. Maybe she had dreamed the whole thing after all.

"You don't have to stay," she said, forcing her tone to be neutral. "You're right. I am tired and I just want to sleep for about a week or so."

He seemed surprised but he didn't try to protest. "I do have some reports to file. Once that's done, I'll explain everything else to you."

She nodded. But she didn't hold out hope on anything.

ADAN DIDN'T KNOW how to take Sophia's reaction to finding him in her hospital room. Maybe he should have left while she was sleeping, but last night he couldn't bring himself to do it. Instead, he'd emailed a few of the particulars of this case to Ranger headquarters in Austin, and he'd talked to the sheriff about his suspicions regarding the Burtons. Once Joe Pritchard was well enough to give a statement, they'd force the truth out of him, too.

In the meantime, Adan did have a lot of work to do.

First thing, he wanted to question Maggie Burton. She had agreed to meet him at the sheriff's office back in Crescent Mountain. So he left the big regional hospital and drove back the forty or so miles to the base of the mountain.

Maggie was waiting in the sheriff's office. When Adan entered, she looked up with both relief and trepidation. "How's Sophia?"

"She's doing all right," he said, not willing to give Maggie any more information on Sophia just yet.

Sheriff Demont greeted Adan and then settled back in his chair. "Got a report on Pritchard. He came out of surgery and he's in the recovery room. He'll be put in a private room later today with two guards at the door and only official visitors allowed."

Adan nodded on that. "Let's get this over with," he said.

The sheriff indicated he was ready. "Mrs. Burton, you ready to give your statement?"

Maggie nodded, but she looked lost and scared. Adan didn't want to feel sorry for the woman, but he did in a way. He waited to hear her story before giving in to that notion.

Maggie shifted in her chair. "You know Arnie and I love to hike. We've walked and explored just about every inch of Crescent Mountain."

"I get that," Adan said, impatient to get to the truth.

"So we were walking along the western ridge of the mountain, up this old logging road—"

"When," Adan asked. "What time of year? How long ago?"

She looked down at her clutched hands. "About

a year ago." Shrugging, she said, "We hadn't gone up that particular road in a while because it was dusty and…kind of boring. But it was a nice spring day, so we decided to give it a try."

Adan glanced over at the sheriff. "Go on."

"We got up to this level spot—probably where the trucks used to turn around—and saw this big mound of branches and shrubs. We went to investigate and then we remembered—this was where we'd helped Sophia hide a car several years ago. It was covered with vines and saplings."

"And you realized it was Sophia's car?"

"Yes." She bobbed her head. "We tugged at some of the vines. Arnie loves old cars, and he got the idea that maybe enough time had gone by that he might be able to buy the car from Sophia and restore it."

Adan was beginning to see the picture. "And…"

"And…we checked the car out, front to back. He even popped the hood and looked in the trunk." She lowered her head again. "We found a hidden compartment cut out of the trunk near where the backseat was. There was a dark bag inside. We opened it and found all of this money."

Adan let out a sigh. "What did you do after you found the money?"

Maggie shrugged and wiped at her eyes. "We…uh…decided that instead of restoring the car…we'd just…skim a few dollars off the top…

here and there." Lifting her head, she glanced from the sheriff to Adan. "We shouldn't have done it. We should have told Sophia we found it or we should have reported it, but…we had some bills to pay and…we got greedy. Each time we'd come up here, we'd hike to the car and… take more money. Finally, when we arrived here this time to celebrate Christmas and heard about Joe Pritchard being on the mountain, we figured he'd come to get his money and that if he found some missing, he'd kill us or he'd hurt Sophia."

Adan felt sick to his stomach. "So you took all of the money?"

She bobbed her head again. "We thought if we could find Pritchard and convince him that Sophia had taken the money, he'd go after her and not us. But I wanted to be sure we'd get out this alive, so I tried to convince Arnie that we should just take the money and go. We'd never have to come back here again. He didn't like that idea, and so we argued down on the path near the stream.

"We were standing on a ridge and he grabbed my arm and tried to convince me that we needed to do the right thing. He was so worried about you being here and about Joe Pritchard hurting Sophia." She sniffed and shook her head. "I was kind of jealous of Sophia. Not that Arnie cared about her. He's always loved me. But I made a big fuss and when he grabbed for me, I pushed away and he hit some loose rocks and…he slipped."

She burst into tears then. "I was so afraid I'd killed my husband. But it was an accident. A terrible accident."

Adan leaned close. "So you lied. You never saw Joe Pritchard on the path that day or anytime at all, did you?"

"No," Maggie said. "Never." Then she gave Adan a resigned glance. "But… I do know where that money is."

CHAPTER TWENTY-NINE

SOPHIA GOT OUT of the car and glanced around.

She was home and it was the night before Christmas Eve.

Bettye and Karen both gave her reassuring smiles.

"C'mon, now," Bettye said, her eyes bright. "Let's get you inside out of this wind."

Karen held Sophia's elbow, making her feel like an invalid. "I can walk on my own, you know."

"We want to pamper you," Karen said. "We'll get you nice and tucked in and then you can rest all you want."

"I don't want to rest," Sophia said on a petulant breath. She wanted to walk and to laugh and to cry and to whine.

Adan had gone home to his family.

Without even telling her goodbye.

And these two dear friends who'd spent time with her and brought her home in time for Christmas weren't telling her anything. All she'd heard was that he had to get home.

Not a word about telling her goodbye or if he'd

ever come back. Not a word about all the questions she still had about Joe Pritchard and everything that had happened in her life because of one misguided youthful decision to marry a cruel, nasty man.

She needed some answers and she intended to get them.

But when Bettye opened the door to Sophia's cabin and stood back to let her inside, Sophia was immediately greeted with cheers and laughter and a large sign that said, "Welcome Home, Sophia."

And waiting there beside her tiny Christmas tree stood Texas Ranger Adan Harrison. With a smile on his face.

"I THOUGHT YOU'D be long gone by now," she said a few minutes later when the others had given them some space.

They stood by the fireplace while Bettye passed out food to the others. Bettye and Jacob played host along with Karen and David. But she didn't see Maggie. She surely must be at the hospital with Arnie.

Adan leaned close and whispered into her ear, "I couldn't leave just yet. I had to make sure you got home safe."

Giving him a look that had to show her confusion, Sophia said, "Well, I'm here and I'm safe. You're relieved of your duties, Ranger-Man."

"Seeing you is not a duty, but a pleasure," he retorted.

Sophia had to be brave, probably even braver than she'd had to be out on that mountain with a killer. "Seriously, you don't have to stay."

Adan touched a finger to her bangs. "Seriously, are you trying to get rid of me?"

"You need to be with your little girl."

"And I will be," he said, his expression changing from joyful to concerned. "Do you want me gone so fast?"

She shook her head. "What I want, as someone once said to me, is the truth."

"Oh." Understanding washed through his gold-hued eyes. "Come with me and I'll tell you everything."

An hour later, Sophia could only shake her head and wonder. Cuddled with Adan underneath a heavy quilt, she sat on a bench on the back porch.

And while she felt warm and safe in his arms, a chill went over Sophia. "So...all this time, I was so careful not to spend that drug money, but Maggie and Arnie didn't have any such qualms."

"Apparently not," Adan said, his chin resting against the top of her head. "The so-cute couple wasn't so cute, and they weren't so honest, either. They put on a good show the day they helped stall me down by the stream because they really *were* trying to stall me. They'd been busy hiding the money before Jacob got there, in the spot where they fell in love."

"So romantic," Sophia said, her mind still reeling with this twist out of left field. "No wonder they never hung around with the rest of us too much."

Having heard that Maggie and Arnie might face charges or at the least probation time for spending stolen money, she wondered about her own future.

"So what will happen to Melissa and Sean… and me?"

He kissed her temple, which gave her hope. At least he hadn't cuffed her when she'd entered the front door.

"Community service for Melissa, and once we've cleared the way with the proper authorities, hopefully Bettye will become her legal guardian and she can live here. They're already talking about enrolling her in the high school down in town."

"That would be so wonderful for Bettye. She deserves a second chance and so does Melissa."

"And that leaves you," he said on a smile.

"Do I deserve a second chance, too?"

"I think so," he said. "You didn't spend the money because you didn't even know it was there at first. Your only crime is that you didn't report it when you discovered it."

"And I stole that car," she reminded him.

"It ain't much of a car." Adan didn't seem worried. "But you're willing to testify to most of Pritchard's crimes and that will go a long way with the DA back in Texas."

"And you're willing to put in a good word for me?"

"Yes, and why can't you believe that?"

She wanted to believe, but she was so afraid she'd wake up again and this part would go away. "I'm trying to believe," she said, her hand touching his face. "But Adan, we have so much to work through. You wanted honesty and I didn't give it to you."

"And you wanted to trust me and I didn't convince you to do that."

"So how do we make this work?"

"Let's start with this," he said. Then he kissed her and held her close. "I know we have a lot to work through, but now we can take our time and get it right."

"I'd like that."

"Good," he said. Then he lifted her up and kissed her again. "Now, I do have to go. I'm gonna drive all night to get home...but I will be back."

"When?"

He grinned down at her. "Maybe next week?"

"Next week?"

"Is that too soon?"

"Not soon enough," she said, deciding she'd

worry about all the variables later. As he liked to say.

"And I might bring someone with me, if it's okay with you?"

She drew back. "The sheriff?"

"No, someone much sweeter than him." He turned serious. "I'm thinking Gaylen might enjoy seeing a mountain or two."

Sophia gasped. "You want to bring your daughter here?"

He nodded. "My two best girls together. Just to test the waters."

"What if she doesn't like me?"

"How can she not like you?"

He had more confidence than Sophia felt, but she kissed him anyway. "What will your parents say?"

"Hallelujah?" he said on a laugh. "They want me to be happy again and in spite of you tying me to the bedposts, and all the other stuff that happened over the last week, you do make me happy."

Sophia wanted to cry with joy. "You make me happy, too." But she still had one question. "What about the logistics? You live in Austin and I live here."

"Who says we can't have both?" he asked. "A home in Austin, where I can watch you like a hawk, and a vacation home right here, where I can still watch you like a hawk."

"Because you don't trust me?"

"No, because I don't want to let you out of my sight."

Then he reached into his pocket and pulled out a colorful bundle. "Merry Christmas, Sophia."

It was a new scarf, knitted with several breathtaking colors. "It reminded me of you," he said.

He kissed her one more time and then he left for home.

One week later

SOPHIA HEARD A truck coming up the mountain road.

It was bitterly cold and the weather people were predicting snow again. Didn't look as though anyone would be leaving this mountain over New Year's Eve or Day.

Or coming here to get stuck, either.

So she steeled herself against disappointment and hurried to the window to see.

Then her heart stopped.

Adan had kept his promise. He was back on the mountain.

"I told you so," Bettye said behind her. "Now I'm gonna get gone before y'all have your big reunion."

"We're just going to see how it goes," Sophia retorted.

"It's gonna go fine, trust me. Remember, Melissa and I can babysit if you two need some alone time." Bettye kissed her and hurried out the back door.

While a tall shadow stood at the front door.

Sophia opened it and saw Adan standing there with a bouquet of colorful flowers, and her heart did a dance of pure bliss. But when she looked down and saw the adorable little golden-haired girl who stood with him, she knew her second chance had finally come.

"She has your eyes," she said to Adan. Then she bent down and said, "Hi. You must be Gaylen."

Gaylen giggled and smiled. "Uh-huh. Are you Soapy?"

Sophia laughed and nodded. "I am. I am Soapy."

Then she stood and smiled at Adan. "Welcome back, Ranger-Man."

He grinned and ushered his daughter into the cabin.

Then he kicked the door shut and pulled Sophia into his arms. "Happy New Year."

"It will be," she said, "now that you're here."

When they heard Gaylen's exclamation, they both looked down. But the little girl wasn't looking at them. She was twirling around the cabin. "I wuv this place," she announced, clapping her hands together in glee. "Is this your playhouse, Soapy?"

Adan winked at Sophia. "Told you so. We both

love this place." Then he whispered in Sophia's ear. "And… I love you, too."

Sophia was so glad to hear that. "Good. I love you, Adan. And this time I won't have to tie you to the bedposts to keep you here."

"I don't know. Might be fun." He laughed out loud and then he ran to show his little girl around their new playhouse.

* * * * *